A CABOT CAIN THRILLER

ASSAULT ON MING

CALIBER BOOKS

Also from ALAN CAILLOU

CABOT CAIN Series
    Assault on Kolchak
    Assault on Ming
    Assault on Loveless
    Assault on Fellawi
    Assault on Agathon
    Assault on Aimata

TOBIN'S WAR Series
    Dead Sea Submarine
    Terror in Rio
    Congo War Cry
    Afghan Assault
    Swamp War
    Death Charge
    The Garonsky Missile

MIKE BENASQUE Series
    The Plotters
    Marseilles
    Who'll Buy My Evil
    Diamonds Wild

IAN QUAYLE Series
    A League of Hawks
    The Sword of God

DEKKER'S DEMONS Series
    Suicide Run
    Blood Run

The Charge of the Light Brigade
A Journey to Orassia

Rogue's Gambit
Cairo Cabal
Bichu the Jaguar
The Walls of Jolo
The Hot Sun of Africa
The Cheetahs
Joshua's People
Mindanao Pearl
Khartoum
South from Khartoum
Rampage
The World is 6 Feet Square
The Prophetess
House on Curzon Street

ASSAULT ON MING
Book Two

For further information visit the Caliber Comics website:
www.calibercomics.com

CHAPTER 1

Under the hot blue sky, the bright colors of the little town were startling.

It's the first thing that strikes you when you hit Macao; a blaze of brilliant reds and blues and greens and yellows, as though a surrealist painter had gone out of his mind and painted the colony in a furious, abstract madness. The painted Eastern and Western characters on the signs over the stores seem to be battling for preeminence, each trying to outdo the other with their colors, as though the Portuguese are saying to the Chinese: We can do better, and better means gaudier.

And I hadn't been there for more than half an hour when some hopeful idiot tried to kill me.

It was the middle of the hot day, and the wash of the waves at Barra Point, where the dark green banyan trees line the waterfront, was a soft and gentle cadence that seemed to murmur peace. I'd walked from the airport, and I'd dumped my bag at the Penha Palacio Hotel, and gone on to see Markle Hyde, which was why I'd come here in the first place. And as I reached the big white house they'd told me about, with the iron gates on the side that looked across the Inner Harbor to the hills of the Chinese mainland; a young Chinese who was idly watching the fishermen mending their nets turned and looked at me and grinned a sort of welcome and shouted out: "Mr. Cain, over here!"

He was a hundred feet or so away, and there was a good-looking outboard skiff drawn up by the stone wall close by him; he was moving towards it, and he looked back and waved and grinned again and shouted: "Over here, a moment, please." His English was quite good, with the touch of an American East-Coast accent. I wondered idly how he knew my name—though my size makes me distinctive enough to anyone who's had a description—and I walked over to see what he wanted, to see if this were perhaps one of Markle Hyde's men who had something to say about my pending interview. His manner was affable, careless, friendly; I saw him reach into the skiff and he came up with a rifle, and not losing that smile of welcome he raised it to his shoulder and fired. The movement was fast, and the sound of the shot came no more than a fraction of a split second after the beginning of the motion. I was fast too—lying on the ground behind that sheltering wall, I heard the bullet smack into the granite blocks and go whining away across the water. And then, as I stared, two men came running out of the iron gates with revolvers in their hands, and I wondered for a brief moment if I was really as smart as I thought I was in never—or seldom—carrying a gun of any sort.

But the moment of fear passed quickly; the two men were firing over my head, over the wall that sheltered me from the man by the skiff. I raised myself up and looked, and he was already lying there dead half in and half out of the water and the fishermen were hurriedly gathering up their nets and moving away, seeing nothing, hearing nothing, knowing nothing; the casual ease of their movements told me that it was nothing new in Macao that casual battles were won and lost in the heat of every day to the tune of the whispering waters. Perhaps it's the only place left in the civilized world where this is so, where the terrors of the underworld bubble up sometimes above the surface of the colony's calm order.

It's a club, Macao, a European oasis that is surrounded, incongruously, by the nostalgic concepts of Oriental individuality, where every other citizen is at one time or another a pirate, or a smuggler, or just a plain old-fashioned gangster. You feel that you're in a sort of tropical Riviera with all the elegance you can imagine; and then, suddenly, you're reminded that this is not only China, but a China that has been left behind in the nineteenth century. It's one of the world's last strongholds of completely overt piracy, where anything, absolutely anything. goes.

The two men were Americans; but somehow, they seemed more distant from me than the young Chinese who had tried to kill me. They were dour, unsmiling, unemotional men and they'd put away their guns already and were standing there looking this way and that down the road. One of them whistled shrilly, and three Chinese came pouring out through the gates and ran towards the dead would-be assassin. They lifted him up and tossed him into his own skiff, and one of them started up the motor and pointed it out to sea, and in a few seconds the whole thing was over with the skiff and its dead cargo veering around the Inner Harbor and vaguely finding its way to the hills on the other side. I watched it as it swung around and steadied itself and seemed to find a course, as though the dead hands were steering it home.

One of the two Americans jerked a thumb at the gates and said: "Inside, Mr. Cain, it's safer. Mr. Hyde is waiting for you."

I'd heard plenty about Markle Hyde, of course. Financier, philanthropist, professional do-gooder; and I wondered what he was doing with such efficient, old-time bodyguards.

I soon found out.

He was a man of sixty or so, tough, agile, very sure of himself except in patches, a short, stubby sort of man who stood on two wide-spaced feet as though daring the world to come and knock him down. And everything about him spelt money.

The house was big and cool and comfortable in the old Portuguese Colonial style, overfilled with Chinese furniture and decorated with Chinese sculptures in stone and jade, some fine pieces among them. A huge and ugly bronze bear from the Han Dynasty, heavily gilded, was the centerpiece of the room I was in; and when I looked at it with admiration—there are only three of these pieces left in the world—Markle Hyde said tartly: "Not my taste, Cain, this is not my house. Now, what's your drink?"

His voice was sharp and imperative, the voice of a man used to giving orders. But he was holding out his hand and saying in the same breath: "I'm Markle Hyde, and you're going to work for me."

I said mildly: "I am?"

"Yes. Yes, you are. Sit down, Cain. Sit down and listen."

I said: "You offered me a drink."

"All right, what'll it be?"

"Back home, this kind of weather, I like to drink gin and tonic. But out here...anything long and cold. Whatever you have."

It was almost an affront to an overly developed sense of hospitality—or perhaps I should say, of the pride that comes from possession and the ability to make it show in even the smallest ways; he was going to put me in my place right away. He said: "What kind of gin? Just name it."

"Gordon's Gin, Schweppes tonic, lots of ice, and a fourteen ounce glass. Please."

He said coldly: "Good. I like a man who knows what he wants." He made no move towards the mirrored bar at the back of the room; but when I turned at the breath of a sound, an elderly Chinese servant was padding across the room in almost absolute silence; I heard the tinkle of glassware, Markle Hyde said suddenly: "And before I tell you why you are here, I'd better ask if you know who I am?"

I said: "I've heard of you. Who hasn't? But I only know what I read in the papers."

"Ah yes, you're a voracious reader, aren't you? They told me."

"They?"

He ignored the question. He shrugged his shoulders and said: "And I'm sorry about that little incident outside. If you'd let my man drive you in from the airport, it wouldn't have happened."

I said: "It's three miles. For me, that's a pleasant stroll. I like to walk."

The elderly Chinese, red-robed and soft-slippered, was there beside me, handing me a fourteen ounce glass on a silver tray, bowing and showing his yellow teeth; I was astonished at the absolute silence in which he moved; I fancied I could hear old bones creaking and nothing more.

I said: "Nobody important got hurt, so it's a trifle. What happens when that skiff runs out of gas and the dead body turns up?"

He shrugged. "This is Macao, Cain. It'll probably hit the other coast anyway, and then it's *their* problem, not ours." He said abruptly:

"Did you ever hear of a man named Ben Stirani?"

"No."

"A gangster, old-style, post-Capone."

"Ah yes. Drugs, I seem to remember."

"That's the man. Did you ever hear what happened to him?"

I frowned: "No...I seem to recall that he just...dropped out of sight."

In the back of my mind, there were bells ringing, announcing little bits of useless information that had long been half-forgotten. One of my students at Stanford had written a thesis on the theories of supply and demand in a permissive society; it was concerned largely with the idea that when society as a whole permits what the law prohibits, then there is a complete reversal of all that the law stands for. Part of his argument dealt with a climate in which the gangsters not only flourished, but became shrouded in an aura of legendary glamour. Stirani had figured largely in his arguments. I thought it was a strange world for a man like Markle Hyde to be interested in, till it occurred to me that a man of his enormous wealth must, from time to time, be aware of the predators around him.

He said now, with a touch of sarcasm: "Stirani was undoubtedly one of the most vicious hoods in history, Cain. If anyone can be said to have deserved the end he was reputed to have met, then Stirani did."

"Oh? I didn't bear about that?"

"According to the files of the FBI, Stirani was dropped into a bath of sulfuric acid. In Geneva, Switzerland."

"Oh? And whose idea was that?"

He laughed. "Almost everybody's. But it's not true, Cain. That was the story that was discreetly passed around to facilitate his disappearance. And his reappearance as someone else."

The bells were still ringing, and all the little pieces were coming back into focus in my memory. They were sketchy; there were only newspaper reports to go on.

I said: "And there was a story a while back that Stirani's old crowd has surfaced again, led by a man named...Ming? Alexander Ming? Are you suggesting that Ming is Stirani? Because if you are, I'll be damned if I can see what the hell all this has to do with me."

Interrupting me, Markle Hyde said sharply: "No, Cain, I'm not. I wouldn't have brought you all this way, I wouldn't have hired you in the first place, if all we're concerned with is...God dammit, gang warfare. I know a great deal more about you than you know about me. I know that you can't be hired for trivia. And to my mind that's all it is when hoods start killing each other off, jockeying for position, coming to the surface and drowning again...It's a matter of the least possible concern to me. I need you for something much more vital, so vital you can't possibly turn me down. So shut up and listen."

He didn't have a particularly disarming manner. But I'd come a long way and wasn't prepared to run off in a sulk just because his manners were offensive. There was something that was worrying him deeply under all that bluster.

As if reading my thoughts, he said:

"I know that you can only be called upon when...when something terribly wrong has to be put right."

My empty glass disappeared in silence; it was refilled and put back in silence.

I said mildly: "As long as so much is understood..."

He switched tacks suddenly and said again, as though checking the extent of my knowledge: "You do know who I am and what I stand for, don't you? Or shall I give you a catalog of my good works? The foundations, the libraries, the endowments, the hospitals?"

The sardonic touch was back again. Somehow, it pleased me. And another bell was tinkling another note. I waited, and he said:

"Yes, atoning for a greedy past, that's what you're thinking, Cain, isn't it? Thirty years of good works, and let's not hide the fact that I've done an enormous amount of good over a very long time. I've put my money where it could help. I'm a respected pillar of society, and God dammit, I'm a good man, a damn good man. And you're asking yourself what this has to do with Ben Stirani. You're also asking yourself where my money came from in the first place, because nobody knows that, and just why I should take such pains to be such a damn fine fellow. You're asking yourself: if Stirani's still alive, then what the hell has he got to do with a man of my fine and upright reputation? Because that's what my reputation is, Cain, and you know it. All right, stop guessing, I'll tell you." He took a deep breath and said: "I am Ben Stirani. Or rather, I was."

I took my drink and wandered over to the big window. There was a fine garden of roses framed in rich turf, out there. And beyond, in the harbor, the fiber-mat sails of the junks were patched in brown and lavender, yellow and orange, looking like futuristic bats'-wings in colors of rust and burnt sienna. Their masts were forward-sloping, their sterns high in the design that is peculiar to the waters of Macao. They would be loaded, I knew, with gasoline that was in transit from Hong Kong to Red China via the Macao harbor, where the officials turned a blind eye to the rusting drums piled high on the time-blackened teak decks. Behind me, Markle Hyde said—and the tone of his voice had changed again:

"I am Stirani, Cain. And I need help. Badly."

I turned and watched him. It seemed that all that strength had drained out of him. I said: "And the police are after you?"

He snorted. "Before I left the States, I told them. I told the D.A., just a few days ago, told him the whole damn story. Alexander Ming used to work for me in the old days, and I told the D.A. all about him too. I gave the D.A. a list of names, of places, a rundown on all Ming's background and current activities."

I said: "Then why didn't they slap you inside?"

He grunted. "You never heard of self-incrimination? Times have changed since the old days. Maybe, if they'd pushed hard enough they could have put me away for a while, if no damned lawyers interfered, and if that was what I wanted. But it wouldn't do any good, so what's the point?" He said sarcastically: "And before you start backing out of this assignment, ask me why it was necessary for Stirani to disappear, why he gave up a racket that was bringing in millions of dollars every month."

I said: "All right, tell me."

"So sit down, for God's sake, and listen." I sat down.

He said shortly: "A man in my position makes plenty of enemies, and one of mine was my old buddy Ming. He turned on me and tried to take over. That wasn't his name in those days, but...I got him put away for life, and he escaped, and he went gunning for me, in his own subtle way. Next thing I knew, my son was hooked on drugs. In brief, it killed him. You didn't know I had a son, did you? How could you? Nobody knew. That's one of the prices you have to pay when you're in the rackets. You keep your kids hidden. He was a good boy, Cain, and they got to him and killed him. So, Ben Stirani retired and put around a story that he was dead, and he came back as Markle Hyde and devoted the next thirty years to helping others, and don't tell me that that doesn't count for something."

I said: "It counts."

"Markle Hyde, philanthropist, the man you could count on if you wanted a hospital built, if a kid wanted an education, if the underprivileged wanted boys' clubs." He said again: "Don't say that that doesn't count."

"And now?"

"Now, the vendetta goes on. When Mark—my son—died, the D.A. got an anonymous tip, thirty-two pages of facts and figures. And Ming, who was just getting to be where I had always been, was put out of business and had to run for his life. He had quite an organization going, and I broke it up for him. And to hell with honor among thieves and all that crap, this was my personal life at stake, my family. And then...then there was peace and quiet, and nobody knew that Markle Hyde and Stirani were the same man, and Markle Hyde went on with his good works, his atonement, until..."

His voice drifted away. He had found a seat in a deep, red-leather sofa and was sitting there, his hands dangling down between his knees, looking suddenly less robust and a lot older. He looked up at me, and his eyes were on fire. He said:

"A daughter too, and they found me at last and got to her. Nearly thirty years later, but vendettas never end, do they? The mixture the same as before. They hooked her on narcotics too. A tough, strong-willed girl, with all of my determination. And still...they hooked her. Oh, they were clever about it. She's a—how shall I put it? She can't keep still for five minutes; she's always off at a moment's notice to the end of the world some place—who knows what for? Give her half an excuse and she's off, at the drop of a hat, to Timbuktu, or Athens, or Lima, or Outer Mongolia for God's sake. She went to Uganda, and came back with malaria, and you know something? In the States we've got the best doctors in the world, but give them a simple case of malaria and they're lost, because it's something they never see, a strange and exotic disease that calls for a specialist. Who gets malaria in the States? So it was a problem. We put her in a hospital, and she only got worse. They gave her Atabrine at first, and then quinine, and still she didn't respond, so I went to the hospital to find out what the hell they were doing to her there. The doctor was puzzled: she was showing symptoms he couldn't understand, coma and short intervals of lucidity, and she said one day that the needle had hurt her arm—only she was being treated orally, no injections at all. The doctor took a quick look at her arm, and promptly gave her some tests, and then just as promptly called the cops."

I'd read about it in the newspapers, just a short, disdainful paragraph two years ago.

I said: "Sally Wentworth, July, the year before last. I read about it."

He said sharply: "You only read what they printed. We stopped publication of what really happened. Wentworth is her married name. It was a marriage that lasted a couple of years and ended in divorce, and he was a vicious, useless son of a bitch with a Boston accent and a taste for good food, a pernickety little bastard who thought the world was made just for him. He married my daughter and treated her badly, so I pulled out all the stops and ruined him, and he dropped back into the gutter where he belonged. Anyway, the cops came, and thank God it was a bright young officer who knew a thing or two. We set a watch on the ward, and that night an intern came in and gave her an injection, only it wasn't an intern at all; it was one of Ming's boys, just a thug, and his hypodermic was full of heroin. God knows how long this had been going on—we never found out because that night he hanged himself in his cell; at least, that's what it looked like. We put Sally on a withdrawal course, the best in the world, with a dozen men standing by her day and night. A specialist from New York, one from India, and another from Japan. She was hooked bad, deep in up to her ears, and they told me she'd never recover—it was too far gone. But she did, by God, she licked it. It took a long, long time, and when she came out, she was so thin and bony that she wouldn't even leave her room for fear of the outside world. She was a skeleton with nothing but dried flesh on her bones. A young and attractive woman, and my God, she looked..."

He stood up and started walking around, gesticulating fiercely. "Have you ever seen a walking skeleton, Cain? I don't mean a very thin woman. I mean a yellow rag stretched over sticks, with black hollows for eyes, a skull that doesn't even seem to have its own skin."

I put down my glass and turned to the window again. There were white puffs of cloud in the blue sky, and the fishermen, the recent danger gone, were back at their nets, their thin, brown hands working expertly with the twine.

Markle Hyde said: "Young and attractive, and as tough as a fresh-cut steak. For a while she was quiet and restrained and withdrawn, and she would look at herself in the mirror and say nothing, And then one day she came to me and said abruptly: 'Alexander Ming is in Macao. I'm going there.' I asked her where she got her information, but she only shrugged and said: 'Information is where you buy it.' And then...then she was gone. She came here, Cain, and I came here looking for her. And there's no sign of her anywhere."

"And Ming?"

He was sharp, the old man. He shook his head and said sadly: "No, all my old contacts are gone, gone a long time ago. I'm out of my depth now."

I said: "But your daughter must have had some. How would she find out about Ming's whereabouts, otherwise? Doesn't that mean she had the kind of friends she ought not to have had?"

He thought about it for a while, fighting back the anger. He said at last: "She's thirty-two now, and that means she had ten or twelve years of at least knowing just who the old crowd was. She must have reached some of them, or she'd have never found out where Ming is, if he really is here. But if he is..." He swung round on me and said violently: "My God, Cain, do you realize what I'm saying? She's gone gunning for the top man of the biggest goddamn racket in history! She's come here, alone, to break up a mob that makes the Mafia look like a Rotarian Convention!"

"Then she's a fool."

"But she's my daughter. And I want her back. I want her back alive and well, and..." All the violence went from his voice, and he said quietly: "If you refuse me, Cain, I'll double the money, and go on doubling it till you accept. I've more money than you'd ever dream one man could acquire in a dozen lifetimes, and I'm giving you a blank check, because you're the only man in the world I can turn to."

I said: "Just tell me what makes you say that. Tell me where you got my name. The man you sent to me in San Francisco was not particularly communicative." He'd been an accountant, the man who had sent me here, a dried-up stick of a man with a bland, persuasive manner; all he had to say meant, in other words, that when a man like Markle Hyde calls for help, you go to him. And here I was.

Hyde said, looking at me shrewdly: "A man I've never met gave me your name. I went to the D.A.'s office for help; and there was nothing they could—or would—do. A friend of a friend put me in touch with Interpol, and they couldn't help much either—how could they? But apparently one of their men knows you...a Colonel Fenrek? He gave me your name and told me about you."

Fenrek was an old friend from Paris, from Interpol's Department B7.

Hyde said: "Fenrek wrote me a letter. He said you could handle this for me if I paid you enough and appealed to what he called your old-fashioned sense of justice."

"Good. Then I know I have nothing to worry about on your account. Fenrek will have had you investigated from top to bottom before he'd mention my name to you." He was a very thorough man, Fenrek; the mention of his name suddenly brought back old, nostalgic memories.

Hyde grimaced. "My past is out now. Markle Hyde is dead, a phantom that served a purpose. Now, we work in the open."

I said emphatically: "No. If you want me to find your daughter, I work alone, I don't want any Stiranis getting in my hair."

"All right, if that's the way you want it."

"Just tell me one thing. You came here looking for her; what did you plan to do? Just make the rounds of the Hotels?"

He sighed. "A man named Bonelli, he owns this house. An old friend, a good friend."

"How careful are you with words?"

"A *good* friend, Cain. For a long, long time."

"Carlo Bonelli?"

He nodded. "You know him?"

"Only by repute. Is he the man you told I was coming here?"

He was suddenly surprised. "Yes, but how did you..." He broke off and said thoughtfully: "Ah yes, that attempt on your life."

"That hopeful assassin called me by name."

"But Bonelli—take my word for it—he had nothing to do with it. I merely asked him, when I got Colonel Fenrek's letter, if he'd ever heard of you."

"And had he?"

There was that old sardonic touch again. "He'd heard. And if you need help, that's the first place to look for it."

It was a famous name in these parts. Bonelli was Italian, an expatriate who'd built up a fortune out of three hundred tons of salvaged potassium nitrate that had found its way to these waters at the end of the Korean War; that's a lot of fireworks in the making, and Bonelli had built a factory first, then switched his interests and founded a chain of fan-tan houses in Macao, Hong Kong, Bangkok, and Singapore; and some said that there were other phases of his business that wouldn't bear too close inspection.

I said: "Am I right in supposing that Bonelli has already made an attempt to find your daughter?"

He nodded. "When I first came here, a few days ago."

"Tell me about him. If he's been a friend for a long time...what about the old days, when you were Ben Stirani?"

"Yes, we knew each other then. He was almost the only man who knew just how Stirani...died, and was born again."

"And he was with you in the rackets?"

Emphatically: "No. As a matter of fact, he hated what I was doing. He'd made his money illegally sometimes, but his trade was not quite as...as vicious as mine, and he tried to get me to give it up. You find that strange, in a man like him?"

"When I get to know him, I'll answer that."

"Well, Bonelli was the man who found Markle Hyde all the papers he needed to start out. My passport, to this day, is a phony; it was made in Istanbul, I believe, by one of those shadowy figures we all used to know so well."

There was a nagging thought at the back of my mind. I said: "Forget the paternal pride for a moment. Just how bright is your daughter?"

He was very sure of himself. He said: "As bright a woman as you'll ever meet, Cain. That's not just a father talking, it's a businessman. If Sally had gone into General Motors, in five years she'd have owned the company. That's how smart she is."

"Then she wouldn't have come all the way here without some nesting place to hide in. Surely she must realize that if she's out to get Ming, pretty soon he'll be out to get her."

"Undoubtedly." He was very calm about it.

I said: "Would she have friends here unknown to you?"

"Maybe."

"And Bonelli knows her?"

"He's never actually met her."

I waved away the silent servant. He came and went all the time, and I wondered why Markle Hyde chose to discuss these private things so openly when the old man was always within such indiscreet distance. I asked him about it, and he smiled and said:

"One of Bonelli's men. I'd trust him with my life. Or with Sally's."

I sat and thought for a while, and Markle Hyde waited and said nothing, letting me take my time to decide. I said at last: "The old organization is back on its feet, now under a man named Ming, and it's a lot more deadly than it used to be, right?"

"Right. In my time, society was against us. Nowadays, it's more permissive. We knew that what we were doing was wrong, and we said the hell with it, look at the money. But these people..." He sighed, "A lot of folks nowadays don't really believe that drugs are all that bad, and so...now, the organization works with much less antagonism, and it's gotten stronger. All they're fighting now is the law, whereas in my time—hell, Cain, you know what it's like nowadays. There's a kind of cynicism around I'd never have thought possible, and good honest folks are saying, well, why shouldn't they experiment if they want to? You know what I mean?"

"And Alexander Ming's headquarters are here, in Macao?"

He shrugged. "He comes and goes, no one ever knows where from or where to. He's refined the art of the sudden disappearance till it's masterly. His poppies are grown in Southeast Asia and Anatolia, but mostly the stuff's refined here. And it's here that the distribution starts, so...yes, his real headquarters are here. But he's everywhere, Cain. And I don't have to tell you what you'll be up against. They've more power than we would have thought possible in my day. And just the same kind of contempt for the life of anyone who gets in their way." He laughed shortly, sardonically, and added: "If it worries you too much, do what I used to do; think of the money."

"Uh-huh." I said: "I'll need your phone number, I'll need photographs of your daughter, and I'll need a rough biography. I want to know her as well as possible, everything you can tell me about her. Take a couple of hours and write it all down. Everything."

"I'll have it by this evening."

"I'm at the Penha Palacio for the time being."

"I'll send it over."

"I want to know her tastes in food, her favorite colors what kind of music she likes, her hobbies."

"Hobbies? She collects stamps."

"She doesn't sound to me somehow like a philatelist."

"One of the best. A very valuable collection, some of them over a hundred and fifty years old."

"The earliest postage stamps date back only to eighteen-forty."

He shrugged. "I don't know about that, I only know what she tells me. Valuable, anyway, does it matter?"

"No, I guess not."

He nodded. "Give me a few hours; you'll have everything."

"And I'll need a good supply of ready cash, quite a lot of it."

"That too."

It was somehow symptomatic of the old man's way of life that we never got closer than this to talking about such prosaic things as a fee. In spite of his lurid, evil past, he was a good man now; I didn't think we should have to go on paying for our sins forever, however bad they were. And one thing was certain; he'd tried hard to make up for it. There was a love there, too, for his daughter that was touching, sad and unsure, and desperate.

I got up and started to leave, and when I reached the door, he said, pleading: "Cain?"

I turned, expecting it.

He said: "Cain, she's all I have in the world. The past is all out now, and Markle Hyde is destroyed, destroyed after all those careful years. But I don't give a goddamn about that. Sally's all that matters. Find her for me, please? Before it's too late?"

I said: "I'll find her."

I used the back door to sneak out of the house, just to be sure, and went over to find Carlo Bonelli.

CHAPTER 2

There are three hundred thousand Chinese and Macanese in Macao and only a couple of thousand Portuguese. But even the latest overtures from the ever threatening mainland, though they had caused considerable change, could not rob the colony of its distinctive Vasco de Gama flavor.

But it seemed to me that in the fan-tan house where I finally ran Bonelli to earth, all those three hundred thousand Orientals were firmly and noisily entrenched. It was called The House of the Seven Hills after the seven hills of the city, and was three stories high, with long, oblong holes cut in the ceilings over the rush-covered tables so that more customers could be accommodated on the upper floors and still watch the games going on below. Upstairs they were shouting out their bets and lowering their money in wicker baskets on long strings, and the huge, brown table tops were bright with the colored metal markers.

The Chinese dealers wore black pajama suits, and they were dipping their brass cones into the piles of button-like, white-bone counters and counting them out in sets of four with small, shiny, ebony sticks; one, two, three, or four buttons would be left over at the end of the count, and great shouts would go up from those who had bet on the right number.

The table was littered with money. I saw Macanese, Chinese, Hong Kong, America, English, and Portuguese currency; I saw a thousand-dollar bill, American, changing hands; and one man was using gold Napoleons and arguing vociferously about their current value.

Bonelli was a tall, thin, elegant sort of European of the old school, a man of forty or so with an easy, watchful smile and an affected manner that did not hide the intelligence in the dark, suspicious eyes. He *swayed* when he moved, and used his long, delicate hands like a ballet dancer. His gray silk suit was impossibly chaste, his mahogany-colored tie impeccably knotted, and he even wore a tiny lilac-colored rose in his buttonhole; it was one of the old Miniature China Roses, of a kind not seen much nowadays, a variety called Sweet Fairy which De Vinck first propagated in 1946, if I remember correctly, and I thought it was a very fitting choice. He carried a long cigarette-holder, and there was the smell of mild Latakia tobacco in the air.

He waved the holder at me, and smiled easily, and said.

"Why don't we go into my office, Mr. Cain?" He wrinkled his delicate nose at the smells here and said: "I really *hate* all this noise, but every shout is another little bundle of notes in the bank, and so I've taught myself to tolerate it."

We moved off, and there were more guards there than there are in Fort Knox. He saw my mild look of surprise and said, as two tight-knit Portuguese in uniform, revolvers at their waists, stepped aside and unlocked a variety of decors for us:

"Really quite necessary, I assure you, Mr. Cain. In my business—unfortunately, wherever a great deal of money is being handled, the undesirables seem to flock in great numbers, and they can really be quite dangerous. But once inside, we're *very* well protected."

The office was a Chinese nightmare. There were ornately carved chairs and benches in polished ebony, with marble inserts and red silk seats, and brass dragons all over, and gilt-framed paintings out of China's ancient history; one of them was a fragment of a fresco that showed a group of *arhats* feeding the poor, a splendid painting on silk that dated, I guessed, from the late twelfth century; I thought it might be by Chou Chi-chang. I asked Bonelli about it, and he smiled and said: "No, his pupil, Lin Ting-kuei. You know about these things?"

I thought that was a damn fool question, so I said nothing.

Over a beautifully sculptured divan, there was an old map that attracted my attention, a delicately painted map in fine black line and water-color. I looked at it for a while and said: "Robert Hart, surely? No one else ever made maps quite so beautifully."

There was a little silence, and when I looked round, Bonelli was examining his fingernails and saying: "They told me you had a rather varied knowledge, Mr. Cain, but, *mannagia la miseria*, what makes you think that's a Robert Hart?"

"It's not?"

He said smoothly: "Just a fake, I'm afraid. A counterfeit."

He gestured at one of the hard chairs, and took one himself when I sat down, and clapped his hands once with the imperiousness of the old-time aristocrat. Two astonishingly attractive young Chinese girls came in, one of them carrying a brass tray with a bright green porcelain teapot on it and two blue porcelain cups. She bowed and set it down beside us and began to pour, and the other girl bowed and waited, half-smiling; Bonelli said: "A little music while we talk, would you like that?"

He spoke to her in a dialect I did not recognize, though I know Mandarin and Cantonese, of course, since I once taught a seminar in Advanced Oriental Studies at the Sorbonne, while I was on loan from Stanford.

The girl bowed again and picked up a dulcimer, the sixteen-string dulcimer they call the *yang ch'in*; she sat down on a silk pillow in the corner and began to strum the instrument softly. It was a pleasant, drowsy sort of sound, almost hypnotic in its soporific effect. We sipped the tea—it was red-leaf congou from South China, and delicious—and Bonelli said:

"Well, do you want to talk about Sally Hyde, or about the man who took a shot at you this afternoon?" Before I could answer, he asked: "Did you get a good enough glimpse of your assassin to see that he was a Northerner?" He somehow made it sound very important.

I grunted noncommittally, and Bonelli said: "Although there's an amusing little game going on that I really must tell you about first, *una cosa molto delicata*." He was sipping his congou tea with. his pinky held out, moving his ballet dancer's waist a trifle, in a gentle, swaying motion, as though he were floating on the delicacy of the room's fragrance.

"Oh? What's that, Signor Bonelli?"

He said carefully: "My business is gambling, Mr. Cain. A few factories here and there which I keep as a reminder of the past and as a cushion against the future. But mostly, my business is in fan-tan houses. We play fan-tan, we play mahjong, we play bird cage, we play the lottery game. The Chinese, as you know, will bet on anything, and at this moment there's a very *exciting* game being played, for quite large bets." His English was delightful, fluent and easy with just the touch of an accent and an unlikely word thrown in here and there with almost a sense of deliberation, as though he did not want to be accused of being English. He said: "The name of this game is: How long before Cabot Cain is killed? And the favored numbers this afternoon are between eighteen and thirty-two. Not days, Mr. Cain, hours. Does that intrigue you?"

It was a shocking thought. I had not been over-disturbed by the futile attempt on my life a little earlier; because somehow—perhaps because of its casual manner—I sensed that it was a warning more than anything else; and warnings always come in threes; it's historic. But I said: "You mean the whole damn colony is interested enough in my presence to make book...Well, I'll be damned."

"Not in your presence, no. But in your death."

The sound of the dulcimer was a comforting, tinkling, drowsy sort of sound. The girl began to sing softly, one of the old love songs in an ancient five-tone scale, and Bonelli, cocking his head to one side and raising his hand for silence, said in a moment: "Did you know that the twelve-pitch scale for the pipes was fixed as long ago as the sixteenth century?"

I said sourly: "Yes. That was done by Prince Chu Tsai-yu, and if you want it, I can give you the complicated mathematical formula he used, though I don't suppose you'd really understand it. But I'd much rather hear why I'm not supposed to last out more than a day or so."

He smiled. "Perhaps you'd like to take one of the bets yourself? A lot of money is going to change hands at the appropriate time." He walked over to the beautifully carved desk, took a little notebook from a drawer, and said earnestly: "If you were to take the number twenty-two, I think you'd stand to make the most profit. Twenty-two is going for eight thousand American dollars just now, and the price will rise very quickly." He checked his watch and said: "It comes home so to speak, at ten o'clock tomorrow morning, and by ten-thirty or so, you would have picked up nearly four and a half times your investment. Twenty-eight will pay more, but its current price is prohibitive, and I wouldn't really recommend it." He snapped the little book shut and smiled delightedly and simpered: "An investment of eight thousand, and tomorrow morning you'd stand to win thirty-five. You could even use some of the money that Hyde is giving you."

I said: "You're getting carried away, Bonelli. Just tell me why, and who."

"The why is easy. The who is easy too, really. Only..." He sat down again on his chair, sitting straight and slim like one of the emperors who had used it before him. He said, holding the tips of his fingers together and frowning at them:

"The most marketable product of Macao, Mr. Cain, is rumor. Accept that, and you will understand everything. We're cut off from the rest of the world here, under constant threat from the mainland, and rumor is our life's blood. All right? Now...Sally Hyde came here a few days ago, went straight from the airport to a bar named The Essence of Heavenly Light, and told the barman that she was looking for Alexander Ming. That's all. She did not even buy herself a drink. She walked over to the bar and said loudly enough for anyone to hear: 'Tell Alexander Ming that Sally Hyde is in Macao, looking for him.' And then she walked out, went round to her hotel, waited for dark, went out again, and she's not been seen since."

"Her exact words?"

"Her exact words."

"And just how surprised was the barman?"

Bonelli smiled. "A good point, Mr. Cain. But unhappily, my informant merely said that the barman just stared at her. Perhaps he is, perhaps he isn't, one of Alexander Ming's men. Her intention might have been for someone else to hear the threat. My informant stressed the fact that she spoke loudly, rather deliberately."

"But you were talking about rumors."

He said gently: "So far, we're dealing with fact. Another fact is that nobody, at that time, was particularly worried by her threat." He shrugged. "An impetuous woman dramatizing a personal neurosis. But then Markle Hyde himself turned up, and the colors began to change. Green to amber. For all his age and his good works, Hyde is still a formidable man." He said discreetly: "No doubt he told you all about his unhappy past?"

I nodded.

"And the past dies hard. So does the formidability. And still, the color was only amber. But then Hyde sent for you, and the color changed to red. A few inquiries were made about you, and nobody really liked the answers that were supplied. So Ming gave out a casual order, kill Cabot Cain; it was as simple as that. And now...now we start with the rumors. Your escape this morning led to an amusing circumstance that is particularly Macanese. Everyone knew, of course, that the young and inept assassin had been put onto you by Ming, and they knew that he had failed. So Ming's office, so to speak, was flooded with applications from ten, twenty, who knows how many, lesser hoodlums, professional killers, pirates, smugglers, all the riff-raff that hangs out here and wastes its time waiting for the chance to turn an honest penny. *I'll do it, Mr. Ming, for a thousand dollars. No, take me, I'm better skilled. We have the best men in the murder business, Mr. Ming, and we'll undercut anyone else's price by twenty percent...*You get the picture? Ming must have sighed to himself and agreed to let whoever was handy handle the job, and then he must have gone back to more pressing business. Intrigued? Yes, I thought you would be."

"It sounds a little casual, wouldn't you say?"

He raised a hand and smiled. "Ah, but so very exciting! A little stimulation to enliven a colony that suffers from the acutest possible boredom. The whole town knows about it, and is delighted. And it's something to bet on. How long will Cabot Cain last?" He sighed and said again: "Are you sure I can't interest you in number twenty-two? I'll make you a special price."

I said: "Just how well informed is Ming?"

"A sparrow falls in Macao, and Ming knows it."

"And he's worried enough about me to put out orders like those?"

"But very casually. So far, you haven't hurt him at all, have you?"

"It might surprise you to know that all I plan to do is find Sally Hyde and take her back to the States."

"Ah, that is the intention. But we all know, don't we, that it's not likely to stop there. One thing might lead to another...The earnest do-gooders are the people who start wars, aren't they? And that's what you are at the moment, Cain, a knight in shining armor ready to do battle for a damsel in distress. You really think it will stop there?"

I said mildly: "No, I don't really. I suppose there just might be complications. Take a wild guess and suggest where she's gone to ground?"

He shrugged. "A very wild guess, that's all it would be. Once she's here...she could be on a junk in the harbor, she could be in Hong Kong, she could be in Red China for all I know. People have a habit here—they come and go as they please, and to the devil with the authorities. So there's really no way of checking."

"In other words, your men haven't been able to find her."

"I didn't really look very hard. Even if I'd found her, the chances of my persuading her to give up her dreams are rather thin."

"You weren't, by any chance, *persuaded* not to look too hard?" I was very polite about it, but I had to know.

He had the grace to laugh. "No, Mr. Cain, nothing like that at all. I pay a token percentage of my profits to Ming's outfits. That's part of the custom too. But it doesn't really mean very much. It's simply that this, for all of us, is the easiest way to survive in the comfort we're all accustomed to."

"The king of the rackets—just suppose Ming knew where Sally was; what then?"

Again, that elegant, I-could-care-less shrug. "In that case, she'd find herself snatched on the streets, bound and blindfolded, and taken to him—or perhaps to one of his lieutenants. He would want to know just why she was so sure that she could find him so easily. That's the crux of the matter, isn't it? I mean, if the police don't know where he is—and I assure you that they don't—then, how come *she* knows that he's here in Macao? This is only one of his little outposts. In other words, Sally Hyde must have information that we don't know about. And Ming would want to know precisely what that information is and where she obtained it."

"Or again, he might just have her killed."

"Perhaps. Life is cheap here, Mr. Cain. I run a fairly respectable chain of houses, as these places go, but there's not one of my staff who wouldn't cheerfully drop you in the bottom of the harbor with an anchor chain round your waist for the promise of a raise. But in this case..." He frowned, "No, in this case it would be necessary to prolong the life just long enough for Ming to find out what he really *has* to know. There's a leak in his organization somewhere, or Sally Hyde would never have come here. And he surely *has* to find out where that leak is. It is not a pretty prospect, is it?"

"No, it's not. We'd better do something about it, fast."

Not exactly backing off, he said: "They tell me you're staying at the Penha Palacio. A comfortable place."

I felt he was trying to tell me something, and I waited.

He said: "But a trifle vulnerable, perhaps. So many people coming and going."

The thought had occurred to me too. I asked him: "Where can I rent a reliable junk with an equally reliable crew?"

"Ah yes, of course, a moat round your castle. I wonder..." He thought for a while, and said at last: "One of my junks is coming into the harbor tonight, en route for Red China. There's no reason why I shouldn't keep it here for a while."

"If you're sure it's nothing urgent."

He said gently: "Just a few guns. Someone stole them from the harbor in Taiwan, and they seemed to finish up in my possession. I can get a very good price for them on the mainland, but there's no great hurry. I don't really like the Red Chinese, and it will do them good to fume for a while."

"That's very kind of you."

"If you anchor below Penha Hill, you'll be in less frequented waters, but there'll still be a sampan or two to watch out for."

"And the crew?"

"My men." It seemed to say everything.

I said: "All right. I have to go to Hong Kong, so as soon as I get back..."

"Hong Kong? How very fortuitous. I'm going there myself. Perhaps you'd like to honor me with your company? A small plane, a

Bellanca, quite comfortable."

"That would be very pleasant. The only thing is...I would like to go fairly soon."

"Now?" He was on his feet, gesturing towards the door.

"Well, I don't feel I should put you to so much trouble."

"Trouble? I wish it were indeed trouble, so that I could more easily deserve your approbation. But it is a pleasure, and you are my guest."

Well, that seemed friendly enough. I said: "If you're sure it won't tear you away from...all this." I made a gesture at the little Chinese girl, and he smiled and said: "She'll still be here when I get back, Mr. Cain." I had a feeling I was being pressured, but he was so impossibly gracious about it that I couldn't refuse. He said cheerfully: "Remember that the longer you live, the more I stand to make on my bets, Mr. Cain. If anyone should be waiting outside for you, I won't make half as much, so let me show you a less obtrusive way out."

I said: "My God, secret passages?"

He shook his head gravely. "Not even secret passages are very secret for very long, not in Macao. This way."

We passed through the noisy fan-tan room again and went down a narrow staircase to the mahjong room, which was even noisier. The black counters were being shuffled loudly to the accompaniment of raucous yells from the winners. And nobody paid us the slightest attention. We went through a long, dark corridor and down some more stairs; and Bonelli opened an iron door with a heavy key; and we found ourselves in a cellar where Bonelli pointed to sacks of carrots piled high along the brick walls.

"Carrots from the mainland," he said. "Imported whisky fetches such a high price here that I prefer to make my own. And there's always the danger that legitimate supplies will be hijacked on the way in. All those junks you saw in the harbor—those that are not engaged in smuggling their own supplies are just as busy holding up those who do. So...we learn to provide ourselves from our own sources wherever we can."

I said: "You're a very enterprising man, Mr. Bonelli."

He inclined his head gracefully, "We live in a criminal world, I'm afraid. It would be absurd not to profit from it, wouldn't you say?"

"That's exactly what I would say."

"And I promise you that you will never drink carrot whisky in *my* house. We make it exclusively for the paying customers, whose tastes are sometimes a trifle provincial."

The long, low room with its whitewashed walls and stone arches could have been one of the great wine cellars in the South of France. There were rows of stacked bottles, and great oak casks, and copper measuring pots, and a dozen *pipettes* hung on the walls, their long glass tubes reflecting the light from small, iron-barred windows. Ten or twelve Chinese women wearing the black pajamas cut from the cloth they call "Fragrant Cloud Linen" were busy pasting labels onto the bottles, and I stopped and read one of them. It was Johnnie Walker's Black Label, and when I raised my eyebrows, Bonelli said smoothly: "Well, the labels are genuine. We have them printed in England; the local printing really isn't very good."

We went down a small flight of stairs again and along a corridor of whitewashed brick, and Bonelli said: "Mind your head." I'm six-foot seven, and low doors are always a nuisance; this one was of heavy iron. He unlocked the door, and we went outside.

We were under one of the wharfs at the edge of the harbor. Across the bay I could see the island of Taipa and, beyond it and a little to one side, the hills of the island of Coloane. The whole colony consists of a mere six square miles, and it is hard to believe that there are over three million people living there; from coast to coast, Macao itself is only a mile across and three miles long.

Away to the northeast, the bright lights in the harbor of Lantao, Hong Kong's "outer island," were just coming on in the dusk. I could hear the shouts of the sampan men close by as they guided their fragile craft over the smooth waters, their women standing straight and slim in the stern with their long, shining, wet poles. I noticed that Bonelli was looking around carefully, peering into the shadows, a slight frown on his handsome, effeminate face.

I said: "Anything?"

He shook his head and then said gravely: "No, but don't take my warnings too lightly, Mr. Cain. You should know that this is a terribly dangerous place for you just now. You are showing an interest in an operation that brings its organizers literally millions of dollars every month. It's a continuing and highly efficient organization that has some of the best executive brains anywhere in the world. Their intelligence setup would put the CIA to shame, though perhaps that wouldn't be very difficult; if you know what I mean. And their terror squads are as well drilled and competent as a Marine Commando. But with one difference: they have no one to answer to for their methods. In the last three months there've been eighteen murders in this little area alone, and God knows how many there were across on the mainland. Not all of them were caused by Ming's outfit, of course; but many of them were, without a doubt. We're back in a seventeenth-century jungle here, and it behooves you to remember that. All of the time."

I said: "I wasn't very impressed with their first attempt. If I'd carried a gun, I could have gotten that would-be assassin before he'd even picked up his rifle."

He said easily: "And doesn't that presuppose that they know you *don't* carry one? I wonder how much they know about you?"

"You've got a point there."

A small motorboat was approaching, a blue and white beauty, with a big outboard motor. A small, wiry Chinese was at the tiller, and he expertly brought the boat close by. He was a small, wiry man. Bonelli looked at him and smiled and said: "You know you have to watch out for the big men, don't you? Yes, of course you do." I wondered what the hell he was talking about.

A few moments later, we were stepping ashore at the tiny airstrip half a mile along the green coastline; and half an hour after that, Bonelli's red and white, single-engine, six-cylinder, fuel-injection Bellanca was touching down at the brightly lit airport of Hong Kong.

Before Bonelli left me to my own devices, we arranged to meet again at midnight, and I went off to see my old friend, Superintendent Mann-Crawford, Special Detail, Her Majesty's Hong Kong Police.

CHAPTER 3

Harry Mann-Crawford was British, of course, and the kind of empire-officer on whom the sun never sets. But he'd been an exchange student at Stanford when, for a short while, I was detoured from my studies of theoretical mathematics to teach physics there. And later, when I was attending the International Conference of Teachers of Oriental Languages in Calcutta, I'd run into him again. I'd told him, back in the old Stanford days: "Forget about physics, Harry, you haven't got the brain for it. Stick to languages, or politics; there's an aptitude there that shows through the veneer of empire..." He was a bright and cheerful young man with a restless sort of *reise-fever* in his blood. He'd taken a job with the Hong Kong police, at first to teach Mandarin and Cantonese, which he spoke marvelously well; and then, after a few years, he'd taken on the semisecret Political Department, and Harry had found his niche at last.

We'd corresponded once in a while over the years, and he was always insistent that he was in my debt because I'd changed his tracks for him.

We sat on the open balcony of the Knoc Chai restaurant and watched the bustle of the hopelessly crowded streets below. Harry said happily:

"It's good, good to see you, Cain. How long is it, five years?"

"Damn nearly. I hear you're a very successful policeman now."

He grinned. "Well, at least I head the department."

"And you know everybody within a hundred miles of here. I need some help, Harry."

He said promptly: "Anything, Cain. Just don't ask me to break too many laws too fast. I don't mind bending them a bit for you."

"I need a woman."

"My God!"

I said patiently: "An English, American, French, German woman—doesn't matter a damn as long as she's not an Oriental. Preferably about thirty years old, preferably skinny and blonde, and preferably intelligent. Essentially, she must he prepared to risk her life in return for a handsome payment, and she must know which side is up. An off-duty policewoman would be ideal. She'll be in great danger for a few days, and then she can go home and spend her tax-free money."

Harry said: "The policewomen here are all Orientals, or I'd have just the gal for you. What sort of danger? That's the first question, isn't it?"

"Mortal."

"Oh."

"I'll be sticking close to her myself, and she'll have an unobtrusive bodyguard as well, but—well, the danger's acute. It needs a woman who has learned the hard way how to take care of herself, who won't panic, and who's been trained at least in some of the arts of survival. Is that too difficult?"

He grumbled: "Bloody impossible."

He stretched out his long legs, and sunk his boyish chin onto his chest, and frowned darkly for a while, and then said: "A Eurasian, would she do?"

"No, she's got to look like an American, even if only superficially."

"There's a tough bitch of a woman who runs a sleazy bar down the road. I'd trust her with my life, but she's fifty years old and looks ninety."

"Won't do, Barry. Thirty, thirty-five. Preferably attractive, preferably sophisticated, and essentially...very tough."

"Does she have to, well, look like anyone in particular? I mean, she's obviously supposed to take someone's place, isn't she?

And doesn't that mean she's got to look like a specific person?"

"Don't guess too hard, Harry. As long as she looks as if she *might* be an American, might *possibly* be thirty-five or 50, might *perhaps* be this other person—but I want it found out pretty damn quickly that she's not, if you get what I mean."

"Before she gets killed off?"

"Something like that."

"Sounds a little unappetizing, old boy. For her, I mean."

"That's why toughness is the prime quality I need."

"Y-e-e-s..." He thought for a while and said at last, perhaps more to break the silence than anything else: "And the fee would be fairly generous, you suggest?"

"She can name her own. There's a hell of a lot of money behind this operation."

"That's going to make it a bit easier, of course. Suppose you tell me what she'd have to do, or is that too indiscreet?"

Harry was never quite sure what I was up to, ever. He had a vague idea that I was in some sort of obscure government service, and my denials didn't help a bit.

I said: "First she'll have to be given a passport in the name of Sally Hyde. You can take care of that, can't you? Yes, of course. Then, she'd have to take the ferry over to Macao, register in a hotel, take in a few nightspots, be seen around, ask a few dangerous questions, and then...Then she has to wait for someone to kidnap her. And that's the someone I'm interested in."

He pulled out a long, curved pipe, a Charatan straight-grain, and began thumbing tobacco into it. He said: "A woman who gets kidnapped always seems to get either raped or shot. Or both."

"Yes, there's always that danger. Probably, the shooting is more likely; sex is cheap enough in these parts. But the likelihood— and likelihoods are the things I deal in—is that this someone will want to find out what the hell she's up to. And, while he's finding that out, I'm finding him. Simple."

"Simple, and dicey as all get-out." I waited for him to translate, but he didn't. He sighed. "I'm going to have to ask it, Cain, Who's the *someone?*"

I said: "Alexander Ming."

He sat up straight and stared at me and said at last: "Good Lord!" I told him that wasn't a very apt comment, and he said: "Yes, but...Good God, that means the drug business. Or one of his other rackets?"

"Just Ming, personally."

"Good God. I hope you know what you're doing."

"Yes, I do. Two things. First of all, with a phony Sally Hyde wandering around, the real one, who's in hiding somewhere is going to surface."

He said quickly: "You can't be sure of that."

"It's a likelihood. And secondly, Ming is going to try and find out what she's up to too. That much is certain. And that means in the last analysis, that he's got to show at least a part of his organization. That's all I want, a lead that's concerned with this particular part of his operations." He was a very worried man, Harry, and I leaned into him and said: "Alexander Ming and Sally Hyde are on a head-on course towards a bloody battle, and I've got to stop it before it starts, for obvious reasons. The real Sally Hyde has gone to ground, and if I dangle another one under Ming's nose, he's going to show his hand even if she doesn't. And, with any luck, they both will; and then I can step in between them. It's all very simple."

"My God."

There was a long silence. He said then, moodily: "Your generous fee has just shot up by about five hundred percent. That is, if she has to know the score."

"She has to know it. It's not only necessary; it's also only fair that she should."

"And how soon do you want her?"

"The sooner the better. If she could get to Macao in a day or two..."

"The passport will take a few hours. Does it have to stand inspection?"

"Superficial."

"We have a department for that sort of thing. They're very good." He said suspiciously: "And we'd need it back when you've finished with her."

"Sure."

"No problems of resemblance? Look-alike, that sort of thing?"

"Skinny and blonde is enough. They'll find out soon enough that she's not the real Sally Hyde, but that's what I want. I just want the name floated around. I want someone to say: *this woman might or might not be Sally Hyde, and if she is not, then what the hell goes on?* A little confusion always seems to confuse, doesn't it?"

He nodded absently. There was something on his mind. I called for more drinks to fill in the gap; and when the waiter had brought us Courvoisier in the thinnest snifters I had ever seen and had gone back into the shadows, Harry took a deep breath and said: "All right, I think I've got just the gal for you."

"Ah. Do tell."

"She's twenty-seven, sophisticated, attractive in a dangerous sort of way, and thoroughly armor-plated. You may have quite a job handling her, but for the right kind of money—it would have to be quite a lot."

"No problem. Promise her the sky if she wants it."

"And how much can I tell her?"

"Everything I've told you. The more the word gets around of what I'm up to, the better I like it." I looked at my watch. "I'm due at the airport at midnight; is there time to go and see her now?"

Harry smiled and shook his head. "Where she lives, no visitors this time of night. She's in jail."

"Oh? On what sort of charge?"

He laughed. "Here, we call it pandering. You probably call it white slavery, or something equally dramatic."

"I didn't think that was very illegal in the Orient."

Harry said rather pompously: "British territory, old boy. Anglo-Saxon morality, all that bloody nonsense. I'll have her on the ferry tomorrow afternoon. Fair shakes?"

"Fair shakes, whatever that means. What's her name?"

"Bettina. Bettina Harkan."

"Nationality?"

He grimaced. "None. One of the unfortunates. No known nationality. Born in Canton of Armenian parents. Her home is Hong Kong, and she lived a long time in the States. A long time."

"Ah, then her English is at least good."

"Hardly, old boy. An American accent as ripe as your own."

I sighed. That's the trouble with the English. Surround them with the panoply of empire, Sam Brown belts, and khaki shorts, and they can't remember that they lost that war.

He said: "She's an attractive sort of woman, Bettina, if a little highly polished. But she's been tied up with almost every racket in these waters at one time or another, and we've constantly warned her to keep out of trouble or get picked up. But we've never really been able to pin anything on her until recently." He said, suddenly suspicious: "I'll get her back when all this is over, won't I? She's got a three-year sentence to serve."

"Suppose we talk about that when the time comes?"

He hesitated, a trifle worried, and then he said cheerfully: "Oh well, it's the first favor you ever asked of me. All right, when the time comes. Just remember that a Queen's pardon isn't normally given for service to individuals. I'll be sticking my neck out a long way."

I said gently: "That's what necks are for, Harry."

We had some more Courvoisier together and talked about old times, and then I asked him: "What do you know about Carlo Bonelli?"

He shrugged. "No businessman who makes Bonelli's kind of money in this part of the world can really be very honest. Fireworks factories, gambling houses, a bit of smuggling on the side. Nothing really too bad, though he's inclined to be *non grata* here too. Just inclined a little, we've never really tried to bar him from the colony."

"Can I trust him?"

"No."

"Well, that sounds hopeful. My life seems to be in his hands at the moment."

Harry said earnestly: "Well, watch him carefully, Cain. Very carefully."

"And if you had to look for Alexander Ming, where would you start?"

Harry said piously: "I'd resign my commission and go and breed chickens somewhere. Never did want to finish my life floating face down in the harbor. But for what it's worth, Ming comes and goes with the most absolute impunity. Hong Kong, Macao, Istanbul, San Diego. Nobody ever knows where he is until he's not there anymore.

There's a rumor around that he is in Macao at this moment, but that probably means he's gone already, if he really was there. He has an uncanny knack of just dropping out of sight."

"The masterly art of the sudden disappearance?"

"Yes. And then, unexpectedly, he turns up again from nowhere, just when we've decided he's back in the States or somewhere."

"Doesn't that presuppose a hideout close by?"

Harry shrugged. "Of course. One of the junks in Macao harbor, probably. Or even in Red China, who knows? But there's some backing this time for the rumor. That he's in Macao, I mean."

"Oh?"

"The word is that the outflow of prepared heroin is somehow getting much heavier."

"Just recently?"

"Yes. It might mean that Ming is settling down over there, taking a more personal control."

"Good. Just as long as it keeps him there."

"And you might like to know that a very large load of heroin has just left these waters for the States."

"Oh?" I said: "Shouldn't we tell someone about that, while we're here?"

Harry leaned back and said dreamily: "An informer has been scheduled to tell your narcotics boys precisely where it's going to be landed. On the islands off Santa Barbara, California. Then it's to be taken in small bundles to the mainland in lobster boats at a later date."

"An informer? One of yours?"

"No, dear boy. One of Ming's."

"Oh. And the real landing point?"

"W-e-l-l...under that cover story, there's another one which won't reach their ears quite so readily. Has to do with a group of American draft-dodgers in Canada who think they're merely carrying marijuana. But *that* story isn't true, either. The truth is that it's to be landed in Los Angeles itself, hidden inside the hollowed-out blocks of eight brand-new Japanese motorcars." He said glumly: "Unless that's a cover story as well. We can't be sure. But we've given all the versions to your fellows; let them sort it out; they're better at that sort of thing than we are."

"So business for Ming is looking up."

"And for a thousand miles around, every police force is girding its loins for trouble. Watch out, Cain. I'd hate to see you tangle with him too closely."

We got up and wandered out onto the noisy nighttime street, and Harry said, worried:

"I'm not going to mention Ming to Bettina. If you want to, that's your pigeon. But I won't, or I'll never get her on that ferry. If she thinks Ming's involved in this, she'll never touch it with a ten-foot pole."

"All right. Send her over, and I'll tell her myself."

"And she'll come smartly back on the first boat."

"We'll see. There's at least a likelihood that I can persuade her."

"You're an incurable optimist, Cain."

I told him: "No. But I know what a woman can do when she has a reason to do it. I'll supply the reason."

We found Harry's police car, and he drove me over to the airport. Bonelli looked at me a trifle hard when I made the introductions. Harry treated him with a great deal of respect tinged with a certain touch of one-day-we'll-get-you-too. I asked Harry if he were a betting man, and he looked surprised, and I said:

"Do you play the horses?"

He grimaced, "Sometimes. Can't really afford it, not on my salary."

I asked him: "How much money do you have on you now?"

He fumbled and came up with a hundred Hong Kong dollars, and I took it from him and said to Bonelli: "A hundred dollars on twenty-two for Superintendent Mann-Crawford." Bonelli beamed and wrote out a little receipt, and I said to Harry: "A good horse coming in at ten o'clock tomorrow morning; it pays odds of nearly four and a half to one."

For a moment, he looked suspiciously as though he thought I was trying to bribe him; but then he realized that this couldn't be so, and said: "Good, long time since I backed a winner."

We made our farewells, and in a moment we were airborne

again.

And by one o'clock in the morning, we were passing once more through the noisy mahjong room on the way to Bonelli's office. We found out that the junk he was expecting had been delayed 'by the need for evasive action' and would not be arriving until the morning, and Bonelli insisted that I spend the night in his quarters; he had an investment to protect.

"By tomorrow night," he said, "you'll be taking your own chances on your own junk with your own crew of bodyguards. And chances, Mr. Cain, are what brings me in the fortune I have become accustomed to."

The room he gave me was a wild chimera in scarlet silk and black ebony, and it contained a huge carved bed covered by a shining teak canopy and framed with ivory-inlaid screens. The walls were hung with landscapes, one of them by no less a personage than Ma Yuan, and there was a splendid tapestry by the artist-Emperor Hui Tsing. There were two young Chinese girls to bring me drinks and run my bath in a magnificent room of highly polished red teak that was as smoothly worn as old alabaster and that reflected the dim lights of the sweetly scented candles. I luxuriated in the bath for an hour, with the two girls pouring in more hot water as I needed it. Then, later, I did pushups for thirty minutes and sat down to study the file that Markle Hyde had sent over on his daughter's life history, her foibles, her dreams, her whims, and her talents. And with it, there was the thickest bundle of currency I had ever seen all at once. When I had finished reading the file, it seemed to me that I knew her quite a lot better; he'd done a good job, her father. The last page of the file was a plea: "Please, Mr. Cain, get her back."

I slept in a pair of borrowed pajamas of bright blue Shantung silk and did not wake up till ten in the morning.

And at noon, when I was sipping the tea that one of the girls brought me—a semifermented oolong from Foochow—Bonelli came in and said excitedly:

"Sally Hyde has turned up, Mr. Cain. She came in on the ferry half an hour ago and has gone to the Pesha Palacio."

I said: "Came in? From Hong Kong?"

He looked at me very suspiciously, and thought for a while,

and stroked his nose with a delicate finger, and said: "Ah...I see. Then perhaps I shouldn't go over and see her? Or even call her father?"

I said happily: "Why don't we let her unpack her bag first."

He looked at me shrewdly and said: "You're a devious man; aren't you?"

"Just planted a couple of seeds to see what would sprout."

"Dragon's teeth, perhaps? You realize that, whoever the young lady is, she's not likely to last for very long, don't you? I hope you consider her quite expendable."

"Just as little expendable as I am myself, Signor Bonelli."

"Good, that's a comforting thought. I was worried momentarily. Perhaps I should have known better. Did you sleep well?"

"Excellently, thank you."

"And the girls took good care of you?"

"Splendid care."

"And your junk is ready. After lunch, I'll run you over there. It's not far. And, oh yes, your friend Mann-Crawford."

"Harry?"

"His horse came in at ten o'clock this morning, didn't it? I've sent over his winnings."

"Good old Harry. He's going to twiddle that mustache all day and wonder if it's a bribe of some sort. And then he'll pay it to the Police Benevolent Fund, just in case."

Bonelli said, with great sympathy: "It takes all kinds to make a world, doesn't it?"

We walked over to the Palacio together, and I noticed that he was keeping a very sharp lookout. And I also noticed that we were being followed. There was an unattractive man keeping his distance behind us, a roughly dressed Portuguese with more scars on his visible body than I would have thought possible to acquire in a lifetime. A sailing man, by the looks of him. I was about to tell Bonelli about it, when suddenly two youths on bicycles appeared from nowhere and came swooping down towards us, moving quite fast, as though they were racing each other; one of them swerved and almost, but not quite, collided with me, and I saw that there was a long knife in his hand and a wild and greedy look in his eye. The hand went back and up; and I was on the verge of picking him up and throwing him away, when the unattractive man behind me stepped forward; and I thought for a moment that I might be in trouble. But then, the two cyclists were suddenly caught together in the thick arms of the sailor type, and their heads were smashed hard together, and they were pushed bodily out of the way; but both recovered quickly and got up and ran, hard, and then the sailor was just as suddenly gone before I could even begin to ask him what was happening. I looked at Bonelli.

Quite unmoved, he was examining the rose in his buttonhole, a beautiful little white cup-shaped Soulieana; he raised his eyes to me and said: "I wonder if I should have told you? That was Ericeira."

"Ericeira?"

"The skipper of your junk. He's keeping an eye on you. I felt sure you wouldn't mind. You don't, do you?"

I said politely: "Let me just tell you how impressed I am with his competence. I'm a competent sort of man myself, but four fists, no doubt, are better than two."

"I'm so glad you feel like that."

The skipper had faded away, completely. Bonelli left me at the hotel, and when I asked for Sally Hyde, I was shown up to a top-floor suite overlooking the magnificent panorama of the harbor.

And there, sitting at the dressing table in a marvelously ornate kimono, brushing her long, fair hair in front of the mirror, was an attractive, svelte, and impossibly well-poised woman. I closed the door behind me and leaned against it, and she looked me over from head to foot, very slowly and completely, with a hard, controlled expression in her eyes. The hand that held the brush had stopped, and now it moved on again in long and rhythmic sweeps. She said nothing, and she did not take her eyes off me, and it seemed that she was sizing me up at her leisure.

But behind her, a little to one side, the door to the other room was open. And there, a shadow moved slightly, and a young girl came forward. She stood in the doorway and looked at me. She was holding a revolver.

She looked about sixteen or seventeen years old, though it's hard to tell with the Cantonese women. And she was undoubtedly one of the most beautiful women I'd ever seen, and I've seen a good number of lovely women in my time. She had the slender, willowy hips of the Cantonese, and smooth ivory skin with a not quite Chinese look to it.

She wore the tight silk sheath with the slit skirt that they call the *cheosonq*, with a rather higher collar than was correct—a style usually reserved for the prostitutes. Her waist was so slight that I could easily have put my two hands around it, fingers touching. And her hand was steady as a rock, with a long-barreled Bayard .38 pointed straight at my groin.

The woman at the dressing table said at last: "Well, you're the biggest goddamn son of a bitch I ever saw, and I suppose that makes you Cabot Cain. I'm Bettina Harkan."

She turned to look back in the mirror, and looking at the young girl's reflection, she said casually: "All right, Mai. This couldn't be anybody else. Piss off."

The young girl tossed the gun casually to the woman at the dressing table and moved towards me, heading for the door, her eyes cast down as though she didn't want to look me in the face. She was very tall for a Cantonese, but she moved in absolute silence in her cloth shoes, like a cat. As she reached the door, I stepped aside and put a hand on her shoulder gently. She stopped and looked up at me, her deeply slanting eyes expressionless. But I felt an inexplicable tensing of her body.

I said: "Mai?"

For a moment, she held my look. Her eyes were smiling suddenly, though her lips did not move. She said at last, her voice very soft and musical: "Mai Cho-sing, Mr. Cain." She made a little gesture that was almost a bow, and opened the door; and before she went out, she looked at me again with an almost surreptitious smile; and then she was gone.

And as I watched her moving silently down the corridor, I heard Bettina Harkan say, her voice hard and decisive and sarcastic: "If you can take your eyes off that skinny little tart for one minute, Cain, let's talk business."

I closed the door and went over and sat on the edge of the bed for a chat with Bettina.

CHAPTER 4

The Palacio is a good hotel. The rooms are large and airy, and they have old-fashioned fans in the ceiling that keep the air moving and give at least the illusion of cool in the stifling, humid heat.

The pastel-painted houses along the Praia Grande, pale blue, pale pink, and pale yellow, and shaded by dark-leaved trees, could be seen through the big, open windows.

Beyond them, the water was green and shining, and the saffron-colored junks were painted on canvas as they swung at anchor. Somewhere, a brass band was playing on the street; there were always raucous noises in these parts.

I said: "Yes, indeed, I'm Cabot Cain. Who's the young girl?"

Bettina said tartly: "Young girl? She's older than I am. Don't let that milky white skin fool you. She's my *amah*, my servant, my bodyguard, too, and from what that bastard Mann-Crawford told me, I'm going to need one. What about the money?"

"He made a deal with you, the Superintendent?"

She picked up an envelope from the dresser and tossed it to me. It had been opened carelessly, though there was an elaborate red seal on the back. It was a note from Harry:

This will serve to introduce Miss Bettina Harkan, the lady whom we discussed. She has agreed to work for you, in the capacity you outlined, for five hundred dollars a day; American, not Hong Kong, I'm afraid. She's undoubtedly going to tear this open and read it, in spite of the official seal, so I'll say no more except that she's really quite a reliable person in spite of her many faults. Good luck. I hope you get along together as nicely as brother and sister. Harry.

I put the letter away; the image of the young Chinese girl was still with me, somehow more startling now than it had been at first. I said: "For a bodyguard, I'd have expected someone a trifle less fragile."

"Fragile?" she snorted. "She could break you in two, Cain, in spite of those God-awful muscles of yours. Before they shot him for hijacking the payroll, her father was combat instructor to the Canton Security Force, and she could throw him around like a rag doll. What about the money?"

"You know what you have to do?"

She did not answer, but just sat there waiting imperiously, so I made a gesture and handed her my wallet. I said: "A few days' pay in advance? Help yourself, dearie." I was carrying fifteen hundred dollars in cash, and she took the lot and handed the wallet back to me, for which I was grateful.

She said casually: "I'm supposed to show myself around town and pretend I'm this broad of yours. What am I supposed to do when some bastard takes a shot at me?"

I said: "Duck."

She laughed suddenly, and the laugh transformed her face completely; she looked a good deal more pleasant. Then she relaxed again and said: "Well, it won't be the first time."

"It might well be the last."

She was very tense all of a sudden. She said flatly: "Then there's something that bloody cop didn't tell me, is that it?"

"The man gunning for you is Alexander Ming. Does that worry you?"

Again, there was a freezing of motion, and then she went on brushing that long hair rhythmically and with a great deal of concentration. She said finally: "There's always a catch, isn't there? I wondered why you were so free with the money."

I asked her again: "Does it worry you?"

She said easily: "Of course it worries me, you stupid bastard." She looked at me sharply and said: "You don't know much about the seamy side of life, do you, or you wouldn't ask a stupid question like that. In my world, you worry about every bastard who'd like to stick a knife up your arse. Because, if you *don't* worry, you don't survive; but I suppose a thought like that never occurred to you."

I said: "Are you backing out before you've given it a try?"

"No." She waved the bundle of money at me. "Just keep the currency rolling in; it's a mighty cure for all ailments."

"All right. And a fat bonus when we're through."

"Unless I get killed."

"If you get killed, I'll have saved myself that little bit extra, won't I?"

She laughed again, unexpectedly, and said: "You're all right, Cain. I like you. And when this is over, if you want to join my operation, I'll take you in with me. Room and board and the pick of the broads, how does that sound?"

She leaned in to the mirror and started making up her eyes. They were dark, dark blue, almost black. She said thoughtfully: "Alexander Ming...I owe that bastard a turn or two."

"Oh? How come?"

She said with a shrug: "He gets a cut of my operation. He gets a cut of everybody's operation. Pay up, or else look out."

I didn't like the sound of that and said so. "If you pay these dues, isn't it likely that they'll know you?"

She said: "Pooh. One of my minions pays one of their minions; lower-echelon stuff—it's no problem. And that's in Hong Kong, not Macao, and the compartments are kept watertight."

"He must be a very popular man around town, Alexander Ming."

Bettina said: "You want to run gasoline into Red China, or bring girls from Bangkok, or hijack guns outside Takow, you pay a cut to Ming, or the pirates are there waiting for you." She stared at me suddenly and said: "Yes, that makes him pretty unpopular; but don't kid yourself; you won't easily find people to work against him."

"But you will."

"For money, yes. I hate his guts, and I don't like his main

source of income very much either."

"Drugs?" I was absolutely sure I wasn't making a comment.

But she turned on me almost accusingly. "All right, I'm probably the most immoral bitch you ever laid eyes on, but my commodity is sex, Cain, and sex never killed anyone. It never turned a woman into a sniveling, gut-rotted animal; and if you've never seen what Ming's product can do, then don't try to tell me how wicked I am. My business keeps them clean and healthy and happy; yes, happy, for God's sake, because they're no good to me any other way, but Ming—that bastard. Have you ever seen anyone who can't get off the stuff?"

"I've seen. And I'm not trying to lecture you. How well do you know Macao?"

"I've been here a dozen times before." She turned and grimaced at me. "How's that?"

"How's what?"

"The eyeshadow, idiot?"

"The eyeshadow's fine. Then you're known here?"

That shrug again. "Only in the best circles. I usually change my name if I move around too much. In my racket, it isn't always healthy for everyone to know just who is where, when. There's always some jerk trying to move in on me every time some pretty little teenager comes to my nest. It's bad enough with the big boys."

I wasn't about to say a word, but Bettina said swiftly: "They come to me out of the slums, starving, barefoot, and covered all over with lice, without a hope in the world for anything—until I get my hands on them. Then they get fed, and cleaned up, and clothed, and well looked after, and they make good money. And all they're doing is what they've been trained from babyhood to do; only when they're working for me, they're doing it with a guy who washes, and not some filthy, stinking peasant who hasn't had a bath since the day his grandmother dropped him in the stinking harbor. Once they've been with me for a couple of weeks, my girls wouldn't go back to what they came from for all the tea in China. And neither, if you'd seen what that's like, would you."

Well, that was quite a speech.

I rang for room service and said: "What about a drink? Gin?

Scotch? Or whatever?"

"Scotch, dearie."

"Soda?"

"No soda. Soda makes my ankles swell up."

The man came and I ordered a bottle of Haig and Haig and some ice; and when he had brought it and we were sitting there like old friends, I gave Bettina a list of night clubs together with the precise times she was supposed to spend at each one.

I said: "I want to know exactly where you are at each minute of the day. You start at eleven tonight, and you keep it up till dawn, and when it looks right you ask somebody, anybody, if he knows where you can find Alexander Ming. That's all; just—*Where can I find Alexander Ming?* You come home at dawn, and you do the same thing tomorrow night, and the night after, and keep on doing it till we get some action. Play the tables, spend a little money, and don't forget that your name is Sally Hyde. Now, your companion is a problem, Sally Hyde wouldn't be toting a Chinese girl around with her."

Bettina said flatly: "Where I go, Mai goes."

"So I'll see that there's a man handy to keep an eye on you."

"I take her with me, Cain. That's all there is to it."

Well, I didn't think it would matter very much. I said: "Okay, then make at least a pretense that she's showing you around, a guide, a personal friend, that sort of thing."

"That's exactly what she is, a personal friend. And does *that* bother *you?*"

"Oh. Well fine. But I'll have a man behind you anyway. If anything untoward happens, get word to him fast, and he'll get it to me. Unhappily I stand out in a crowd, so I can't stick too close to you."

"I'll bet." She said: "There's just one thing. What makes you think they'll try to pick me up rather than just...knock me off. Mann-Crawford seemed to think you were pretty sure about that."

I said carefully: "Two things. They just might believe you really are Sally Hyde, in which case they'll pick you up because Ming will want to know how come Sally Hyde knows so much about his movements. Or, on the other hand, they might realize at once that you're not; in which case they'll want to find out what the hell goes on and who put you onto them and why. In either event, they'll snatch you and try to make you talk. I don't have to tell you the risk is considerable, so keep your wits about you."

I saw her shudder. She lost her composure for a moment and muttered: "You'd better keep that money coming in, that's all."

I said: "Sally Hyde must have a friend, or friends here, someone who told her Ming was here. She's not the kind of woman to race off on a wild goose chase without some sort of knowledge. That's the bit of knowledge that they'll want to drag out of her."

She was standing in front of the mirror, stroking her fine breasts. She said moodily: "They stick bamboo slivers in you and set fire to them." Her hands stayed on her breasts as she turned to look at me solemnly, questioningly.

I said gently: "I'll take good care nobody hurts you, Bettina."

She was suddenly her old self again, and she said sharply: "Mai will do that."

I said, worrying about it: "I don't want to pull any punches. It wouldn't be fair."

"I know. If you did, I'd get up and go, and the hell with you and your money. So, don't ever hold back on me, Cain. As long as this lasts, keep up the honest boy scout bit, it comforts me. And talking about comfort, you want to take me to bed?"

I said politely: "Not right now, dear."

"Okay, just an idea. You want Mai?"

"Later, maybe."

"Just say the word."

"Tell me about her, Bettina. I can't believe you regard her as...for God's sake, as a bodyguard. All ninety pounds of her."

Bettina slopped some ice into our glasses and filled them with Scotch. She lay back on the bed with her shoulders on the pillows and sipped her drink and said:

"Mai's more than she seems, a lot more. When they killed her father two years ago, she came to me for work. There's not much for a good-looking broad like Mai to do in these parts that pays better than what I could offer her, and she knew it; only...my God, at twenty-eight she'd never been to bed with a man in her life, can you believe that? In this day and age? And she didn't really want to, but I thought what the hell, she'll learn, and then...Well, I found out that she had some unexpected talents, very considerable talents. Her father had taught her how to use a gun, and use it well, and she has a black belt in karate too. Her old man was as tough as a bag of hobnails. He taught the terror squads over on the mainland how to keep the good guys subservient to the bad guys...Anyway, just about this time one of the secret societies was trying to horn in on my business, and they'd sent one of their thugs round to see me. This jerk was going to rough me up because I told them all go to hell. He had a knife, the ugly little bastard. Well, Mai was there, and the moment he pulled out his blade she snapped his arm in two places with the flat of that tiny little hand, ruined him for life with a sharp kick in the balls, and then threw him out, clear through the second-story window. So I figured there might be better things for her than tarting around with the rest of them. She's been with me ever since. Companion, bodyguard, call it what you like."

Was I being old-fashioned? I said: "I still find it hard to believe she's all that good."

Bettina shook her head stubbornly. "Whether it makes sense or not, take my word for it. You get into a fight, and in my business that happens all the time, Mai's worth any ten men I know. I don't care what the opposition is, or what they're fighting with, Mai will take them, but good. For God's sake, you've never heard of warrior women before?"

"All right. And what happens when she learns that the opposition is Ming?"

Bettina said sourly: "You don't have much of an opinion of women, do you, Cain? First me, then Mai. Take my word for it, neither of us is going to wet her pants on account of Ming."

"So that's all right then." I got up to go and turned back to look at her lying there with one arm behind her head and sipping her whisky. I thought that at this moment, at certain angles, her hard face was quite attractive, even beautiful; it was a face with past agonies etched deeply into it, agonies that had been overcome but never quite forgotten. The softness had gone, and it is the touch of softness in a woman that makes for true beauty. She looked terribly vulnerable, and I hoped I wasn't being too optimistic about her chances.

I said: "Start out at eleven this evening, but wait till I come back here first. I want you to see that man who's going to be close behind you, the man you yell for if anything happens."

She nodded gravely.

"So...see you around ten-thirty or so. Don't leave this room till then. Chances are it's all over town that Sally Hyde's in port."

I went outside, and there, sitting on a window seat at the end of the corridor was the fragile Mai, backlit with her lovely face half in shadow. Her deep brown eyes watched me as I walked away towards the wide stairway; when I looked back, she was still watching me, not moving at all, just sitting there demurely with her hands in her lap. On an impulse, I went back and spoke to her.

I said: "You know the danger you're liable to be in?"

Her childlike face was solemn, composed, unemotional. As I looked at her, she smiled and then laughed, showing her very even teeth shining brightly against the red of her mouth.

She said: "Yes, I know the danger, Mr. Cain, for all of us. You too. For you more than anyone."

"Oh? Why so much for me?"

"This is our life, Mr. Cain. We move all the time among people you probably never meet except once in a lifetime. Not nice people. This is a very hard place, and I don't think you know that yet."

"I know it." It was hard to talk to her; she looked like a child.

She said: "Remember it always. It is better."

I wondered if she knew more than I did about all this. Come to that, I wondered if *everybody* knew more than I did. As I went back to the stairs, I reflected that, in this evil place, I was working for an ex-narcotics king, and my allies were whores and panderers and a man whom the Hong Kong police would dearly like to get their hands on. But in this sink of iniquity, these were precisely the people I needed. But I was, I thought, none the less the gullible newcomer ready to be stepped on the moment he got too worrisome.

It seemed wise to take the back way out of the hotel. I went through the kitchens, where a number of eyes were raised in surprise, and out onto the narrow passage that ran down behind the hotel.

But getting into the habit can be a bad habit. I should have used the front entrance, where there were crowds and the relative safety that crowds imply. Because the moment I stepped out into the bright sunlight, I saw that I'd made a mistake. That's where they were waiting for me.

There were four of them. Big men, from the North. Big, that is, for Chinese; not one of them came up as high as my chin, nor came within thirty pounds of my weight. And I remembered, inconsequentially, Bonelli's cryptic remark: *You know you have to watch out for the big men, don't you?* It hadn't meant much at the time; but now, with the clarity of sudden panic, I remembered one of those tinkling bells—Ming was an American, of Chinese origin. But the Chinese part of him came from the North, from Shantung, where the men, unlike the small and light-footed Cantonese of the South, are big and burly and muscular. Look out for the Northerners, Bonelli was saying. They're liable to be Ming's men. They stick together, these men from the North.

And there they were, all four of them. Not a weapon in sight, but somehow full of menace. Their leader, a barrel-chested man who wore khaki shorts and an off-white T-shirt, had arms like the legs of a cart-horse; and tattooed on one of them was the cypher that meant, in the old language of Shantung: *One hundred and seven.* It all came back to me at once.

There was a lot of history in that symbol; and it was terrifying history.

As I looked from one to the other of them, they began to move in on me.

CHAPTER 5

You probably don't know about the Wuh-keis. They're a fighting race of Chinese from up North, somewhat akin to the Sikhs of India, the dissenting sect of the Brahmanical Hindus, in that they have long regarded their vocation as fighting and not much else. But there, all similarity ends.

They were a Chinese tribe, the Wuh-keis, who lived beyond the Great Wall some two thousand years ago, a tribe that the Chinese Court historians, because they were never subdued, called barbarians. They devoted their entire lives to combat, and specifically, after the beginnings of the Great Legend, to unarmed combat—a form of fighting called *Sha-hai*. In modern Chinese, *Sha-hai* has come to mean 'killing', and with good cause.

The Great Legend said that in the eighth century, the Wang-ti, or Emperor of China, had conferred the title of Prince on the surviving head of the Wuh-keis after nearly thirty years of constant fighting; this was meant to be a noble gesture in admiration of the Wuh-keis' skill and obstinacy. But the Wuh-keis had regarded the title as imposing some sort of vassalage, had called their forces together, and had gone on a terrible rampage, breaking out of their valley-state on the banks of the River Liao and taking on the rest of the world in general. The Emperor's armies had invaded the river valley and had almost wiped out the Wuh-keis in a battle that raged for one hundred and seven days. But when he was finally victorious (with an army of two hundred and eighty thousand men behind him), the Emperor had made another noble gesture; he spared the lives of the hundred and seven best Wuh-kei fighters, one for every day they had held out against him, and had formed them into a special cadre of personal bodyguards. But he had taken the precaution of issuing an edict that their weapons were to be locked up at night—another insult the warriors weren't about to tolerate. So, for a hundred and seven token days, they had submitted to this indignity; and then, on a given signal, they had risen up and slaughtered every man woman and child in the Emperor's Court. With their bare hands.

Under their chief, Ha-to, they had escaped back to the Shan-a-lin, the Long White Mountain, and taken refuge in the high gorges. And ever since, the Great Legend went, the Wuh-keis had scorned the use of any weapon.

When I was conducting a course at the Institute for Oriental Military Studies some years ago, I had met one of the still legendary Ha-to family who now called himself Jennis Hatto and had learned from him a great deal about the old tradition. He told me, Jennis, that male babies in the Shan-a-lin were exposed on the bare mountain, naked in the snows, in a process that seemed, with some success, to weed out the weaklings. And before puberty, they were set out naked in the forest a hundred miles from home and expected to return before the moon changed, fully clothed, riding a horse, and carrying a spear or bow that was then ceremonially broken at the puberty rite itself.

And even today, the few surviving Wuh-keis still carry on their forearm the mystic and now much-dreaded symbol *107*; and each one of them still spends his entire life practicing his own specific art of combat, the *Sha-hai*. It consists, quite simply of reliance upon muscular efficiency developed to an astonishing peak of speed and power. The classic killing format, for example, is a grip with the left hand on the opponent's throat, a grip with the right of his thigh, a raised right knee and a smashing, downward blow that quickly breaks the poor bastard's back. It is called the *Sheng-ta*, and is numbered six in the *Sha-hai* progression. It demands, of course, a fantastic strength and coordination because, while all this is going on, the opponent probably isn't exactly standing still for it. He could be wielding a gun or a knife or a sword; but that doesn't matter very much to the Wuh-keis; it's there fast; one, two, three, and drop the body.

Strength and coordination? Jennis Hatto showed me. He wrapped a half-inch Manila rope round his right fist and smashed it into an ordinary, standard American brick wall. And while I watched, astonished, it took him fifteen minutes to batter a hole clean through it. I learned a lot from Jennis about the Wuh-keis. And now, I was getting a chance to watch them in action, but from quite the wrong standpoint.

They stood there, the four of them, with the leader ahead of the others, one to the left, one to the right, and the fourth man standing in reserve. It was the leader I was concerned with: the others, I knew, would not raise a hand unless their leader went down, and at the moment that didn't seem very likely. He stood there with his feet well spread, his body crouched, his hands resting lightly on his knees. The hands were flexing rapidly in a butterfly sort of flutter; though with hands as big and red and fleshy as an Arkansas ham, this is not a very good analogy.

I tried to remember exactly where I stood. The main street, with all the comparative safety it implies, was on the other side of the building. The passage I was in led—ahead of me and beyond the Wuh-keis—to the old wharf area where the broken down fishing docks were. Behind me, it led to a cul-de-sac where all the garbage from the hotel was stored. I was cut off; they bad chosen the spot well, though the choosing was mostly mine. I tried to count the advantages I might have: height, weight, and speed in running, though not in immediate movement, and speed in the water too, if I could get to it.

His bullet-like head was thrust out temptingly for a blow, and I knew that if I made the mistake of trying to hit it, this would be the last move I'd ever make. Instead, I put my own head down low, and thrust out with my feet, and dived between his widespread ankles. I had two things in mind: either to knock him off balance, which I didn't really expect to do, or to get between him and the water.

And I was right in my expectations; he moved aside with lightning ease, just simply not being there any more when I shot along the ground; and he put out a foot as I went by. It caught me in the groin, a glancing blow because I, too, was moving fast. I felt the pain sweep over me, but I wasn't seriously hurt; not incapacitated anyway. I didn't stop to see exactly where he was, but did a sort of neck roll and landed on my feet, and I knew that he'd have turned to face me, ready to take the next, more careful charge.

But I didn't turn round to look and see; I just ran.

Once I ran against Louis Jones in the four hundred meters, and damn near beat his time of forty-five point two; and now I had only a matter of a hundred and twenty yards to worry about. I hit the wharf in just under twelve seconds and heard them all behind me as I raced along it to the end and dived. And where I landed, there was less than two feet of water with heavy, wet sand and hard, barnacle-covered rocks scattered about like so many blackjacks. I caught my head a crack that sent stars shooting across the bright red sky, and I rolled under the rotting timbers as I saw the first man, the leader, leap lightly over the wooden railing and land in the shallow water close beside me. He landed on all fours, like a cat and I threw myself at one of the heavy teak stanchions that were supposed to hold the wharf up; it was hanging loose on its iron bindings, its water-end long rotted away but solid up there where the business end of it was. It swung loose with the force of my two hundred pounds moving at speed, and crashed into him and we went down into the water, and then two of the others were there, coming straight at me among the floating cans and rotted garbage and broken planks that were the underside of the wharf.

One at a time, I thought, that's what the Wuh-kei rules call for.

And indeed, one man did hang back when the other got there first. His left hand shot out like a bolt of greased lightning heading for my throat, and I could see the other hand striking downward. And then, suddenly, he seemed petrified. All motion stopped and he just hung there, both hands out and one knee raised; and on one leg, he toppled over slowly into the water. There was a red mess on the side of his head; and I had not even heard the shot.

He was out of action, but I was passing out myself. When you weigh as much as I do and dive onto a mass of barnacles from a height of ten feet or more, the pain, not insupportable, starts at the head and works its way down to the spine, and then on to the soles of the feet; that's not too bad, but then, if you're not careful, you black out; and that's not a good thing to do when someone at that moment is trying to kill you.

But there were two of them in the water, and there was blood all over; some of it, at least, was my own.

The other two were there now, just moving in and frozen in motion; they were staring off to one side, and then they were gone: In one split second, there was no sight or sound of any of them; and I fell in the water and floundered, trying to find water deep enough to swim in; I was heading out, away from the shore because I didn't know what had happened. The body of the leader was in my way, his head cracked open by the great timber I'd hurled at him; and I was blacking out in that terribly dangerous moment of semi-relief that comes when the danger seems, but might not be, past. You can hang on, half-dead, while the danger's still there, like a chicken that prances around with its head cut off; but once it seems to have gone, then the natural weaknesses all sweep in on the flood, and you pass out, if you're not mighty careful. I struggled for sanity in a black world of red darkness, and hands were trying to hold me and I was trying to fight them off, and a voice was shouting: "Senhor Cain! Senhor Cain!"

There was an urgency to the voice that had in it none of the casual calling of that would-be assassin with the rifle. And the urgency told me all I wanted to know; somewhere, out of the haze and the darkness and the yellow, bursting stars, a genie had materialized to come to my rescue. I wondered foolishly who was rubbing the lamp, and when I woke up I was lying on hard, polished wood that shone redly, and a saffron sail was high above me, patched with great sheets of pink and lavender, and there was the creaking of a gently swaying ship. A scarred face was peering into mine, and suddenly it grinned.

I put a hand to what seemed to be my head, and I heard myself groan, and the face said politely: "El Capitan Theophilo de Ericeira, Senhor Cain...*Todo ben agora?*" Somebody's hand was under my shoulders and trying to pull me up into a sitting position, and someone else was holding an enameled mug of hot soup to my lips; it was made mostly of peppers, and I spluttered, and the *capitano* grinned and said in a sort of English: "Best thing for bad head, Senhor."

There were eight or nine of them gathered around me, Chinese mostly, with the Portuguese captain who'd been following me back there, and a big, flabby-stomached Arab who turned out to be the cook who'd made the horrible broth they were offering me.

I pushed the boiling mug away and said: "A damn fool question, I know, but what happened?"

The captain grinned. "Four men come to beat you up. Somebody shoot one of them. I don't know who." The revolver was sticking in his belt like a pirate. "Somebody else break one man's head. I think maybe that was you, no?"

I said: "Ah yes, I remember. I hit him with the wharf."

And then there was a bustling of noises, and Bonelli was there, climbing over the side and hurrying forward. The others made way for him respectfully, and he stood there looking down at me. He was dressed in a blue blazer and white slacks, with an orange-colored Bayadere rose in his buttonhole. There was an anxious look in his eyes, but I heard the skipper say, cheerfully: "Nothing, Senhor Bonelli, nothing bad. Little bump on head is all."

I tried to get to my feet, and Bonelli put out a hand and helped me up, and I swayed for a moment or two and heard him say briefly: "A drink. Some brandy, down in the cabin, can you make it?"

I asked him: "What kind of brandy?"

"Courvoisier. Remy Martin if you'd prefer it."

I said: "I can make it."

It was one of the oceangoing junks from the Fukien coast, of the type known as *ningpo*, with two large eyes painted on the sides to keep a lookout for the omnipresent water-devils.

It was duck-shaped, with a high, carved prow painted in brilliant colors, and what is called a balanced rudder in the stern—the rudder that continues for a further third of its length forward of the steering post, where the impact of the water is one third greater, to permit a single helmsman to manage the huge tiller even in the heaviest seas. I recalled that this was an arrangement that the West had finally latched onto only after the Chinese had been using it for more than a thousand years. The twin sails were made of fiber matting, and the holes punched into them by the winds had been left unpatched because perforated sails are supposed to allow more control in a typhoon: The deck was a hundred and ten feet long, with shelters built of rush matting, and a huge wicker-work basket hanging from a cage over the stern. The fish basket assured that the day's meals would be kept at water-freshness till it was time to eat. On the deck, there were wicker baskets lined with oiled paper and smelling foully of diesel oil, and when I went below, I discovered the reason for them—the junk had been fitted with a large and powerful diesel motor. The name of the junk, THE CRIMSON GARDENIA, had been painted in crimson and gold along the sides, in both Cantonese and European letters. The sour smell of oil mixed with the ripe scent of drying fish that hung in ropes along the decks was overpowering.

But below, the cabin we went to was clean and neat and comfortable. It was not very big, but the timber-work was polished teak, and it had been fitted out in a style that didn't seem to jibe with the ship's occupation, which was smuggling among the coastal ports.

Bonelli waved an airy hand and said: "Sometimes, I must travel on this junk myself; why should I be uncomfortable?"

I fitted myself carefully into a corner and accepted the drink he gave me. My head was pounding savagely.

He said accusingly: "You told me you didn't think it was necessary for my man to keep an eye on you."

"And I've changed my mind. But I've got a better job for him. Can he come with me over to the Penha Palacio? I'd like him to exercise his talents on behalf of the Sally Hyde we have there."

He looked at me and said nothing. His eyes were sharp and alert, and I told him about Bettina. And when I'd finished, he lit one of his Turkish cigarettes and stared up at the red-shining ceiling of the cabin for a long, long while; and then he said slowly:

"I agree with all your reasoning except for one thing. A man in Alexander Ming's position must, surely, be constantly in danger of betrayal from his own men? Wouldn't you agree with that?"

"Probably. And so, he'd be constantly on the alert for any indication of betrayal. In the case under scrutiny, *somebody* led the real Sally Hyde to Macao. Ming's got to find out who that might have been."

"I'm suggesting that he just may not bother. You're forgetting that his original intent was to get at Markle Hyde through her. And now she's made it easy for him by offering herself as a target for him. The fact that this isn't the real Sally Hyde merely suggests that the target will be hit mistakenly. But it will still be hit. And your Bettina will be dead." He shrugged. "Perhaps that doesn't matter very much. I don't know. But what does matter is that you will have had her killed uselessly."

I said stubbornly: "He's *got* to find out where she got her information."

"But it's a risk, none the less."

"Yes. Yes, it is. That's why I want your man on her tail day and night, as close as he can get. A lot closer than I could get without giving the game away."

I was beginning to like Bonelli very much. His concern for Bettina Harkan was somehow unexpected, and I didn't believe his casual disinterest in her death one bit.

He said: "And you're taking the efficiency of my man on trust too, are you not?"

I said: "How can you say a thing like that? Before, perhaps, I was. But now I've got good cause to know just how bright he is. The way he handled those cyclists was enough in itself, without the other. Against two men, he used his hands; when there were three or four, he started shooting; that points to a nice comprehension of the odds. I know he can be relied upon. I wouldn't be here if he couldn't."

"A junk load of Northerners arrived in port this morning, does that interest you?"

"It might mean the enemy's getting worried already. Is every Northerner in Macao working for Ming?"

"No, but the more there are of them, the more we can be sure Ming is gathering enough forces for a quick and easy settlement of whatever problem he decides you might present. They all stick together here, these men, a clique that is never really quite at home among the more gentle Southerners. They band together for jobs, for mutual protection, and to help each other. And for them, Ming is a Northerner himself, in spite of his American upbringing."

The Courvoisier was good and my head was improving. What sort of a world would this be without good cognac to sooth its horrible little ills?

I said: "I've got to keep out of sight wherever Bettina is, because I'm too noticeable, and I don't really like that very much. But if Theo Ericeira can keep an eye on her, I'll feel a lot happier."

He sighed and said: "The chances you take...And yet, my

whole life has been predicated on the philosophy of the calculated risk, so I cannot disapprove of what you are doing, even though I don't believe it can succeed. All right, as soon as you're fit we'll take him over and introduce him to his new charge."

"I'm fit now."

"And when should he start? Tonight?"

"Of course. The moment she sets foot out of that hotel she's in danger. Tonight and every night, he must stay within a few yards of her, ready to grab for me anyone who tries to grab her. I don't care how low on the ladder he is, he's the man who's got to lead me to Ming."

"If you're sure you can walk?"

"On my ear. Let's go."

We went back on deck and found Ericeira and took him over to the hotel, and the two of them waited in a sidewalk cafe while I went on up the broad, white-painted stairs to Bettina's suite.

I knocked, and there was no answer. I put a foot against the door and smashed it open, and went inside and found Mai stretched out on the floor, unconscious, with a broken glass beside her. There was a lot of blood about her arm, and I thought at first she'd been stabbed, and I wondered about her legendary prowess; and then I saw that she'd fallen on the glass, broken it, and cut herself.

I fixed a quick tourniquet with my handkerchief and slapped her face a trifle, uselessly, and carried her to the bed in the other room and set her gently down on it. She was as light as a feather and seemed impossibly fragile and helpless, her body bending as I hefted it as though there were no strength in it at all. Of Bettina, there was no sign; not that I expected any. And when I examined the whisky bottle, the one I'd left there with them, there was the faint but distinctive smell of $CCl_3CH(OH)_2$ coming from it. I went back to the bed and put a hand on Mai's forehead; she was quite cold; she'd taken a large dose and would sleep for a long time yet. I took off the tourniquet and improvised a bandage, and closed the window to raise the temperature in the room, and covered her over with blankets to keep her warm, and went down and told Bonelli they'd got Bettina.

He looked shocked. He said: "My God, Cain, already?"

"Yes, already. They didn't waste any time at all, did they?"

There was a terrible feeling of guilt deep inside me. I should have known; I should have guessed; I should have even suspected...and not left her alone for a second. I said, as angry with myself as I've ever been, as fearful too: "I chose the time and the place and didn't have enough sense to know they wouldn't necessarily accept my terms."

He said: "But *how*, for God's sake? In the middle of the Palacio?"

I told him: "Chloral hydrate in a bottle of whisky, the bottle we'd already been drinking from. Someone got in there after I left, and then, it was just a question of time. Do you know any venal policemen?"

He stared.

I said impatiently: "Every police force has its rogues. I want the best of them, fast. Now, within the next ten minutes."

There was just that shrewd look in the sharp eyes while he asked himself, rather than me, what I was up to. He said thoughtfully: "Yes, the best thing, of course. A man named Melindo, a lieutenant. But whether it will work or not..."

I said: "It's got to work. It's the only likelihood we have to go on, isn't it?"

I thought of Bettina, of the momentary terror in her eyes when I had explained the dangers so carefully, so callously, to her. I'd told her of all the risks, and I'd known that the danger would not really be very acute because I was there to protect her. Only I wasn't.

I could feel that I was trembling. Bonelli looked at me and said quickly: "*Corraggio*, Cain, we will do this thing together, both of us."

I said: "It might be too late already."

CHAPTER 6

Lieutenant Melindo, when we found him, was busy supervising the exchange of pigs: eight pigs with tails for twelve pigs with no tails.

It was all very complicated. Bonelli explained. He told me that on the Red side of the border, the peasants were permitted to export their pigs to Macao, and were given a token which permitted them to reimport, in exchange, any article of more or less equal value—a length of cloth, or cooking utensils, or spare parts for broken-down vehicles, or whatever. But the Red peasant, though politically confused, is no idiot; and soon after the token system started, he found out that the token was worth more to the Macanese trader than any amount of pork, since imports into China proper were heavily restricted. And so, he would drive his pigs over the border through the normal checkpoints, sell the tokens, and drive his pigs back over the hill when no one was looking, then repeat the process the next day.

The next step was equally simple: the Red guards simply cut the tail off any pig being exported to Macao so that it could not be used again. Check; but not for long. Now, in Macao, tailless pigs were exchanged on a prorated basis that fluctuated daily like any other market. The peasants received pigs that still had their tails and could be smuggled back into China and have *their* tails removed at the checkpoints.

And one of Melindo's little rackets was the procuring of tailed pigs for exchange on the Macao side of the frontier.

I had chosen the word "venal" well; and Bonelli had equally well chosen the man. Venal was right. Venality was heavily scored in every line on his weather-beaten, used-up face. He was a tall, stooped man with a shock of black hair, and sallow complexion, and a sense of withdrawal about him, as though he felt the need for curling up inside himself and springing out when the occasion arose. His gray-blue uniform was soiled and frayed, and his small house on the slope of the hill was overrun with children, ten, twelve, thirteen of them. He looked them over and said to me broodingly: "How can a man stay honest with so many mouths to feed?"

I got the impression that he had long ago given up the battle and was letting things come his way as best they might. Later, Bonelli told me that he was paying Melindo a reasonable salary to keep him informed of any police activity that might, conceivably, interest him one way or another.

We sat in the small living room, in which the dominant piece of furniture was a huge, old-fashioned bed, while his wife made tea for us in the outside kitchen. She was Chinese, the wife: a squat, prematurely aged woman with a shiny, leathery face and a permanent smile that seemed to tolerate all the indignities that poverty could pile upon her. The whitewashed walls were scribbled over with ill-spelt words in childish Portuguese and neatly formed Chinese characters, and told of everything from nursery thymes to telephone numbers to simple mathematical sums. A tiny stream was running past the open doorway, and there were bright red poppies and wisps of pale blue lobelia growing on its bank.

I said: "Well, now's your chance, Melindo. You can work for one of the richest men in the world. No need to know just who he is, but somebody kidnaped a woman in broad daylight out of the Penha Palacio. And I want to know where she's being held. I want to know fast. It was some time this afternoon. Suite a hundred and two on the third floor. It overlooks the old wharfs, and the only way she could have been removed is out the window and down the fire-escape. That means that somebody must have seen what was going on. You don't lug an unconscious woman down three flights of fire-escape without somebody or other seeing it. The word will get around, and for my money the whole underworld will know all about it and know that it has to keep its mouth shut. But for your money, they can damn well open up." I said: "You can name your own price, Melindo. And I'll pay more for speed."

Bonelli said smoothly: "An easy twenty dollars, Melindo. Twenty dollars American."

I threw him a look and said: "Let's think in terms of hundreds, Melindo. With a big bonus for speed. And another big bonus because I know who took her."

Melindo's black eyes were quite without expression. He said: "You better tell me, Senhor, just who it was, if he deserves such consideration."

I saw Bonelli silently hoping I'd hold my tongue. I didn't. I said: "Alexander Ming, one of his men."

Melindo's hands were twitching slightly. His wife came in and put down the tea things and poured from a chipped and dirty pot; she dropped a few violet petals onto the hot tea, then sat in a corner with two young children on her lap. She began to feed one of them, pulling out a huge breast and suckling it, smiling and cooing gently.

I said again: "Name your own price, Melindo."

He looked up and said softly: "Can I trust to your own generosity?"

With all those kids around, a childhood story came back to me, of a boy in a candy store who was told by the owner to help himself, go on, take a big handful. The boy refused, and the generous owner reached into the barrel and came out with a handful. Later, the boy said gleefully to his pal, explaining the strategy: *You see, his hands are bigger than mine.*

I said, looking at the soiled and ragged children: "Yes, you can, and my hands are indeed bigger than yours."

He stood up then, his tea unfinished, and said: "Tell me, Senhor, where I can find you in an hour. Will you wait here, perhaps?"

I looked to Bonelli, and he nodded, and I said: "Come to the fan-tan house, The House of the Seven Hills. I'll be there. And if you need men to help you...put them on the payroll."

He left then, a sad and crafty man heading for riches and mortal danger, climbing over the garden fence and taking a short cut down the hill to the bay where the sampans were. We watched him go and saw Ericeira standing in the shade of a banyan tree, watching and waiting. And when we walked along the hot macadam surface towards the town, I knew that the skipper was still there behind us, keeping out of sight and remaining watchful. His competence was a great comfort to me.

Below us, the city was a panorama of brilliant colors, the pastel shades of its houses brightened by the gaudy flags and the glaring signs of the stores. There were bamboos there, and vines and flame-trees, with hibiscus and bananas, great rhododendrons and azaleas, and bright patches of green bracken. The sounds of the city came up to us here as we wound our way down to meet them.

Across the blue water, the ferry was puffing towards Hong Kong, a white tail of water behind it. There must have been a hundred junks in the tiny harbor. And across the bay, the hills of China were blue in the evening light. I looked at my watch; it was half-past five.

Bonelli was moving delicately, like a woman, down the steep slope, his body swaying gently. He seemed strangely out of place here, his elegance exaggerated and unseemly. He stopped abruptly, looked down on the town, and said broodingly: "How long will it take them to find out that she's not Sally Hyde?"

I said: "They'll know that right away. What they won't know is why she's posing as Sally Hyde."

"She'll tell them, of course."

"At once, I hope. My hope is that they won't believe her."

He frowned, puzzled, and I said: "It might take some time before she convinces them that I'm the only one they have to worry about."

He said: "Some time...and some energy, and some pain."

"Yes." The thought was enough to make me shiver. I remembered how Bettina had stroked her breasts and told me: *They stick slivers of bamboo in you.*

Bonelli said: "He can't just let her go, you know that, don't you?"

"He could, without any damage to himself. But I don't suppose he will. A question of teaching me to mind my own business."

"And you feel that Markle Hyde's money can pay for all that woman's agony?"

"No. I don't." I couldn't help being short with him. He was drawing away from me because they'd acted faster than I'd expected. It was a mistake, and I was horribly aware of it. I said, excusing myself and not feeling at all comforted by my excuses: "I assumed that the word would have to be passed around for quite a while before anyone would rise to the bait. Instead, the real Sally Hyde made that one comment in the Essence of Heavenly Light, and that was enough. So when she apparently turned up a couple of days later, they moved in. That can only mean that the barman she spoke to had a direct line to Ming, it wasn't just a fortuitous contact. And Sally Hyde must have known that. That's why she spoke just once and then went smartly into hiding. The ball she started rolling moved faster than I thought it might."

"And now?"

"Now we wait for Melindo."

I filled in the time by taking Bonelli to the bar they called the Essence of Heavenly Light. It was hard to restrain my anger as I marched up to the barman; I wanted to kill him there and then, but instead I said to Bonelli: "Is this the man?"

He shook his head, "No, not he."

It wasn't worth asking where the man had gone that Sally had spoken to. He'd be well away from there by now, in one of the rabbit warrens of the city, or on a sampan in the harbor, or perhaps lying dead on its bottom.

We went back to the fan-tan house and waited. Melindo turned up an hour and a half later while we waited impatiently in the office. Waiting is always the hardest part, and I felt I wanted to get something, anything, in my fists and twist the life out of it. It was an ugly feeling. He showed no sign of fear, but there was a hesitancy about him which made me think he might not be of much further use. But he'd done well. He said, eyeing the bundle of bills I took out of my pocket:

"A woman from Hong Kong, Senhor, who is not what she pretends to be."

So they knew already. I said: "Go on."

"A chambermaid, a servant from the hotel put something in her whisky bottle while she was making up the beds, and a little while later two men went in through the fire-escape, just as you said, and took her down to the wharf. Another woman, a Chinese, was left behind unconscious."

I said sharply: "And I want to know why they left her there."

He shrugged. He could not take his eyes off the money. "The one they wanted was the European woman."

"Well, I'll find out about that later on. Do you know where they took her?"

He nodded eagerly: "A storehouse, Senhor, on the Rua Querenta, where they used to keep fireworks. There is a cellar there, and the Senhora is there now with three men and some geese to guard her."

I knew all about the geese, but Bonelli said: "A hungry goose is the best watchdog there is, a very popular system in Macao." He said to Melindo: "A fireworks storehouse...number eighty-five? There are no others, I think...?"

"The same, Senhor. On the south side of the street."

"I know it." Bonelli turned to me and said: "I know it well. I used to own it."

"How well?"

"Well enough for your purpose, and more."

"Good. Can I get in there?"

"Yes. A skylight, if you can reach it. It won't be easy."

"I'll reach it. I'll need some of your grain."

"My grain?"

"Sour mash from your distillery, a handful or two."

"Ah, that is good."

It was a question I had to ask. I said: "Has she been hurt?"

There was a terribly tight feeling in my stomach.

Melindo said: "She has been hurt, Senhor."

"And Ming? Alexander Ming?"

He shrugged. "There is never any word of Alexander Ming, Senhor. No one ever sees him, or hears him, or knows where he is. It is even said that he is not in Macao at this moment, but in Tangier."

"And how good is that last bit of information?"

"Not good. A rumor, no more. The kind of rumor a man would spread if he wanted it thought that he was not here."

"And is she likely to be moved? From the cellar?"

"You mean, no doubt, before dark, Senhor?"

"Don't try to read my mind, Melindo. Just tell."

"They will move her if they find out that I have learned that she is there. But they will not find this out."

"You sound pretty sure of yourself, and that's the whole crux of the matter."

"My source of information is very secure."

Bonelli said: "Tell me who it is, Melindo." He was sitting alone in a dark corner, Bonelli, detached from us and listening, his pointed fingers touching each other in an attitude of prayer.

The lieutenant wriggled hesitantly, shuffling his feet and looking at the ground, but he said at last: "Hu-san, the blind one."

Bonelli said: "An old, old man who begs on the corner of Rua Figueroa Magalaes. A man who knows everything and says nothing." He looked at Melindo and said, more curiously than anything else: "How did you get him to talk?"

Melindo smiled slowly: "He owes me a favor. Many favors. I helped him once to bring his family over the border."

"And they go back if he doesn't help you once in a while? You're an evil man, Melindo."

Melindo said: "We are all evil men, Senhor Bonelli. It is only a question of degree, is it not?" And I said: "Let's leave it at that. Thank God for the evil. We'd get nowhere without it."

I said: "And now?" Melindo looked at me, and I said impatiently: "They won't just let her sit there."

"No, Senhor, they will not. But they will not kill her either, not yet." It was a straw to seize on. I looked at him, and he went on: "She told them that it was you who persuaded her to do what she did, and they think that she is a weapon they can use against you if they have to."

"In other words, I'll go looking for her, and then...But in that case, they *expect* me to find out where she is. Is this *o jeito*, Melindo?" The *jeito* is a game the Portuguese play; it means, simply, trickery, the outsmarting of one man by another for the sheer exhilaration that knavery can provide when it's used as a game of skill. If I was supposed to go looking for Bettina, then they would have to let me know where she was being held, one way or another. They'd guess I'd try to find out for myself; could they so quickly guess I'd find a man like Melindo and use him? Perhaps they would: they knew I was with Bonelli, and Melindo was Bonelli's man. On the other hand, perhaps it would be safer for them to let me know some other way, in which case I could expect a message of some sort. Or could I? Would they be so straightforward as to send a simple messenger saying: *Come and get her. She's here or there*. Could they have told Hu-san, the blind man: *Make sure that Cain learns this or that*. Or was Melindo also one of Ming's men?

O jeito, the game of trickery.

But Melindo shook his head. *"Nao e o jeito, Senhor*. It's not the game."

Somehow, I believed him; and trust was all I had working for me at the moment. But the message was drilling itself into my mind: if Melindo is telling the truth, there's got to be a message coming from another source. Please God it comes in time, or I'm dead too, and then Bettina, whom I threw to the wolves.

And then, there was a commotion in the anteroom that led to the office. It was the sound of a shuffle, and a shriek of pain, and the sound of running feet, and Bonelli was on his feet in an instant, heading for the door, white-faced all of a sudden. But the door flew open before he got there, and there was Mai, her dress torn, her eyes dark with fury. Behind her, one of the guards who worked out there was getting to his feet, clutching his shoulder and grimacing with pain, and another was running forward towards Mai with a look of shocked surprise on his face, and a gun in his hand. Mai thrust Bonelli aside like a wilted flower and burst into the room. The guard was aiming the gun, and I yelled: "No! For God's sake no, it's all right!" I was physically stopping the sentry from shooting, and I swung round to Bonelli and said. quickly: "It's all right, Bonelli. I know her. More, I was half-expecting her."

Bonelli closed the door and stood leaning against it; adjusting the immaculate set of his tie. He said: "If you would perhaps be kind enough to present me..." His voice was cold with anger; and I supposed that it wasn't often that frail little things like Mai burst into his office and almost put a half-nelson on him. And there was also the destruction of a cherished image; he'd told me that his office was safe, well protected, and who should burst into it, throwing the guards about, disarming them, and putting an arm-lock on the boss himself? None but a frail and pretty little thing he must have thought he could have blown over with a good puff. Soothing his ruffled feathers, he opened the door again and said savagely to the men outside: "All right, get back to your work." One of them started, ashamed, to explain, but Bonelli slammed the door in his face and turned and said viciously: "A virago!"

"Yes, I suppose you could call her that. But a nice one. Senhor Carlo Bonelli. Miss Mai Cho-sing." Bonelli recovered his composure, but not enough to do more than bow imperceptibly. I said: "Sit down, Mai, I know why you are here."

Recovering some more, Bonelli made a slight gesture towards a blue and green silk-covered ebony chair, and Mai hesitated, then sat there almost sulkily. She glared at me for a moment with more venom in her lovely face than I'd ever expect to see on one so young-seeming; and then she said, puzzled:

"You were expecting me?"

I said: "Sooner or later. Didn't they contact you?"

Melindo was hovering there in the background, not quite knowing what to do. I gave him a thousand dollars and said: "I may need you again, Melindo. And thanks." He stuffed the money into his shirt, down by the waist, and pulled his belt over it; he bowed politely and left, and I said to Mai: "All right, they called you? Sent a messenger?"

She took a deep breath, looked at Bonelli, and half-smiled. She said: "I'm sorry. I was very rude, was I not? But I was worried. I do hope I didn't hurt you." Smiling at him, she said, as though to justify his helplessness against her: "I am trained in these things. It's not always easy to accept, I know."

Now, he bowed more graciously. The aplomb was all back in its proper place again. He said: "I'm sure you will forgive me if I pour myself a large glass of cognac? May I offer you one, Mai Cho-sing?"

She shook her head and looked at me. She said slowly: "Yes, a phone call, how did you know?"

I said: "A link to me, and thank God for it. That's why they didn't take you too. I was worrying about it. They wanted a sure way of getting a message to me. And proof positive that Bettina didn't just get up and go."

She was busy trying to fix her torn dress, and Bonelli, a gentleman again, clapped his hands for one of his girls. She came in and made a polite little bow, looked at the high collar of Mai's dress and wondered about it; then Bonelli said shortly: "Needle and thread." The girl went out and Mai said: "Fifteen minutes ago, I was sleeping. They drugged my drink, did you know that?"

I nodded. "Chloral hydrate. It was I who put you to bed and wrapped you up."

"Oh. Well, a man who spoke Mandarin called. He said Bettina is with them, a hostage, and that they will exchange her for information they want from you."

"Did they say what information? Not that it really matters very much."

"No, they did not. They said you should come to the Tang-si tonight at ten o'clock. That's one of the junks in the harbor."

"Sailing for China tomorrow," Bonelli said promptly.

I asked her: "And that's where Bettina is now?"

"Yes. She's on board the junk."

"Then we know what we have to do, don't we?"

Mai looked at me uncertainly. "It must almost certainly not be true. They would not tell you where she is."

"Uh-huh. How do you feel?"

Surprised, she said: "Fine, why?"

I said: "I'm wondering whether to let you sit here and sweat it out...or to take you along with me tonight."

"To the junk? But surely you don't believe..."

"She's in a storehouse on Rua Querenta, and tonight I'm going to get her out."

Mai got to her feet and said sharply: "Then let us go there now."

Bonelli was looking at her suddenly with a great deal of admiration. He said: "There are three men guarding her."

Mai said: "Then we will need guns, perhaps."

"And geese."

"Oh." She looked at me, and I said: "No problem with the

geese. And no guns, we can't litter the colony with corpses. It wouldn't be proper. Do you know anything about the Wuh-keis?"

She frowned. "Y-e-s...an ancient sect of fighting men." She said sharply: "The guards? Wuh-keis?"

"Probably."

There was a long silence. At last, she said: "I believe Bettina told you that I am expert in many of the...the arts of self-defense. For karate, for judo, for all the others...for me, these things are very easy. But it is not possible to fight against a Wuh-kei. You should know that. We must have a gun, and even then..."

Bonelli said: "She's right, Cain. You're a big man, a strong man, but don't imagine that you can do anything, anything at all, with your bare hands." He said smoothly: "But I believe you have already learned that, no?"

I felt the bump at the top of my head. "I've learned it."

He went to the door and opened it, and turned and said: "I'll be back in a moment."

And then, the two of us were alone. There was a little silence, and Mai sat down again and waited, her eyes cast down, as though the intimacy of just the two of us meant something and that she had to be demure. The savage little wildcat who had burst into the room was gone, and in its place there was just a lovely young girl looking shy and alone and half frightened. The sudden change was quite charming.

She said at last: "Will they have hurt Bettina?"

"Yes, they hurt her."

There were almost tears there. "And you too? The Wuh-keis?"

I shook my head. "Not me. This afternoon, when I left the hotel, they jumped me. I ran and dived into the water off the wharf."

Suddenly, she was laughing. "You did not know that there is not very much water there? That is why the wharf is no longer used."

"I found that out. One of Bonelli's men came to my rescue."

Now she was serious again. "And now, we go to Bettina. How did you find out where she is?"

I said: "I'm not sure that I have found out. We'll know when we get there."

"It is my fault that they took Bettina. Is that why you want me to come along with you?"

"No. And it was my fault, not yours."

"Why then?"

"I don't really know the answer to that one. I just feel I'll need help. And if half of what Bettina says about you is true, then you might be able to provide it."

"Is that all?"

"Well, I can't think of anyone else I'd rather have along to hold my hand. Is that what you want me to say?"

"Yes. That is what I wanted you to say."

Bonelli came back looking rather sheepish; but he carried two guns with him. A nine-millimeter Luger, which I took, and a .32 Walther, which I gave to Mai. He had a well detailed blueprint too of the store he used to own. I thought it was lucky that Bonelli was the type of man never to give up possession of anything that might, just conceivably, one day come in handy.

I wondered about Mai. It seemed strange, conspiring with one so fragile for what was ahead. But Bettina had almost convinced me. *Worth ten men in a fight*, she had said, *any kind of a fight*. I remembered, too, what Bonelli had said about the impregnability of his private quarters, and the look on the faces of the two guards when Mai had unceremoniously burst past them, not even deigning to look round at the man she'd thrown over her slender shoulder. There had been indignation in their faces, and surprise, and shock; but most of all, there'd been a very wary respect.

And creeping around in the darkness with that slender, scented body close beside me in the silence was something that just had to be tried out.

I once saw a 1932 eleven-liter V-12 Hispano-Suiza rusting away in a garage. It was the legendary Type 68 that weighed three tons and could eat up the roads at a hundred and fifteen miles an hour without exceeding three thousand rpms—which was pretty fast in those days. A glamorous beast of a car, it had hanging sidemounts and a body made almost entirely of strips of tulipwood fastened with copper rivets. It was smoother and shinier than the deck of an expensive yacht; the leatherwork was like silk; and the lines were those of a thoroughbred racehorse. I remembered drooling over the car and wondering about its historic potential, wondering if it was still as magnificent as the myths about it claimed. I longed to get my hands on it and test it, revel in the sheer frightening luxury of its performance. And now, that's how I felt when I looked at Mai, not believing entirely in the legend, but somehow feeling an overwhelming urge to find out for myself, to see if the legend were true and perhaps to revel in the astonishment of its being true.

I'd like to have told her, but I thought it wasn't a very flattering analogy.

Bonelli spread the blueprint out on the beautiful, carved desk and touched it with the back of a delicate finger. He said: "The cellar is here, under the main storeroom. There's a heavy iron door in this corner, with a flight of, what, ten or twelve steps going down."

"The door to the cellar—what kind of a lock?"

"Old-fashioned, Yale type."

The Chinese symbols on the print were hard to read and semi-obliterated with age. I asked, indicating: "A skylight here, is that it?"

"Yes. Twenty feet above the floor."

"And this gimmick here?"

"An air vent. Just a simple tube leading in from the roof. It's about eight inches across. Far too small to enter."

"A filter under it, can you remember?"

"No filter. The cats used to fall through it and kill themselves on the concrete floor below. When someone was cooking food down below, they'd slither through it and find there was no way to back up, so they'd jump and fall the twenty feet. And, sometimes, a bird would fly in. But it's only eight inches across. The skylight is your best way in, but there's a bell hanging from it. Just a simple device, an old ship's bell that rings once or twice if you lift the panel."

"Let's look at the other ways in. The doors?"

"Good locks on them, heavy timber doors. And the windows are barred with iron straps."

"A rope then, from the roof, through the skylight. It seems a trifle simple, but the simplest way is usually the best. The bell should be no problem. Is it hooked on? Removable?"

"Yes, it is."

Mai was peering over our shoulders. She said: "And their first line of defense will be the secrecy. If, that is, you are sure she's there, if you're sure the other story is a lie."

I said: "I'm not sure. I'm just hoping she's not on that junk where they're expecting me to look for her." I asked Bonelli: "What about lighting on the street? What about a way up to the roof?"

"No street lighting at all. And there are two ways up to the roof. There's an iron stairway up one of the walls, but a gate at the bottom is kept locked, and the staircase is unsteady and not very safe. We used to use it in the old days when we stored tools up on the roof. But there's no weather protection up there, and so, ever since the place has been used for firecrackers, the stairway has not been used. Or kept in repair."

"And it's therefore noisy. The other way?"

"The water-piping. A cast-iron pipe leads from a reservoir on the roof to a large wooden barrel on the alleyway, bolted to the wall."

"Strong enough for my weight?"

"It was only put in a few years ago. It should still be strong. Up at the top, there's a protruding grille of iron spikes to discourage anyone from climbing it—like the rat-preventive discs on a ship's hawser. But it shouldn't stop a determined man. And, after all, there are always guards in the building, even if it's only the usual sleeping watchman. And the geese, of course."

We talked for a while about the possibilities. We checked this, eliminated that, and made little mental notes about the other; and soon, I knew exactly what we had to do, and how we had to do it.

CHAPTER 7

The little cul-de-sac called Rua Querenta is one of those dingy industrial streets that die at dusk.

It is a street of go-downs, of warehouses, of broken down stores and battered fences and discarded rubbish. At dark, the workers go back to their wives and their children and their gambling, and there are only the huge scavenger cats to give the blind alley a breath of life. And these are not cats as you and I know them; they are huge, and scraggy, and appallingly savage. During the day, no one sees them, because they're down in the sewers looking for the rats that are almost as big as they are, but at night they come out and scour the slum streets for a change of diet. They are well fed but always, it seems, on the verge of starvation; it seems there just isn't enough food lying around to feed their vicious, demanding tempers. You can hear them snarling and fighting, and the sounds are the sounds of the jungle.

And yet, less than a hundred yards away, on the other side of the barrier that the buildings are, the nighttime noises of the Avenida Almeida Ribeiro had scarcely started; it was only nine o'clock. The tourists were always told here: *Keep to the brightly lit streets. Stay away from the dark alleys*; and the warnings were justified. Even the police would not cross that barrier without first calling, on their helmet-radios, for backup support.

In these dark side-streets, the drunks were rolled, the unwary were slugged; and death was much a part of the colony's daily ritual as life itself.

We moved silently together, Mai and I, moving quite slowly, staring into the darkness and listening for any alien sound. A cat snarled and spat, a great behemoth of a beast with shaggy, clotted fur and rib-cage bones, drawing back on its hind legs and baring its white teeth, ready to pounce on me like a tiger. I kicked out at it with my foot, and it seized my shoe and bit hard, then turned and scampered away.

Mai said: "There is someone ahead of us."

Her sight in the dark was incredible. All I could see was a shadow in the gutter fifty feet ahead. We moved closer to the stone wall and crept on. There was a red glow over our heads, a glow from the lights of the main street; we could hear the traffic over there. But here, all was pitch black, and silent, and smelly. There were cobbles under our feet, and they were wet with running garbage. The shadow in the gutter moved, and we both froze. I took Mai's arm, pulled her silently behind me, and moved on a few paces; the shadow keeled over and snored; it was a half-naked drunk from one of the ships, and someone had taken his clothes. I hissed a signal to Mai, and she rejoined me; I heard the safety-catch of her little Walther go back on.

And then, as I turned to her, there was a flurry of violent movement; and there was just time enough for me to know that I should not have turned my back on a seeming drunk. A small, lightweight bundle of savagery crushed onto my face, an astonishingly soft bundle that wasn't like a weapon at all. Something ripped sharply through the shoulder of my jacket, and claws dug into my flesh, and white teeth were tearing at the bag of wet, sour-smelling grain I was carrying, the grain from Bonelli's distillery. A starving cat. The claws ripped my clothes as I hurled it away from me, and it snarled and screamed with a most un-feline noise. I took another look at the drunk; he hadn't moved.

A match flared, and we moved into a dark corner and watched as a beggar settled into the stinking corner that was his home, lighting a joss-stick to keep the night-devils away with the scent of the fragrant, clay-smoldering incense.

We found the barrel and the pipe Bonelli had told us about, and the pipe was comfortingly strong as I tugged at it. Mai said, whispering: "Me first." I shook my head in the darkness, and she insisted: "There'll be no danger at the top—unless the fastenings are not strong enough." She was already climbing before I could argue.

I stood there and watched her silhouette against the warm, red glow of the sky as she negotiated the spiked iron-grille that jutted out from the wall around the pipe. She swung over it lightly and easily, like an acrobat swinging her fragile body out and up and over. She whistled, and I followed her up there, climbing hand over hand and ripping my trousers on a spike as I passed the grille; it wasn't very difficult. We could see the lights of the *avenida* on the other side of the building throwing up their bright reflections, red and white and blue and amber and green.

A tile rattled as I moved my weight across it, and I felt that Mai, beside me now, had frozen at the slight sound. We waited for a raucous sound of the geese down there below us, but nothing came, and in a moment I moved on and found the skylight. It was locked, and I peered through the greasy glass to try and find the bell that Bonelli had said was there; I could see nothing.

Over to the left was the air vent, a tube of galvanized iron canted at an angle of thirty degrees; it was six inches or so across and still emitted the foul, daytime stenches of the unwashed bodies who worked below. I untied the neck of the canvas bag and stuck my fingers into the uninviting mess to stir it around and make it friable, and then dribbled it slowly, infinitely slowly, down through the tube, I put my ear to it and listened for a long, long time, then dribbled more of the sickening mash down there. I listened again and heard a solitary squawk; there was no anger in it, no panic even, just a faint, inquiring sound of curious interest. I fancied I could even hear the shuffle of webbed feet on the concrete floor, I dribbled the rest of the grain down, checked my watch, and whispered: "Now, we wait."

Mai nodded in the faint glow and pulled my arm to- wards a solid protuberance that might have been an old stanchion of iron set in the rubble walls to hold them together and prevent their toppling in a typhoon. I unwrapped the rope from around my waist and fastened one end to the protuberance and gave it a heavy tug to make sure it was safe.

Mai whispered: "How long?"

I have figures at my disposal for almost everything, but not, unhappily, concerning the time it takes for a goose to get incapably drunk on sour-mash grain; I thought about it for a while, wondering about the metabolism of geese, and decided it was a question of likelihoods again. I whispered: "We'll give them twenty minutes."

We lay down on the hard tiles by the side and stared up at the sky in the cold night air. Mai looked at me somberly and said softly; "She might be on the Tang-si in the harbor after all."

"No. It's not likely."

"But possible."

"No, not even possible. They knew that you'd come to me, and they couldn't know, I hope, that I'd have access to a crooked policeman. So, his story is more likely to be true than the one you were given. They're waiting for me on the junk, and Bettina's down there in the cellar."

"You sound very sure." Her voice was troubled.

I said: "Don't blame yourself, Mai. It was bound to happen, one way or another. You couldn't have stopped it."

"I should have stopped it. That's what I was there for."

"Ssshhh..."

There was a scuffing sound at the edge of the roof, and then, the most God-awful scream; another pair of those damn cats. We watched them at work for a moment, and then the male, satisfied, leaped lightly away and left the female there, preening herself in the darkness.

Mai leaned in towards me and put a hand on my chest, saying nothing, but just lying there silently beside me, her body very close. Her dark, slanting eyes were on my face, and when I looked at her, she put her head on my shoulder and moved a trifle closer. In a little while, smelling her perfume and knowing that this was a good time for cats but not for men, I checked my watch again and said, very quietly: "Time now."

Three men in the cellar, Melindo had said, and I guessed there'd be a watchman too on the main floor, though, in keeping with the habit of the place, he would probably be sleeping and relying on his geese to wake him if an intruder called.

I strapped some masking tape to the pane of the skylight and cut it out with a glass cutter, then removed it carefully, leaving a hole big enough to reach through and grope around for the bell. I found its clapper and unhooked it, then unlocked the panel and opened it up. I waited a long while, just in case the sudden draft down there might cause concern, and then I dropped the rope down into the void, signaled Mai to follow me, and went down it quickly, landing silently on the dark floor twenty feet below. Mai was beside me almost before I got my bearings.

There was almost no light at all, and we waited a long time to get our eyes accustomed to it. But at last we could make out the shadows of crates piled one on top of the other, and a pile of heavy lumber of the type they use for the spars of junks. We moved among them, searching; we could hear some quite stentorian breathing somewhere, the heavy, rasping breathing of a man with asthma. Guided by the sound and by the smell of a burning joss-stick, we found a glimmer of light in an angle formed by some boxes; and there he was, the watchman, lying curled up on some old sacks, his mouth wide open and a dribble of saliva on his chin.

By the light of his little burner—a clay statue of a seated bodhisattva in which pounded clay mixed with dried verbena was smoldering—I watched him for a while to make sure that the sleep was real.

It was time to find out a little bit more about my companion and her legendary abilities. I whispered to her; my mouth very close to her ear: "Can you put him to sleep, harmlessly? An old man...Don't hurt him." She nodded.

We both crouched down beside him then, one on either side, and I watched as her fingers played, light as feathers, with the auricular and the occipital nerves, one thumb touching the posterior scapular and the other applying light pressure to the nerve that leads to the trapezium; not the combination I would have chosen myself, but adequate for an old man whose arteries had probably hardened. He stirred once—he wouldn't have done that if she'd used the posterior thoracic as well, but I suppose that her hands were not big enough for the proper reach—and then his old eyes opened briefly as though there were just one split second of consciousness in which he knew what was happening and was powerless to do anything about it; and then, suddenly, he stiffened with a jerky, spasmodic movement, and was out like a light. I felt his pulse, which was moving fast, and knew that he'd be all right.

There was a slight, indefinite sound over to our left, on the other side of the crates that had formed the old man's bedroom. Mai slipped away while I moved in the other direction, both of us reaching cover in the flash of an eye; and then I heard the unlikely sound of her well-stifled giggle. I went over silently to warn her, and found her looking down on the ghostlike bodies of the two geese; one of them was snoring, and the other, lying on its side in a most unlikely posture, was staring at her with a solitary, unblinking eye; the eye closed as I moved in, and all was quiet. We crossed together to the cellar door.

Now, I knew, the difficulties would start.

I oiled the huge lock from the tiny vial I carried, and then oiled the heavy hinges as well. I waited a few seconds, then went to work on the lock with the pick Bonelli had given me. The sound of the tumblers dropping into place seemed thunderous, and Mai drew a quick breath as the last one fell into position. She looked a warning at me, and I nodded and put my ear to the door; there was no sound on the other side, and my common sense told me that the sound had really been quite small, but magnified by our own sense of danger. I gave the hinges a few more squirts of oil for good measure, and then swung the heavy door open.

The warmth that came up from down there told me what I wanted to know; there were living people there—that much was certain. I could smell the scent of their bodies, I could smell, too, the rather gaudy perfume that Bettina had been using too much, and I was glad now of her extravagance with it. And there was the faintest mutter of voices. I pulled out my Luger and signaled to Mai to back me up; she nodded.

I keyed up every sense in the silence. The Chinese say we smell horrible; I wondered if their keen noses could catch the intrusion of underarm deodorants. Down the steps I moved, broken stone steps—no timbers, thank God!—counting them as I went. Nine, not ten or twelve as Bonelli had suggested; I checked carefully for two or three more, but there were none. Ahead of me, there was a stack of sixteen-by-sixteen teakwood beams that reached almost to the ceiling—several thousand dollars' worth of exquisitely grained hardwood that was as tough as steel and heavy as lead and as smooth as silk.

I was in the shadow of an arched embrasure now, a brick projection over my head; I examined the brickwork well, for this was where *someone* should have been, commanding a good view of the cellar and its entrance; nobody; carelessness.

I listened. The voices came again—low, indistinct, but a dialect with the intonation of the North. I moved forward, inch by inch, and the movement brought into sight three heavy-set Chinese in black pajamas. They were sitting at a rickety table and staring at the cards in front of them; I couldn't see what game they were playing, but then one of them threw down his cards and said: "Djinn."

I stepped out quickly, my gun very ready, and said in Mandarin: "Nobody moves, not a movement of any kind." The man who was facing me flickered his eyes and looked at me. His hand, reaching out for the money, froze; he was the one who had called gin.

And then, suddenly, one of the two men whose backs were to me swung round and dropped and flew almost horizontally across the ground towards me, coming for my ankles in a movement so fast that I just couldn't believe it. He was heading straight for me and—to hell with the gun pointing now at the top of his head—diving for my legs with his arms both raised and ready. It was one of the Wuh-keis who had jumped me on the wharf, the third of the little execution party.

There was a shot from above and behind me as I leaped to one side; and he doubled up in mid-motion, sliding along the ground with his own momentum. And clutching at a shattered ankle, he doubled up and grimaced horribly, landing on his back with his leg in the air and his shoulders twisted. I repeated the order:

"I said, nobody moves. Nobody."

Mai said clearly: "I have them." Her voice came from the same source as the shot.

I said: "Keep your eyes on them. Don't even blink."

"Of course."

Only then did I turn to look. Mai had found a perch on the brick abutment, and I wondered how in hell she could have gotten there so silently. I said to the men at the table: "Turn up the lamp, just a little." One of them reached out, not taking his eyes off me, and worked the little wheel; the lamp flared, and I said sharply: "Careful!"

I did not want a sudden burst of flame that would smother the wick and plunge us all into darkness. I said: "Put your hands on top of your heads and lie down on the floor." Two of them did so, sullenly lying on their faces, and I sort of snorted and said nastily: "On your backs, who do you think you are dealing with, for God's sake?" You can't really say 'for God's sake' in Mandarin, so I said *sahu cha mising*, which must have sounded funny to them. But they both rolled over into a position from which it is harder to rise quickly, and still speaking Mandarin so that they'd understand, I said to Mai: "These are the men who tried to kill me on the wharf. Don't take a single eye off them."

Mai did not answer. She merely laughed, and the laugh chilled me to the bone. The injured man, his face tight with pain, was still lying there at the edge of the circle of light, moaning and grimacing so much that his intention was quite evident. A shattered ankle with bits of a .32 in it hurts like hell; but a Wuh-kei? Groaning? He was a brave man, but not much of an actor, and the groan was as theatrical a bit of business as I'd ever seen; he was just trying to fool me and not doing very well at it.

I said: "You too, Charlie, get with your friends unless you want something you can really groan about."

He glared at me, and for a moment I thought he was going to make trouble, but then he dragged himself across the floor to the others, the look of pain replaced by a stolid stoicism now that he knew it wouldn't work. I took my finger off the Luger's trigger and laid it along the guard, and began a search of the cellar.

It wasn't much of a hunt. There were water barrels and cans of oil, and coils of rope, and a dozen or so boxes of explosives, and a great stack of colored paper lanterns, and fuse wire by the ton, and thirty or forty crates of fireworks. There was also a small stack of expensive, American-looking baggage, a trunk and three suitcases, with a rather interesting name and address on them, which I made a mental note of.

And then, I found Bettina.

She was moaning softly, lying between two huge piles of lumber. She had not been tied up; instead, there was a sickeningly heavy beam lying across her stomach, pinioning her to the ground like a squashed butterfly. It was nearly a foot and a half thick, and thirty feet or more long; one day it would be carved as the central pillar of a *tien*, the oblong, column-divided inner room of a temple; and when I stooped to lever it off her, I found it weighed almost more than I could lift. I heard her rasping sigh as the pressure came off her stomach, and she rolled over and vomited, half-conscious, half in a coma. Her face was mass of bloodied bruises, and her clothes were in shreds, no more than rags, her breasts bare in the dim light of the distant lamp. I ran my hands over them; the slivers of bamboo she had feared so much were not there, though there was blood everywhere.

But her eyes came to life, suddenly, and she gasped and turned away, and then she looked at me and said, half-choking: "You son of a bastard bitch, Cain, if you offer me more money now, I'll kill you. So help me God, I'll kill you." She started swearing then, using every kind of obscenity I'd ever heard. It was a good sign; I knew she was going to be all right.

I said: "Mai's here, we've come to take you home."

Her voice was a hoarse whisper: "I know. I heard her. I knew she'd come."

She pushed my arms away and staggered to her feet, and then fell back as I caught her; and the swearing went on, and I picked her up and carried her to the steps; and Mai said cheerfully: "Hi, Bettina," as we passed her, not moving her eyes or the little Walther from the straight-ahead position.

I said to Mai: "I'll get her onto the street and come back for you."

She shook her head: "No. Take her out, I'll follow when you're clear."

"All right."

I went up the steps fast, crossed over the unconscious watchman, slid the bolts on the door, and went out onto the street. Behind me, I heard a recovering goose flapping its wings. He came towards me and staggered in the doorway, and then fell flat on his back, squawking. I stood there with Bettina in my arms. She was unconscious now that the fresh air had caught her, and I waited for Mai. In a few moments, there was the sound of a shot down there, followed by two more in rapid succession, and I put Bettina down on the pavement quickly and ran back into the building. And then, there was the most God-awful explosion and the sound of bursting crackers, and Mai came running through the cellar door, slamming it behind her and reaching for a timber to prop it shut with. I heaved a beam into position and said:

"All right? Did they give you trouble?"

She shook her head. "I just couldn't resist the sight of all those explosives."

"The Wuh-keis?"

She shrugged: "Here they come now."

The sound was enough to tell us, and they were yelling their heads off on the other side of the door, hammering at it with their bodies. There was smoke coming out from under it, the choking blue smoke of cordite. The door shuddered and held, and I said:

"They'll get through it in time, perhaps. Let's get out of here."

Mai was already running out onto the street to look for Bettina, and I dragged the unconscious watchman out, then, on an impulse, dragged the two geese out too—it wasn't their fault they'd goofed—and saw Mai crouching down beside Bettina. Mai had Bettina's head in her arms and was crooning to her like a nurse with a baby. I picked Bettina up, and ten minutes later we were back in Bonelli's private quarters. Bettina was stretched out naked on the bed while two young Chinese girls and Mai sponged her cruelly treated body with warmed and perfumed oil. Her eyes were open now, and she looked at me and almost laughed, a short, angry, bitter laugh. She said chokingly: "Well, Cain, was it worth it?"

I said: "Yes, it was worth it. Are you going to be all right?"

She was recovering fast enough to snarl at me: "No thanks to you, yes, I'll be all right." And then she said heavily: "I told them about you, Cain. I had to."

"I know. I wouldn't have expected anything else."

"As soon as they saw I wasn't Sally Hyde..."

"I know. You want to go back to Hong Kong now? When you're better?"

"Back to that God-awful jail? Not likely."

"Her Majesty's pardon is waiting there for you. They won't jail you."

She looked at me strangely, "A hell of a time to tell me that,

Cain. You haven't finished with me yet. I know that. So why do you tell me there's nothing to keep me here now?"

"I felt I should."

"Okay. But it's my turn now."

"Your turn?"

She gestured at her bruised body. "It's not the first time I've been beat up, and it's not likely to be the last, either. But I want my turn at them, Cain. I don't care what it costs. With or without you, you bastard." She turned painfully under the caressing hands of the girls and said somberly: "I've some payments of my own to make now."

"Just one thing I want to know. Tell me about the man who...questioned you."

"An American. Small, dark, a good, Boston sort of voice, a man too goddamn fastidious to lay a hand on me. He left that to the others."

"The others who were there when we broke in?"

"That's them." She said, whispering: "Don't ever get yourself raped by a Chinese, Cain. They're too cruel with it."

I said harshly: "Give me a day or two and I'll find your American for you. I'll bring him to you."

She turned away, disgusted. "You sure as hell don't know much about Macao, Cain. You'll never find him."

"I know his name. I know where he lives."

I could feel surprised Mai's eyes on me, but I was watching Bettina. She held my look for a while, and then she turned away and began to cry. She said through her tears: "You bastard, do you have to watch me cry? Get out of here, for God's sake!"

Through the open windows with their heavy, curlicued bars, the sound of a siren was loud and insistent. It was only a half-mile or so to the warehouse, and the flames were taking good hold now.

I went and stood on the tiny veranda and watched the glow of the fire; the firecrackers were all going off, and we could hear the shouts of people in the streets. I turned and found Bonelli beside me.

He said, watching: "My old warehouse—we had a fire there once when I owned it. An insurance fire. Only the rains came and put it out before it could really take hold. It cost me a lot of money, that rain storm."

He was making conversation, aware that I felt for Bettina more deeply than he did and not wanting to tell me again of the warnings he had given me.

He said: "Some people can stand anything if they know that sooner or later it will end. But at the time, she could not have known you would save her. Even after the things they did to her down there."

"And how can I make it up to her, can you tell me that?"

A bright red rocket went sailing across the sky, trailing a plume of white magnesium smoke, and burst into a million golden stars. I always liked a good firework display.

Bonelli was silent for a while, and then he repeated Bettina's question: "Was it worth it, Cain? Was it really worth it?"

I perched myself on the iron railing and turned to look at him. I said: "Do you know a man named Wentworth?"

"No. But if he has any interests in this part of the world, I can soon find out about him. It shouldn't be too hard."

"If you don't know him, it presupposes that he has no interests in Macao?"

"I'd say so. Unless he operates under another name."

There was a sudden light of intelligence in his eyes. He said sharply: "Wentworth? Yes, I remember now. I never met him."

"Sally Hyde's ex-husband." He was watching me, waiting. I said: "In that cellar, there were some suitcases with his name on them, and a note had been scrawled on a slip of paper wedged under one of the handles: *Deliver to the Blue Orchid.* A junk presumably?"

"No." Bonelli shook his head: "The Blue Orchid's a fisherman's restaurant in the sampan harbor. There are a couple of hundred sampans there, all wedged in together; and among them, there is an old barge that serves as a restaurant, a club, a hideout—the Blue Orchid."

"It doesn't sound like a very salubrious place for a man like Wentworth to be staying at."

"If it really is the same Wentworth. Surely, a common enough name in your country?"

"Yes, it is. But how many Wentworths do you suppose there are in Macao at the same time? With expensive luggage, the kind of luggage Sally's ex-husband would have? And here at the same time she is here, hiding out somewhere? And tied up, one way or another, with Ming? Too many coincidences, Bonelli. It's the same man. And it answers a lot of questions, doesn't it?"

He stroked his chin delicately with one thin finger, an affected gesture, and looked at me thoughtfully and said:

"If Wentworth is working with Ming, could it possibly be that Sally Hyde got to Ming through him?"

"Precisely what I was wondering. But there's one thing..."

"Only one?"

"Markle Hyde told me a little about Wentworth...Not a great deal, but nothing that suggested he was Ming's sort of caliber, There's a glimmering there of light; a bit vague at the moment, but—have you ever been to The Blue Orchid?"

He raised an elegant shoulder. "To a place like that? Hardly."

I went back to see Bettina. She was covered now with a silk-and-down comforter, a gold and red dragon sprawled across her body. Without makeup, her face shining with oil and seeming paler than it was, she was really quite lovely. Mai was pouring her some green Japanese tea. I sat carefully on the edge of the bed and said: "I've got to be sure about this American, Bettina. I believe I can find him, but I don't want to get the wrong man."

She stared at me for a while and said at last: "Very slight, not much more than...what, a hundred and fifty or sixty pounds. Dark hair brushed across his forehead, a bit long. Brown eyes, with thick eyebrows, sort of level, not curved. And a bit of a queen," I tried hard not to look at Bonelli when she said that, but she noticed the slightest flicker of his mouth and said with a snort, looking up at Bonelli with almost a smile on her face: "Oh, not a flaming, bloody pansy like you, just a touch of it." Bonelli was shocked.

I sighed and said to him: "I'll have to go to The Blue Orchid, of course."

I knew the sampan harbor; some years ago I'd met a man there who made a respectable living by fishing corpses out of the water every morning and selling off the bodies to the hospital across the bay on the Chinese mainland.

I said: "It won't be too hard to get on board, but it won't be so easy to get off again. Any suggestions?"

Bonelli said promptly: "Yes. Keep away from it altogether."

"I've got to find out if Wentworth is really there. And also to make sure he is the man who...who did that to Bettina."

"Then winkle him out."

"That won't be easy, either."

"Not easy, but safer. Meet him on your ground, not his. I tell you, friend, if all the people who want you dead could choose a place to find you fortuitously...that place would be the sampan harbor. You wouldn't get within fifty feet of the barge."

"Maybe. But once he knows I'm interested in him, knows that I'm even aware of his existence—no, he's not about to be winkled out of a safe hiding place."

He was pacing up and down, tall and slender and willowy, the white cuffs showing a broad swath under the sleeves of his black silk jacket. He took a tiny rose from his buttonhole—a violet-scented White Banksia—and sniffed it for a while, turning it round and round between his thumb and forefinger; he began to stroke the side of his long nose with it, delicately, like a man touching his mistress's breast with a peacock feather; I wondered if he got as much of a kick out of it. He turned to me at last and said:

"Why? That's the question, isn't it? Why should Sally's ex-husband suddenly turn up out of the blue?"

"There's another why. Is this why Sally came here? Was she really looking for him, and not for Alexander Ming?"

"Or, is he looking for her too?"

I shrugged. "There's only one way to find out, isn't there?"

He said urgently: "Don't try it, Cain. You'll never get off that barge alive. You'll never even get on it."

"We'll see." Mai was looking at me strangely, a questioning sort of look. I said to her: "By myself, this time."

She said coolly: "I will stay with Bettina, Mr. Cain."

"Good." I said to Bonelli: "She can stay here? She'll be safe?"

"She can stay, and she'll be safe. But I think you're a fool." He sighed. "I'll have Captain Ericeira and a couple of his men right behind you all the way."

I checked my watch; it wasn't even midnight yet.

I said: "If I'm not back here by three o'clock, can you get

Melindo to raid The Blue Orchid? And find me?"

"Or find your body. Yes, I can do that. Try and hold out till two o'clock, will you?"

"Two o'clock?"

"The numbers game. My number comes up then, and if that should be the hour you die...I stand to make quite a lot of money, Cain."

Mai was looking at me with that somber melancholy look in her eyes again. I smiled at her and leaned over to touch Bettina's cheek with the tip of my fingers. Her eyes were closed, and she opened them and looked at me unsmiling, and I said: "I'll be back soon. With the man you want to meet."

Bonelli was looking down at her, wondering how he could help and knowing there was nothing he could do to ease the pain. And then he did something that endeared him to me forever; he said suddenly: "Just a moment."

He left the room without another word, and when he came back after a few moments, he was carrying another of his roses; I wondered just where he was growing them. It was a brilliant apricot color with a golden base to the heavily veined petals, and the scent of it was sweet and strong. He held it out to Bettina and said, almost shyly:

"For you, Bettina. You know what kind of a rose it is?"

She didn't want to show that she too was touched. She shook her head, and Bonelli looked at me and smiled delightedly, and I told her:

"One of the best roses Meilland ever brought out. In 1953, I think. A cross between Peace, and Demain, and Mme. Joseph Perraud. It's called Bettina."

I could feel them all watching me as I moved away. I looked back and saw Bettina smiling now.

CHAPTER 8

The water was warm, but it was cooler than the air above it. And it stank. Its top three or four inches seemed to be composed entirely of week-old garbage that was too rotten even for the fish of the harbor to devour.

The sampans were crowded so closely together that there was scarcely room to move. There were a few stretches of open water not more than thirty or forty feet across and then more sampans lashed together and open water again, and another cluster. The shallow-draft boats were joined by ropes of crudely woven fiber and swung from the four-pointed anchors that kept them permanently in position. These were not boats for traveling; they were the homes of people too poor to find a space to live on the land.

Two acres of land, they say, is all that a Chinese needs to support a family of five or six; but land was scarce in the overcrowded colony, and most of these families were refugees from the mainland; and they were ever watchful for the Cantonese secret police, who came over once in a while to drag or beat and carry back home some helpless mainlander whose criticism of his old homeland was too vociferous. They disappeared at an alarming rate, the refugees; but nobody seriously worried about this; there were too many people in the colony anyway, and there were always new arrivals to fill up the already overcrowded sampans again. Life went on, with the children playing on the narrow decks. They wore gourds tied round their waists—it was part of their everyday clothing—as a protection against drowning should one of them fall in; these water people were almost all non-swimmers.

A Yangtze boat, Bonelli had said, would be my guide. I swam around in circles for a while, looking for the odd-shaped craft, and found it at last, its high teak prow rising up out of the water at an angle of twenty degrees off vertical, its sides twisted, one concave, the other convex, as though a giant hand had taken the finished boat and twisted it like a *croissant*. More than eight hundred years ago, a mariner had built the first complex Yangtze boat with mathematical precision, an extraordinary shape that, somehow, kept its course in the swift and tortuous river; and ever since, the Yangtze folk had built their boats this way, blindly following their ancestor's lead. Here, among the tightly packed sampans with their rush shelters, it was a landmark that could not easily be missed. I swam around it, guided by the lights that were bright behind me, the lights of the town where the rich folk lived.

Over the stink of the garbage, I caught the pungent smell of wood-smoke, of fish frying in oil; I heard a child calling for its mother, and the reed-like intonation in reply. Over to my left, an old, old woman was punting her craft toward me, and there was a thick-set man in the prow, crouched on his heels and trailing a string in the water; I trod water for a moment, my head among the rotting watermelon rinds, waiting until he had passed.

Another sampan passed, an English sailor sitting in the stern, being paddled to one of the floating brothels by a tall, thin woman whose face caught the reflected yellow lights as she passed me in near silence, with just the faint sound of her pole in the water to mark her passing. My bare toes tangled in a sunken net, and I struggled to free them, then swam on slowly till I located the barge that was called The Blue Orchid.

It was low in the water, a converted barge of the kind used to carry brushwood on the mainland, the brushwood they used for flood control, wedging it into the banks of the flooding rivers. (If anyone took this wood to use for fuel, he was imprisoned and soundly beaten.) The tall center-mast was still there, but the sail had long since rotted away, and only a few shreds hung there, gray as a shroud. The bamboo-and-rattan shelter along two-thirds of the deck was high and spacious, with a line running from its rear end to the short and stubby aftermast, and some singlets were hanging from it. Along the side I could see there were seven small portholes, an unusual design here; I wondered how much of the barge would be below the surface, and why it was so low in the water. It was about eighty feet long and fifteen feet wide, and its keel, I knew, would be recurved, the better to ride the troughs of the waves at sea.

I swam carefully round it, listening to the sound of the chatter on board. There was a powerful little outboard motorboat swinging from the stern—a fast and luxurious little boat of a kind I would not have expected to find here; it was a good sign. There was also a clear, bright light streaming out of the high cabin windows in the stern, much brighter and cleaner than the usual kerosene lamps would have cast; another good sign; I made a mental calculation of just where that cabin would be. I swam on.

Someone had once loved this boat; the heavy timbers were ornately carved and painted in bright colors. A replica of the God of Anger, one eye closed in a fierce leer, carved in wood and painted brightly, was scowling into the water, peering down at me from the prow. I took a deep breath, and plunged under the surface of the dark water, and went down deep, fifteen feet or more, before I found the underside and came up on the other beam. More cabins, then, below deck, the old holds converted to make sitting room for the customers and perhaps a private room or two as well, with sand for ballast to hold her low down in the water. I scratched my bare back on barnacles as I came up, and a spike caught in my bathing trunks and ripped them.

I swam aft, and then up forward again, listening to voices; they were all aft, where the scent of a charcoal brazier was strong; I beard the clink of glasses, and a man's strong laughter. I checked the sampans close by; they were crowded with the silhouettes of twenty, thirty, fifty people against the night sky; they were squatting on rickety decks, crouched over fires of smoldering fagots, or wandering about and shouting across the water to one another.

Speed then, to get aboard and below decks quickly, before some inquisitive fisherman should yell a warning. I found the mooring-chain and pulled myself cautiously up it, looking back over my shoulder to the sampans, where the casual danger lay; nobody seemed to be paying attention to anything but his own problems. The moon was bright, but it was low in the sky ahead of me.

I pulled my head up to the thwart and rested there, searching out the deck for a sign of life. I could hear a rhythmic, swishing sound, a strange sound not easily identifiable. Steel on stone? In the darkness, I could make out the shape of a man half-turned towards me, sharpening a long knife with an old-fashioned fid of a stone, easing it along the blade in smooth, straight strokes, like a farmer sharpening a scythe. I pulled my way along a little, leaving the chain and using the heavy teak bulwarks as a hold, inching my way to get behind him. A quick look back over my shoulder again, and then I was silently over the top, slithering quickly towards the cover I had decided on—a tarpaulin thrown carelessly over a pile of plump sacks. I lay on the bare deck there and hoped no one would see the trail of water I must have left behind me. I lay for a long, long time in silence until I felt that I was part of the old boat itself and no longer an intruder. I could hear snatches of conversation in the rough, coarse accents of the North.

"...And no work on the dock except for those *something* Cantonese..."

"There is food. It is not necessary to work. There is food and a place to stay."

Someone else called out: "Bring wine," and soon some bare, female feet padded silently past my hiding place, stepping in the water I had left on the deck; she paid it no heed. I heard the man with the knife dip his stone into a bucket of water and begin honing again; and when the woman passed by on her return trip, I heard her say: "You're splashing water all over the deck." He did not answer her, nor did the rhythmic sound of his knife stop.

Two men, talking quietly, came up from below decks; now I knew where the companionway was. One of them said quietly: "You'll get a better price in the bay, but you'll have to watch out for the police there. They've got new boats, American ones." I wondered how the Red Chinese had acquired American patrol boats. The other man answered the query for me: "Yes, I saw them painting out the Korean markings."

A boat, a gun, a radio is made and sent far away to keep the peace or make a war, the products of the American factories standing out in the harbors all over the earth, and waiting to be off-loaded. Well and good, but a year or two later? Who knows where they may finish up? Corruption, bribery, theft, loss in battle...The chain is never ending; only the artifact is constant, well built and lasting, and it ends up in strange places halfway across the world from its place of origin. It doesn't die easily, a weapon, and there's no power on earth that can keep it where it's supposed to be. We spew them out of our factories, and they get lost, and we spew out more; but they're not lost, they're merely someplace else, serving another purpose, not dying like the men who use them but going from one battlefield to another, sometimes secretly and sometimes with covert and sardonic pleasure.

I lay in the dark and wondered, now that I was on board The Blue Orchid, what the hell was I going to do next. A man in a bathing suit feels naked with only his wits and his muscles for protection; it's as though a pair of pants is a suit of armor. Of one thing I was sure: once I made my presence known, I had to get out of there fast, before the surprise could wear off.

I peeked out from under the tarpaulin and looked at the moon; not a goddam cloud in sight. I studied the contours of the boats, looking for a space of clear water I could dive into quickly without sinking a sampan in the process, or banging my still aching head to a pulp on a half-sunken spar; the west looked a likely direction, and it was the quickest route to the shore.

And if Wentworth wasn't there after all? Well, at least I would have had a swim in the cool waters of the bay, garbage or no garbage.

I crawled out from under, looked around carefully, stood up, and walked quickly to the companionway. I was halfway down it before I heard someone shout, and there was the sound of running bare feet beside me. But I was down there now, in a long, low-ceilinged room with bare teak walls, where eight or nine Chinese were lying down on paillasses against the walls, smoking opium; the air was ripe with the sickly scent of it. One or two of them stared at me with vacant eyes; a young girl, not much more than fifteen, was lighting a little pellet of paste, bending over the pipe of a recumbent old man who lay stark naked across the floor, the yellow skin loosely sagging over skeletal bones.

A young and stocky fellow dressed in the blue tunic of a railway worker dropped his pipe and got to his feet, lunging at me with a movement that was purely reflex; there's something startling about the sudden appearance of a tall, semi-naked man like me—the boards of the ceiling brushed my head in the half-light; with their fear of devils, I must have looked like a strange god rising up out of the sea to damn them all to their own kind of purgatory, and it was with a touch of regret that I put my hand on the man's face and shoved him away. He fell and yelled and dragged out a knife, and then the running steps were coming down the stairs, fast.

There was only one door, and I didn't bother to try it. Instead, I put my foot against it and pushed, and it went flying off its hinges, and there was another room behind it, just as I'd thought, a much better furnished room, with a bright pressure-lamp hissing loudly, the lamp whose light I'd seen at the stern. There was a curved divan here; it was tapestry-covered and running around the wall, with a small wooden platform at one end of it, raised now like a lid to disclose a neat and quite efficient wash-basin and tap. There was a marvelous carpet on the floor, a Ghiordes-knot Chinese from Hupeh in pale greens and beiges, and a couple of leather poufs and a carved-ebony armchair. A small folding table had been set up here, and there were the remains of a dinner on it, what looked like *queues d'ecrivisses* and smelled as if it had been cooked a *la nage*, in court-bouillon and cognac; I remembered Markle Hyde's scornful comments about Wentworth's love of his stomach and a *la nage* is not only the simplest way to prepare crayfish, it's also the best.

He was there all right, sitting at the table and swinging round to stare at me, a white damask napkin in his hand and a very surprised look on his face. I was on him before he could even drop the napkin, and I hit him just once, fairly hard, on the side of the head, and caught him as he went flying across the floor. I scooped him up, a featherweight, and swung round to put a foot in the stomach of the Chinese who was coming at me, knife in hand—a short, ivory-handled knife with a curved blade, the kind they use in Kirin, which lies north of Korea. There was another man behind him, and I used my foot again and caught him under the chin as he dived at me, and then I was stumbling over them as they both tried to get to their feet at once and grab at me in the narrow stairway. But they were behind me now, and I heard someone yell in Mandarin: "Get the gun." And then I was on deck and jumping over the side into the garbage again.

The whole thing had taken maybe sixty seconds from the time I first peeked out under the tarpaulin.

I grabbed Wentworth by the collar and dragged him with me, swimming one-handed, fast, towards the shore. I heard a shot fired behind me, and then another and another, and all hell was breaking loose back there. A bullet plowed into the water uncomfortably close to my head, and I pulled my bundle down under me, swimming underwater for a minute, and hoped that my captive had at least half a lungful of air left in him. I came up on the far side of a sampan, banging into it noisily, and heard a woman yell an obscenity, and then I was streaking out for the shore again, and there was no more shooting.

I heard the sudden roar of the outboard cutting into the night, but they were too late, much too late. I was already at the wharf, and Captain Theophilo Ericeira was waiting for me, with the big, flabby Arab cook beside him. The captain was grinning, and he took Wentworth's limp body from me, and sling him over his shoulder, saying: "*Nao devemos ficar aqui, Senhor*...We better not stay here."

I said: "Take him round to Bonelli's for me, will you?"

He nodded, and the Arab handed me the bundle which was a pair of pants and a shirt and some sandals. I slipped into the clothes quickly and said to him: "You better not wait here, maybe. There just might be more trouble than you can handle." I'm always suspicious of a flabby man's ability in a roughhouse. But the cook threw back his head and laughed, and said:

"*Wallahi, ahssan minni mafish, walleh fi Misr*...There is no one better than I am."

I shrugged and said: "Your head, not mine," and got down under the wharf and waited.

In a moment, the outboard bumped noisily against the timbers, and two men were there, the Chinese who had been sharpening the knife—he carried it now, glinting in the moonlight—and the one whose stomach I had bruised with my foot. They reached out to steady the little boat, standing up in it and grabbing at the mooring-rope. I bent down, took hold of the prow, stood up hard, and tipped it over. They both went splashing into the water, yelling, and I reached down and grabbed the first man and pulled him close up to me, holding him with one hand on his collar and the other on the wrist of his knife arm as he struggled.

I said: "Tell Alexander Ming I'll give him his friend in exchange for ten minutes of his time, any place he wants, any time he wants. You understand? Meanwhile, I'm holding him captive at The Fan-tan House of the Seven Hills. The House of the Seven Hills." I repeated it to make sure the message was getting home, and he stared at me, expecting to be broken in two there and then.

The second man was clambering up out of the water, his hands on the boards of the wharf, so I stomped on them once, just to make sure he knew he was *de trop*; he squealed and dropped back into the water, and I threw the first man down on him and left them there, struggling together in the water. But they'd been given a job to do, and they wanted to do it. They came up again over the edge, not learning the lesson, and I was about to do something about it when the Arab said softly: "This time, *Effendi*, a pleasure for me." I watched. He bent down and lifted the two of them clean out of the water, one in each hand, and held them there, struggling. He turned to me and said: "You see, *Effendi?* What I do with them now?"

I said: "They're undersize, throw them back in." He did just that.

It took me three minutes to run to Bonelli's place. Bettina was sitting up in bed, staring at Wentworth, who lay on the floor beside her, dripping wet and looking up at her in stark terror. Ericeira was there too, standing with one foot on Wentworth's throat; not that he was about to get up and run, he was far too frightened. Mai and Bonelli were there, and Bonelli looked at his watch, making a ballet-dancer movement with his wrist, and said:

"Two o'clock. Have we had enough excitement for one night, Cain?"

Bettina was staring at Wentworth with an expression in her eyes that told me all I wanted to know. But I asked her anyway. I said: "It couldn't be anybody else, but just for the record...?"

She did not take her eyes off him, and there was a look in them that made me glad I was not her enemy at this moment. She nodded slowly. She was trembling.

Suddenly she looked around wildly, saw a tall wine bottle on the bedside table, and grabbed it. She'd just begun to swing it to break off the bottom when Mai took her wrist firmly, arresting the movement, and said gently: "I will take care of him for you, Bettina. I will do it."

I reached over and took the bottle away, and said: "Don't forget you're ladies, both of you. What has to be done, I will do."

Wentworth was dripping dirty harbor-water all over the beautiful blue carpet, and I said to Bonelli: "Can we keep him on ice in the cellar for a while?"

Bonelli nodded slowly, looking at Wentworth thoughtfully. He looked at Ericeira and said: "The empty storeroom, perhaps? You'll find chains and padlocks in the cupboard." He frowned and then turned to me and said: "You don't want to talk to him first? In the course of time, he might recover whatever courage he has. Just now, it all seems to have drained away, wouldn't you say?"

I said: "It won't make much difference. He'll tell me what I want to know, when I want to know it. And I've got some thinking to do first. And I'm hungry."

"Ah yes, of course, you haven't eaten." He was suddenly very apologetic, as though it were all his fault. He clapped his hands loudly and said: "A steak, perhaps? The quickest thing."

I said: "Do you have any crayfish?"

He shrugged. "If that's what you fancy, it's merely a matter of sending the cook down to the docks."

"Good. *A la nage*, then."

He raised a surprised eyebrow but made no comment, and when the young girl came in, in answer to his summons, he told her what was wanted. She bowed and went out. Ericeira was bundling Wentworth through the door, not very gently, with a huge hand tight on his skinny neck, and I said to him: "I need him, Theophilo. Don't lose him." The captain grinned and shook his head. "I won't lose him, Senhor Cain. Trust me."

I sat on the bed next to Bettina and touched her forehead, feeling the heat there. Mai hovered, waiting, her head cocked to one side as though she were listening for a sign of something between us. I said to Bettina:

"Getting better slowly?"

She looked at me, her eyes troubled, and nodded. "Yes. And I didn't thank you, did I?"

"Under the circumstances, thanks were hardly necessary."

"They would have killed me."

"Yes, they would."

"Why didn't they kill me as soon as they found out I wasn't really Sally Hyde? I have been wondering about that."

"They would have used you the way I'm going to use Wentworth. For a trade."

"Oh."

"But now, the shoe's on the other foot."

"Progress?"

"Considerable progress. They're out in the open now. And we've got one of their top men."

"You can't be sure of that. He might be...just a nobody."

"Ming's operation is mostly Chinese, Macanese, Japanese. It's at least a likelihood that an American would automatically be one of the upper echelons. Good old American know-how, all that jazz."

"Yes, I suppose so. And Ming?"

"By now he knows I've got Wentworth. And he'll trade, because I'm not asking much in return. I'm making it worth his while."

Mai said suddenly: "A man like Ming, Mr. Cain, he'll be a better trader than you are. You'll have to be careful, and you'll still get the worst of the bargain."

"The worst is all I need. One step at a time. It all hinges, really, on just how Wentworth figures in all this, doesn't it?"

"And that's something you don't know."

I said gently: "That's what I'm going to find out as soon as I've had my supper."

CHAPTER 9

The *ecrivisses a la nage* were excellent, and they put me in just the right frame of mind for my talk with Wentworth. But first, I stretched out on the floor after my supper and did two hundred quick pushups to aid the digestive system a trifle, and then sat back in the over-decorative chair in the room Bonelli had given me, put my feet up on a silk-covered hassock all decked out with embossed dragons, and did some serious thinking.

My antagonist was a man named Alexander Ming, whom I'd never met. Nor could I possibly know enough about his thinking processes to make more than a guess at what he'd do now, now that I'd got one of his men; the thought occurred to me glumly that perhaps Wentworth had nothing whatever to do with Ming but was merely looking for his ex-wife for some reason or other entirely unconnected with me, and that he was using Bettina brutally because he was a brutal man, and that this was a brutal place where the finer nuances of decent behavior were more easily pushed aside than in most parts of the world.

And yet, if so, what was he doing on The Blue Orchid? They'd made him comfortable there, but it still could be nothing more than a hideout for a man who wanted desperately not to be seen. And if he was having baggage sent there, then his stay was probably going to be a long one; unless—I wished I'd had time to open up those suitcases with his name on them and find out whether they contained the usual ran of two smart suits and a change of socks, or if perhaps...Well, too late now, but I chalked up the mental note of a minor goof: I'd been too worried about Mai holding those Wuh-keis at bay, not knowing how long she would have been able to get away with it.

And another thing. Speed is the best weapon a determined man has, and maybe speed alone counted for my extraordinary success on The Blue Orchid; but were those men, then, Ming's? Would he have had more efficient minions? Perhaps not; the barge was merely a hideout, after all, and a well-enough known one at that. It was never meant to be a closely guarded fortress; and but for the fortuitous fact that I'd seen those suitcases, there'd never have been any indication that Wentworth was there at all, even if he really were tied in with all this.

Back to the starting point again...

I went down to the cellar to find him regurgitating a little because of the *ecrivisses*.

Ericeira had chained him in the storeroom where the overflow of cases of Bonelli's counterfeit Johnnie Walker were stored when the distilling was done; it was a smallish room with whitewashed walls and almost no furniture, and a small barred window high in the wall that gave, on the other side, onto the edge of the water. The window had a length of canvas tacked over it, and hanging down from under it, was a long chain with a padlock; the other end was padlocked around Wentworth's neck, not tight enough to harm him, but not loose enough to be comfortable either; apart from this, Ericeira had made no effort to confine him, but he was sitting outside the small locked room on an apple box, smoking a black cheroot and cleaning a revolver with an oily rag—a British-Army Smith and Wesson .38.

He grinned at me silently, and handed me the keys, and I unlocked the chain from around Wentworth's neck and said pleasantly: "Let's go to my room, we've a lot to talk about."

He was still trembling, and there was a pasty bruise under one eye that had not been there the last time I'd seen him. He said hesitantly: "What are you going to do to me, Cain?"

"You know my name?"

He looked away. "Yes. Yes, I know who you are."

"Good. That already answers one of my questions."

"Is it any good telling you...I'm sorry about that...that

woman?"

"No. No good at all."

"We had to find out who she was, what she wanted. Surely you must realize that?"

"Sure, it's a tough game, isn't it? You're just going to find out how tough."

He was about to answer with a shudder, and then there was the sound of shattering glass, and a scraping sound; and we both looked up at that window together. That damned canvas, stretched tight against the wall, had stopped the bomb from coming right through, and it was lodged there; it might have taken a long time to rip the canvas away, retrieve it, and hurl it back through the window again, and it occurred to me to wonder how long the fuse was.

Not long. I had closed the door behind me, and there was just time for me to charge into it with my shoulder and knock it right off its hinges, so that it went crashing down beside an astonished Ericeira out there in the corridor; and then, as I grabbed Wentworth with one hand and lugged, the bomb went off with a dreadful sound in the confined space. But we were already under the cover of the wall. Wentworth screamed, whether with fright or pain I didn't immediately know. I lugged him to his feet and said calmly:

"You see what I mean? A tough game. Don't say you didn't know that. I wonder what it is they don't want you to tell me?"

Ericeira was staring into the storeroom. The shattered canvas was still burning and had a gaping hole in it, and I said: "Don't worry. No damage." I shepherded Wentworth up the stairs and into my room, sat him down on the floor in a corner, took a comfortable chair myself, poured a drink, leaned back, and watched him for a while as he sat there, looking smaller than ever and somehow lost.

I said: "I can get sodium pentothal, or I can get someone to stick needles under your nails. All that sort of non-sense. Or we can just chat like civilized human beings, even if you're not one. Now, which is it to be?"

He licked his lips. The black eyebrows were a straight, heavy line under his forehead; they were also surprisingly bushy. The dark eyes were alert and cautious, and at the same time reflected considerable fear. He said, shaking: "I'll tell you anything you want to know."

I said: "Good. Just sit there for a moment."

I went out of the room, leaving the door half-ajar, and there was Ericeira standing guard, just as I'd expected. I said to him: "Get Mai for me, will you?"

He went off and I went back into the room and sat down again; I sipped my drink and waited, and when Mai came in—there was a questioning look in her eyes—I found her a chair and said: "I want you to listen to at least part of this, Mai. Pour you a drink?" She shook her head and sat down primly, her hands in her lap; she looked at Wentworth with no expression at all on her face.

I said: "Now, off the top. Who told you to pick up Bettina Harkan?"

He waited a long time before answering, and I wondered if he was plucking up courage to tell me the truth or deciding just how much he could fool me—or might dare to. He was gauging my temper and finding that perhaps I wasn't really a very violent man; but he couldn't be sure. He said at last, his voice a whisper: "Alexander Ming."

"And your relationship with him is...?"

"I work for him."

"Doing what?"

A long pause again. Then: "Marketing."

"Drugs?"

"Yes. I'll make a deal with you, Cain."

"No deals."

"You'd better wait till you hear what I have to offer."

"And in return, you want...?"

"I want out. I want a couple of suitcases I've got hidden away, and an escort to the airport when you've finished with me. If I don't get away...if I talk and stay here..."

"Yes, they'll kill you. Has it occurred to you that I might do that myself?"

"I don't think you will." He was surprisingly sure of that. His courage was coming back slowly, and I was glad of it; more helpful in many ways.

I said again: "No deals, and you'll talk. What you tell me will decide what I'm going to do to you, or with you. First of all, how did you manage to pick up Bettina so easily?"

He told me the truth, "I got one of the hotel girls to slip a mickey finn into her whisky bottle. The girl works for us sometimes." He was talking more easily now, glad he'd planted a seed in my mind.

I said: "Next question. Why did Ming want her?"

"She was claiming to be Sally Hyde. Sally Hyde had said she was here looking for Ming, so...so he wanted to know what she was up to. He wasn't really sure whether she was Sally or not, so...he told me to find out. After all, I was sure to know whether it was she or not. You understand what I'm saying? The only reason I was brought into this at all was that...well, I was the only man who could know, one way or the other." The words were tumbling out now, a comfort to him. He said: "Otherwise, I'd have had nothing to do with it at all."

"And you knew, of course, that she was a substitute. Did you wonder why?"

I think he knew what was coming. He licked his lips again, and his throat sounded dry. "That was what Ming wanted to know. If it wasn't really Sally, then he wanted to know why she was pretending."

"And you found that out."

"Yes."

I said: "How, Wentworth?"

"She told me. She told me that you'd hired her to impersonate Sally, to sit tight till someone picked her up."

"She told you? You just asked her?"

"That's right."

"Willingly?"

Now the comfort had all gone. He said, stuttering: "Well, not...not exactly willingly."

"Tell me what you did to her."

"I'd...I'd rather not. I'm not...not very happy about what...what Ming made me do."

"You mean he was there too?"

"No, but...but if I didn't find out, he'd have...he'd have killed me. It's as simple as that."

"And so?"

"So I had to find out."

I said: "I'm waiting, Wentworth."

He whispered: "I had to hit her a couple of times."

"With your hand?" He desperately wanted to lie; but with Bettina in bed upstairs, how could he? He said, trembling: "I used a stick."

"And you hit her where?"

"On the face...the body. Cain, please, I..."

"How hard?"

"Quite hard. I had to. I was afraid she wouldn't tell me, and I had to know. It was a question of self-protection. Anything I did, I did because I had to."

"And then?"

"Then she told me."

"How did her clothes get ripped off her?"

"She...she fought me. I had to have someone hold her."

"And that was who?"

The first lie now; he was getting overconfident: "Just a couple of Chinese who work for Ming." Not a lie, really; an evasion.

"And then?"

The voice was so quiet I could hardly hear him. "I believe...I believe they raped her."

"In front of you?"

A whisper: "Yes."

"Then you told them to? Or merely...allowed it?"

"Cain, please, I beg of you."

"Did you tell them to rape her?"

"Yes, I told them."

I said: "I can't hear you, Wentworth. Say it louder."

He swallowed hard and said: "I told them to. I told them to."

"To what?"

"To...to rape her."

I looked across at Mai. Her face was composed, quite unemotional; only her hands were moving, the fingers restlessly twining with each other. Wentworth exploded suddenly, his fear and his anger coming together. He said loudly:

"All right! I know it was a terrible thing to do, but...Well, she's not exactly a *lady*, is she? I don't suppose it's the first time she had that sort of...I mean, it wouldn't be as bad for her as it might be for, well, for someone else. I mean…Well, would it?"

I let him talk, not answering him, letting him put the rope around his neck. Mai was looking at me now, and I knew what she wanted; I shook my head.

He said again: "All right, it was a terrible thing to do, but…I had to treat her badly, Cain, don't you understand that? With someone of our class it would not have been necessary, but a woman off the streets—they've different standards from ours, can't you understand that?"

Mai moved, and I sat still. She went across to him and took him by the collar of his jacket, and yanked him to his feet. The surprise on his face was on account of the physical thing: he was a small man, but she was slighter, and yet, she yanked him up as if she were lifting a kitten off the floor. She held him with her left hand under his chin and jabbed the pointed fingers of her right hand into his gut; they were hard, quick, three rapid-fire blows into the solar plexus, and I said: "Don't do that, Mai, he'll be sick all over the carpet."

She took hold of his thin wrist, twisted her shoulder under his armpit, doubled up and yanked, and sent him flying through the air to land with a terrible thud against the wall; I heard his arm break as she let go of it at just the right moment.

I said: "All right, Mai, sit down."

She was moving towards him again, her hands open for a chop at his neck that would have killed him, and I said sharply: "No! Sit down! Sit down, Mai!"

She looked at me hard for a moment, then went and sat down, put her hands in her lap, and looked sadly at the tips of her little black shoes.

Wentworth groaned. He said, stumbling over the words: "My arm…my arm's broken." He didn't know yet the pain that would soon hit him around the gut, but his face was white.

I said: "Go back to your corner and talk."

He staggered to his feet and moved across the room, keeping a wary eye on Mai, and sank down again, leaning his head back, clutching his arm and groaning.

I said: "Now, the big question. Where is Sally Hyde now?"

He shook his head, moaning, and I said again, sharply: "Where is she, Wentworth?"

"I don't know. So help me, I don't know, Cain. If I did, I'd tell you. I swear I would."

"I believe you. Where's Alexander Ming?"

"He's...he's in Macao."

"So I guessed. But it's a big town."

"He...he moves around a lot."

"And at this precise moment?"

He whispered: "He's going to kill me, Cain, unless you get me out of here. South America. He'll kill me."

"Where are the suitcases?"

"The suitcases?"

I said impatiently: "The ones you want to take with you."

"They're in...in a warehouse in town, on Rua Querenta."

"And what's in them?"

"Money. Dollars from the States, I'll split it with you, Cain. Just let me get them. Send for them. I'll split it with you...A lot of money, more than three million dollars."

I didn't think it would be very kind to tell him it had all gone up in flames with the fireworks. I said mildly: "That's a lot of money. No reason why I shouldn't take all of it if I want to."

He doubled up and groaned, the pains coming on now.

"Just let me...let me have...a few hundred thousand of it to get...to get away with. The rest...the rest is yours." His voice was trailing off, and he looked at me with very glassy eyes and whispered: "Give me some of that cognac, for God's sake."

"No. Tell me where Ming is. Now, at this moment."

"He's at...at a bar on the main street, a place called The Essence of Heavenly Light."

"He lives there?"

"No. He's got a hideout somewhere, but the bar...the bar is one of his places, a sort of meeting place for the boys."

I said: "When Sally Hyde first came here, she went straight to The Essence of Heavenly Light to leave a message for Ming that she was after his guts. How did she know where to go?"

He said, gulping in great drafts of air: "I told her."

Well, that was a nice twist.

I said: "That's something I'd like to know a great deal more about. Tell."

He took a deep breath and said again: "Some brandy, for God's sake."

I poured him a glass and gave it to him, and yanked him to his feet and sat him down on a chair, like a civilized human being once more, I said: "All right, talk or I'll set Tiger on you again."

He drank down the cognac and held out his glass for a refill, and when I poured it, he said: "We were married, Sally and I, and it didn't work out, so we got divorced. Her father, Markle Hyde, was against me right from the start. Well, the divorce didn't work out either, and we'd been writing to each other for some time now, but secretly, because of him."

"Or because of his money?"

"Because of both, I guess. Markle Hyde had used his money to ruin me financially. I didn't have a penny left in the world, so..." His voice trailed off, not wanting to tell too loudly of treachery. And the pieces were dropping into place.

I said: "All these years, Ming must have heard of the great philanthropist Markle Hyde. And he never knew that he was really his old enemy Ben Stirani, did he? Until?"

He licked his lips. "That's right."

"Until what, Wentworth?"

He said, stammering: "Until...until I went to Ming and told him."

"How did you know? It must have been a well-kept secret to have fooled so many people for so long. And I'm sure Sally would never have told you. She loved her father too much for that."

As I spoke, it occurred to me that this was only a guess; how did I know she loved him? Because *he* loved *her* so much? And then Wentworth cleared it up for me. He said earnestly:

"No, that's not true. Sally hated her father, though he never knew it. And one day, she told me why—because he was Ben Stirani."

"And then, after the divorce, you told Ming. For money?"

"Yes." His voice was a whisper.

"Well, we do know some nice people, don't we? How did Sally know Ming was here in Macao? How did she know about The

Essence of Heavenly Light?"

"I told her. We were still writing to each other once in a while."

"Did you think to warn her not to try and tangle with a man like Ming?"

"All I knew was that she wanted to get in touch with him."

"A likely story. You must have known she was going to try and kill him, for God's sake."

He tried to shrug, but the effort was too great. His face was white as a sheet. He said: "She's a strange woman. You never know what she's up to, not even what she's thinking. The only thing that's certain is that she hates her father. If he was fighting with Ming, she'd just automatically take Ming's side. That's the kind of woman she is."

It didn't ring true. I knew I would have to sort that bit later on. I said: "You spoke of a hideout somewhere. Where is it?"

He shook his head vehemently. "I don't know, Cain. God help me, I don't know. That's not the kind of information that Ming shares with anybody. He'd kill anybody who even made a guess at where it was." I let him talk. He went on: "I know he's got a place somewhere, because he comes and goes all the time, but, so help me, I don't know where it is."

I said: "A simple *I don't know* would have sounded more like the truth. You're lying, Wentworth. You *do* know, don't you? I'm surprised that you should, but I'm sure that you do. So tell me, and save yourself a lot of grief."

He was licking his lips again, and his throat sounded dry as the bottom of a parrot's cage that hasn't been cleaned out recently. He said, his eyes wide with fear: "I don't know!" But I knew that he did, and I waited. I waited, and then looked at Mai, and she got to her feet and moved towards him slowly, and he said quickly: "No! Please! If I tell you, will you help me?"

"No."

"Will you at least...try to get me away from here? Away from Ming?"

I said: "I'll tell you what I'll do. I promise not to let Bettina Harkan get her hands on you. Now, talk."

His voice was a whisper. "I'm not supposed to know, Ming

doesn't know that I know."

"That's all to the good."

"He'd kill me if he even suspected I know."

"That's all to the good too. Where is it?"

Very low: "The island of Siang-chu." The words were out, and he looked as though the words themselves could kill him, I have never in my life seen a man so scared.

Mai said quietly: "An island off the coast of the mainland, nothing there but ghosts and devils."

And Wentworth said: "Just a barren rock, really, but there is an old fortress there, mostly in ruins. Part of it has been refurbished, built on, and that's where Ming stays when he's in Macao. Three miles off the coast of Red China."

"Within Red China's territorial waters?"

"Yes, of course."

"And the Red Chinese allow the biggest drug supplier in the world to sit on their front doorstep? You're not making sense, Wentworth."

"It's the truth. They leave him alone."

"The Chinese went to war over the opium trade, to wipe out foreigners who were dealing in it. You never heard of the Opium Wars?"

He said, insisting: "I know all about that, but it's true none the less. Ming is useful to them. He comes and goes freely, he deals in other things besides drugs. He's got a hand in every racket there is, and...well, he supplies them with things they need from time to time."

The lights were shining brightly. I said: "Like patrol boats, for example?"

"Patrol boats?"

"From Korea?"

"Oh, that. Yes, Ming and his men hijacked three boatloads of arms destined for South Korea, en route from Japan. He sold the guns to the Nationalist Chinese in Laos, and the boats..."

"In Laos? Aren't your facts getting a bit twisted?"

"No, they are not. There are still more than a hundred thousand of the old Nationalist army in Laos. They've been there ever since the war, with their own generals, their own supply organization. They're quite autonomous. Not soldiers any more, of course, but brigands. They protect the drug traffic that comes and goes; they keep the trails open, and they extract a duty, so much a ton of the stuff that passes through their territory. In that part of the world, in the jungles and the mountains, you can't move without their protection. Anyway, Ming sold them the hijacked arms, and he sold the boats to the Chinese in Canton; they converted them for use with their antipiracy squads. They don't call them patrol boats, they call them chasers."

"Well, learn a little something every day. How high are you in Ming's esteem?"

He stared. "I don't think I understand you?"

"Are you worth a ransom, that's what I'm asking."

The white of his face went whiter still: "Good God, you can't do that, Cain, not after all I've told you. He'd know, he always knows. And he'd...he'd kill me."

I said nastily: "Not until he'd found out just how much you'd talked. I wonder how long that would take?"

"Please, Cain, please! I've played the game with you. I've told you all you wanted to know."

I said: "Not all, not yet. If you've been in touch with Sally, how come you don't know where she is now? Why should she come to Macao and not even get in touch with you? She must have known you were here. And, while we're on the subject, how long have you been hiding out on board The Blue Orchid, and why?"

He said; "I was in Hong Kong, traveling under another name..."

"What name?"

"I called myself Walter Richardson—a passport I picked up in Singapore. The Hong Kong police want me for...for drug smuggling."

"Go on."

"Well, I was in Hong Kong on...on some of Ming's business, and I was in touch with Sally, and she said she was coming here, and the next thing I knew was that she had disappeared. Nobody ever saw her again, and then this other woman turned up claiming she was Sally, so Ming told me to find out about it."

"Have you been on Siang-chu?"

"For God's sake, no! I'm not supposed to know it even exists!

Cain, that's priceless information I've given you. Any police force in these waters would give *anything* to know what I've just told you for nothing! You've got to let me go, do you hear?" He reached out and grabbed me by the lapels, and tugged at me and said again: "You've got to let me get away, Cain! Let me have my suitcase, just one of them, and get me to the airport, secretly. If I can get to Paraguay I'll be safe, and...I've helped you, Cain, you've got to help me. It's only fair!"

A bit of a queen, Bettina had said. He was whimpering now, most unregally.

He said again: "You'll help me, Cain, won't you?" He was whimpering like a sick puppy.

I said: "If I promised you that, I'd break my promise the moment I got upstairs and saw Bettina Harkan again, so I won't promise you anything. I won't even try to help you. And we're not finished yet, either. There's something else I want to know. Give me three names, three men close to Ming, close enough to be in his confidence."

He stared at me, and I repeated: "Any three, as long as they're close to him. Or I'll give you to Tiger here, or to Ming, whichever is worse."

He swallowed hard. "Well, there's Mori Patachiaow, and Gordon Valenski, and maybe Karl Peipin. They're closer than most."

"And what do they do?"

"Patachiaow heads the...the execution squads. If there's any...any trouble, he's the man Ming sends for."

"Where is he now?"

"Now? Now he's in New York, but he's coming here tomorrow. Some trouble with the Chinese end of the operation."

"What sort of trouble?"

"Hijackers. We lost a load of opium en route from Laos. Some smugglers held up the junk and took the load off."

"And Valenski?"

"He's in Hong Kong, head of the distribution end. My boss, I suppose you'd call him."

"Coming here too?"

"Not as far as I know."

"What about Peipin?"

Wentworth's eyes were glassy. I couldn't decide whether or not he was going to pass out from sheer fright at what he was doing or not. He said, gulping: "Peipin is head of the accounting department, the money man. Will you...will you help me get away?"

I said: "Probably not, so don't count on it. Tell me how a man like you ever managed to get any authority with Ming?"

He said eagerly: "I don't have any authority. I'm just a nobody, just one of the salesmen."

I said: "I don't believe all his salesmen would know as much as you seem to."

"No, but..." He said, whispering, more hesitant than he'd ever been before: "He likes me."

I said: "My God." I went to the door and called Ericeira. I said: "Put him back in his cellar, on his little chain, will you, Theo?"

Ericeira said: "And suppose maybe they throw another bomb?"

I shrugged and didn't answer, and Wentworth squealed, and when I closed the door again, the captain was already kicking him down the stairs.

Mai said, her voice very quiet: "Can we go back to Bettina now?"

I took her hand in mine, and together we went back into the other room.

Bettina was sitting on the edge of the bed now, a glass of wine in her hand. She wore a loose silk kimono of pale yellow, and the rose Bonelli had given her was in a small white-ceramic vase at her elbow. She looked up, and I asked: "Are the pains going away, slowly?"

She nodded. "Most of them. Are we making any progress?"

"We?"

Her voice was hard. "*We*. I'm in this too now, and don't try to ease me out of it. Mai and me, side by side behind you, how does that grab you, Cain?"

I said: "I've done you enough harm, Bettina. I'd rather try and edge you away from this sort of thing, rather than deeper into it. Mai, yes, because she's a good man in a fight. But you, no."

"Then just give me a knife and five minutes with Wentworth. I'll settle for that."

"No. Not that either, Bettina."

She said glumly, sighing: "No, I didn't think you'd go along with that. You are a squeamish son of a bastard bitch, aren't you?"

"Am I?"

I'd never really thought that, myself; but it's always good to have someone else's opinion.

Bettina looked at her wine with disgust, tossed it back and said: "I don't know why I drink this goddamn wine. It always gives me athlete's foot. Pour me a Scotch, for God's sake."

CHAPTER 10

Bonelli said thoughtfully: "The clichés, of course, become clichés merely because their truths are inevitable enough to last forever. I wonder who first said: Dead men tell no tales?"

I said: "Wentworth?"

"Or any of Ming's other men. It's absolutely unheard of for a man in these rackets to talk his head off at the first sign of danger. It's axiomatic. The man who talks out of turn is a dead man, and surely Wentworth must know that? Nothing you could do to him would be half as bad as what he'll suffer the moment Ming finds out about him."

"He was scared."

"Of course. But even so..."

"Not scared by what I'd do to him; scared by what he himself had done. There's a very simple explanation. He's not one of the hoods at all. He's a businessman who happens to deal in the product that Ming prepares. For a brief moment, he stepped out of that role and became a terrorist beating up a helpless woman and, no doubt, enjoying it. He just didn't stop to think that in his world this sort of thing is left to others, to the people who, I agree, would die horribly rather than talk to the wrong people. He stepped out of his little world into one he could never really enter; and the terrible thing he did in those few moments scared him much more than any ideas he might have had about retribution. He either had to commit himself, once he'd taken the first step, or seize on any chance to wash his hands of what he himself had done. I agree with you, he's got no courage; but that isn't why he talked so freely."

"You're judging a man with insufficient knowledge of him."

He was absolutely right, of course. But my whole philosophy depends upon the probability of likelihoods; if you wait for truths, then you miss the train.

I said: "But perhaps you'll agree with me about what Ming has to do now?"

He gave me a long, cold look, not liking the upset I was bringing into the smooth functioning of his chosen milieu. He said softly: "There can be only one thing, can't there?"

"Aha! We're beginning to think alike now."

"That careless bomb downstairs." He shrugged. "A childish endeavor that would have come off but for the fortuitous fact that your shoulders are stronger than my door." He sighed and said: "That was a good teak door with solid brass hinges, did you know that?"

"I know that I've got an abominable ache in my back as a result of it. But it's comforting to know, isn't it? That Wentworth is really worth killing off?"

He corrected me gently: "Was worth killing off. Now our shadowy friend, who seems to know everything, probably knows that you've had a chance to examine him, so the situation has changed somewhat. Now it won't be a matter of killing him off; it will be rather a question of kidnaping him back again, so that one little question can be asked and answered: How much did he tell? Am I not right?"

I said again: "We're beginning to think *absolutely* alike."

"He is a terrible danger to Ming now. And something has got to be done about that."

"Even if, as you suggest, Wentworth was carefully telling me exactly what he wanted me to know?"

"Yes, even so. A man as close to Ming as Wentworth seems to be—and even that is moot, isn't it?—is in the hands of the enemy, and has been cross-examined by a man Ming knows is an enemy of some merit. Ming has to know what happened. He has to arrange for him to be rescued, if that's the word."

"Let's play games. Tell me just how he'd do it?"

Bonelli said promptly: "By the oldest method of all. He'd burst in here with a dozen armed men, and he'd find Wentworth, and he'd grab him, and he'd be gone before we knew what had hit us. You said yourself that speed is the only thing that counts in a case like this. The way you got Wentworth—that's the way Ming would get him, fast in, fast out again. Only he'd have a dozen men with guns to back him up."

"Then I suppose you've already taken some sort of precautions against that possibility?"

Bonelli was not the kind of man to sit back and let the tides wash over him. On the surface, perhaps, he was; but a man doesn't reach the degree of success that Bonelli enjoyed without a certain toughness, latent or not; not in these rackets and in this place.

He smiled slightly, as though I'd found out his little secret, and said smoothly, not bothering to apologize about it: "Of course, Mr. Cain. I have instructed Ericeira that, at the first sign of any trouble, he is to tell just where Wentworth is. If necessary, he'll lead them right to him."

I said mildly: "Markle Hyde spoke very highly of your friendship with him."

He shrugged. "Yes, indeed, there's almost nothing I wouldn't do for him. But I'm not going to have my gaming tables raked with machine-gun fire, Mr. Cain. I have a duty to my customers as well. Of course, if I agreed entirely with what you are doing..."

"I half-assumed that you did."

"Not completely. You are dangling a piece of bait for a mouse, but you are hoping to catch a rat, and that doesn't really make sense, wouldn't you agree?"

I sighed. Perhaps I'd counted too much on Bonelli. I said: "Well, at least I'm glad you told me."

He inclined his head a trifle, over graciously, and said politely: "I could hardly do less, could I? So, whatever plans you have for Wentworth, you'd better put them into execution soon."

I said: "I just want to hold him for a few hours, long enough for Ming to decide that he'd better play it my way."

He frowned.

I said gently: "I told Ming where I was holding Wentworth, that I'd trade a body for a talk. I sent him a message."

For a moment, he stared at me, horrified. "You told him?"

"Yes indeed. He'd have found out in time, but I prefer not to wait unnecessarily. I'm sorry about your nice teak door."

"My God." He thought for a while and burst out: "Cain, you're impossible! I wondered how he located his man so quickly! After all, I have always regarded this building as quite...secure."

I really was sorry he was so upset. I said: "Until I know just where Sally Hyde is, I can only regard every hour as another hour of acute danger for her. So..."

He threw up his hands with a gesture of resignation. The phone rang and he turned to look at it, worried. He waved his delicate wrist and looked at his watch and murmured: "At this hour? That's a special line."

"A special line?"

He nodded, reaching for it. "Nobody knows the number except...Markle Hyde..."

He hesitated, looking at me, and I said gently: "It's Ming."

It was, too.

Bonelli took the phone, listened for a moment, and then said: "Yes, he's here. But first I want to speak to Markle Hyde." I looked a question, but Bonelli paid me no attention. He listened again and said sharply: "Yes, I know you are. We were expecting to hear from you, and he's here. But first...I want to speak with Mr. Hyde." He waited a long time, looked at me with an expression of exasperation, and handed me the phone.

I took it and said: "I'm glad my message reached you, Ming Sin-san."

The voice at the other end was surprisingly cultured. Somehow I'd been expecting something quite different. It said very slowly, very low, very carefully: "Am I talking to Mr. Cabot Cain?"

"You are indeed."

"Then listen carefully, Mr. Cain. I understand that Mr. Wentworth is still alive, in spite of the recent attempt on his life. I understand you've been talking with him, and I want to know just what he told you. I want to know now, and at any price. So, whatever your price is, I'm prepared to pay it. If you were quoted correctly, your price is merely conversation, is that correct?"

"The answer to a few questions. Where are you?"

"Bonelli will tell you that." He sounded amused. He said:

"Come here now, and we'll talk. I won't ask you to come alone, because I do not really think you'd do that. Bring Wentworth with you, all right?"

I covered the mouthpiece with my hand and asked Bonelli: "He's at your house? With Markle Hyde?"

He said urgently: "Yes, but you can't go there."

I said: "I'll come without him, Ming Sin-san. Quite alone. I'll send him to you after we've talked, if I think that's a good idea."

I could hear the chuckle at the other end. "All right, I suppose that's fair enough. Will you come now?"

"I'll be there in thirty minutes." I put the phone down and said to Bonelli: "Will you go just a little further with me?"

He said stubbornly: "Ming doesn't want Wentworth, Cain. He wants you. You're not safe on the streets, so how do you think you'll manage face to face with him in a private house?"

I must confess that the prospect was not too exhilarating, but it was a question of alternatives and there just weren't any.

I said: "Why would he go to Markle Hyde?"

"That's what I want to know." He was frowning, his mind nibbling at an unpleasant problem. He said: "Markle Hyde for Wentworth? Is that what he's up to? Or is Markle Hyde already dead? The enmity between those two is unbelievable."

"And yet Hyde has taken no pains, apparently, to protect himself while he's here. All I saw at your house were two guards. Against Ming he'd need an army. That can only mean that he knows he's in no danger himself, not of that sort anyway."

Bonelli looked at me, puzzled. I told him: "All this started because Ming wanted to get at Hyde through his daughter. Vendetta. Just killing him off wasn't enough, you remember? He caused the death of his son and tried the same thing with the daughter. It's essential for him that Hyde remain alive to see just what happens to Sally. And Hyde knows that. He told me so in almost as many words."

Bonelli said thoughtfully: "Yes, perhaps, though you may be reaching for a conclusion you hope is the right one. And there's no reason for him to favor you with the same treatment, is there?"

"No, I suppose not. It's a nasty business."

"Then you won't go?"

"I must. But you didn't answer my question."

"A little further? Yes, I'll go a little further. What is it you want?"

"While I'm gone, that's the time Ming will try to get Wentworth. I suggest you get every one of Ericeira's men together and mount a really heavy guard."

He sighed. "All right. But I'll do better than that. I'll move him."

"Machine-guns raking your tables?"

"Precisely to avoid that, I'll put him where Ming won't be able to get at him, and yet will know where he is."

"That can be only one place. A police cell. You're sure he can't be kidnaped there? Or simply murdered?"

"No, I'm not sure. But it might take just a little longer."

"All right, I'll leave it to you and Ericeira." I was glad that he was on my side again after that moment of indecision; and all over a busted cellar-door! I knew he'd go along with me now, too; he was thinking that his old friend Markle Hyde was probably dead. I said: "Move him as fast as you can then. Don't let him sit still long enough to get grabbed. Or even shot. I might just need the fact that he's alive to get myself out of your house in one piece."

"Ye-e-s. It's a terribly dangerous thing you're doing."

"It always has been."

"But now there's absolutely no reason why he shouldn't just kill you off the moment you show your face."

I said: "There is. You said that truths become clichés when they're good enough to use all the time." He looked at me puzzled. I said: "There's a cliché about insurance too." He didn't know what the hell I was talking about. I said: "Is Melindo to be trusted? With Wentworth, I mean?"

"No, of course not.

"More money, then, by the hour. Every hour that Wentworth stays alive, another bundle of notes for Melindo."

He said sadly: "All these years I've been paying Melindo so very *little*. It seemed wise that he should never show signs of sudden affluence, or he'd be suspect and lose his value to me. And now the careful rationing of my bribery has come to nothing, hasn't it?"

I said sympathetically: "You may have to find yourself another boy, but just now I want Wentworth well looked after until I'm safely out of that house."

He said: "I'll hold him as long as I can. I wish I were sure about Markle."

"We'll soon find out."

He was resigned to my going. He looked at me as though he never expected to see me again. He made one more attempt: "There must be some way to persuade you."

"No. No, there's not. I hate it as much as you do, but there just isn't an alternative. I came here to find Sally Hyde, and Ming is the only lead we have."

"He might be just as much in the dark as you are."

"Yes, he might, but there's a chance he knows. He is her target, and it's a likelihood that she'll reach him, that she's already reached him, I'm working in the dark, and I've got to make the most of any glimmer of light."

Mai was standing at the door that led into the bedroom. She was looking at me with a sad, lonely look in her eyes. I had not heard the door open. Beyond her, I could see Bettina stirring in the bed, sleeping restlessly.

I said: "All right, Mai?"

She nodded, not taking her eyes off me, and I left her standing there and went out through the fan-tan rooms and down through the main door of the house and into the cold early-morning light.

It was five-thirty, and the sky was red in the east. The sounds of the town were muted, the streets deserted. I went down the *avenida* and turned onto the esplanade, and ran fast all the way to Penha Point, filling my lungs with the fine scent of the sea and watching the fishermen coming in with the sampans of seafood, dragging their nets behind them with the night's catch.

The house was an armed fortress. There were three men at the big iron gates, three more patrolling the grounds in the front, another pair at the front door, and I counted no less than seven in the house itself before I ever reached the big lounge where, on that first day, I'd met Markle Hyde.

Nobody tried to stop me. They shepherded me all the way

through, and there, at last, was Alexander Ming.

He was a big, big man (from the North, I remembered), looking not at all Chinese, except for a certain flatness to the nose. In spite of it—or perhaps because of the touch of alien blood—he was a handsome man, with silvery white hair and good, solid features. You'd have said he was a successful businessman, perhaps the head of a giant corporation back in the States; he was well dressed with a great deal of conservative care in a Brooks Brothers suit of fine blue wool, with a blue-striped white shirt and a dark silk tie; the polish on his alligator shoes shone with a remarkable lucidity, and he wore a single diamond ring on the little finger of his right hand.

He stood up as I was ushered in, and offered his hand with a genial smile, the kind of man you instinctively like; it was hard to realize that this was one of the ten most dangerous men in the world today, perhaps the most dangerous of all of them. His smile was reserved, courteous, just a little patronizing. He stood about six feet four, and he looked at me as we shook hands and said genially:

"Are you sure you've no Kirin blood, Mr. Cain? We're all big men in Kirin. How do you do."

"Mr. Ming."

"When we spoke on the phone you called me Sin-san."

"Yes but..." I couldn't resist it. I said: "No lookee Chinese. If you'll forgive me."

He laughed. "Sit down, and let's have a comfortable chat, shall we?" He clapped his hands—and now he was an Oriental—and the silent old servant was there, looking not nearly as inscrutable as he was supposed to be; there was an expression of tight fury on his face. Ming said: "Tea? Coffee? A drink? I hear you're a hard drinker."

I said politely: "Nothing, thank you. Just tell me first where Markle Hyde is."

"Markle Hyde? In his bed, fuming. Two men standing guard on him to make sure he stays there. Next question?"

"All right. Tell me why you came to this house?"

He shrugged. "Surely it's obvious. I could not resist the opportunity of telling Markle Hyde just how useless all his very expensive plans were. I was sitting there thinking about Ben Stirani, and I thought to myself: *He's here now, Markle Hyde in person. Why don't I go and say hello?* So, I came to this house to—how shall I put it?—to wave his helplessness in front of his miserable face, to tell him how badly things are going for him. And, I must admit, I derived a certain pleasure from the encounter."

He said piously: "There's so little of joy in life, we should seize all that we can find. Next question."

"I'd like to be sure he's alive."

"You have my word for it." His tone was deprecatory, shrugging it off as though it didn't matter very much whether or not I believed him. He added: "I have other plans for Markle Hyde. We were partners once, and partners make the best enemies, did you know that?"

"I know. Where's Sally Hyde?"

"Ah, Sally Hyde! I was hoping that perhaps you could tell me that. I'd like to know where she is too."

"Then suppose you tell me why?"

He leaned back in his chair and interlaced his fingers, resting them on his heavy stomach. He said carefully: "She came here to kill me, didn't she? Under normal circumstances, of course, that would not cause me very much concern. It's too frequent an attitude, I'm afraid. But she knew where to find me, knew that I was here. And in my organization, Mr. Cain, there are only two men who are constantly aware of my movements, so it's essential that I find out just where she got her information. I run a very tight little company, and if my secrets are being bandied abroad to anyone who asks for them, I must know exactly who to silence."

I said: "It was Mori Patachiaow. Does that surprise you?"

Surprise is hardly the word. He stared at me with his mouth open for a moment, and then his face was suddenly taut with anger. He held my look and blinked at me, and was about to speak, but closed his mouth instead. And then the fury was gone and he said gently: "Wentworth could not possibly have told you that."

"Wentworth? He didn't even mention Patachiaow's name. Though he told me a lot of other things."

"I see." He pulled a white cambric handkerchief from his sleeve and blew his nose loudly, and said at last: "Well, I suppose that establishes a basis for our talk, was that your intention?"

"It was my intention to let you know a little of what *I* know."

"Add a little to it. Why should Patachiaow betray me?"

I shrugged. "A man in your position—betrayal must be a constant worry. Ambition, greed, money—who knows? Who'll even care?"

"I care. I care very much, Mr. Cain. I wish I could take your word without question."

"You expect me to take yours that you don't know where Sally Hyde is."

"And you don't know either?"

"No, I don't. Why did you choose to meet me here?"

He laughed shortly: "I was here, *in situ,* and why should I look for another meeting place? And where? I certainly don't want you poking around my own quarters, and I'm not prepared to meet you in, say, the lobby of your hotel. Too many people would like to get their hands on me, Mr. Cain. I have a great many enemies. Most of them are small men, but then, death at the hands of a small man is a very miserable affair, isn't it? If I am to be killed, I'd rather my assassin were a man of comparable stature. Someone like yourself, perhaps?"

"And talking of assassination, I wasn't very pleased with the reception you had waiting for me when I arrived in Macao."

"No. I hardly expected you would be." He had recovered from the shock that Patachiaow's name had given him, though I could sense that his mind was turning the possibilities over and over. It showed itself in little inattentions, hardly sharp enough to be noticeable, but there none the less. Something was puzzling him, and he came straight to the point: "And you had no qualms about meeting me here tonight? With fifty men on the street after your blood?"

I mustered all the calm I could manage. I even shrugged. "I was fairly sure nothing would happen to me here."

He leaned forward, genuinely interested. "I know why, of course."

"Do you?"

"A letter, a tape recording, something of that nature? Everything Wentworth had to tell you, in Bonelli's capable hands with instructions to hand it over to the police if you don't return? Am I right?"

The oldest cliché in the world, the insurance. I wished Bonelli could know how well it was working. He'd feel happier for me.

I said: "As you suggest, something of that nature." A little more formidable, perhaps." The image of nothing is always *more* than nothing.

I said, frowning: "I could always find out precisely what it was that seems so formidable. And then get it."

"Could you? Oh, you'd find out all right. I've no illusions on that score. But you'd never get it."

He stared at me, wondering hard what it was that I'd done that was so clever. He grunted, at last, a short, angry sort of grunt. He stood up and walked around, moving in behind me; I did not turn to look at him.

He said: "My organization is probably the most powerful of its kind in the world, Mr. Cain. If I raise my hand just a little, you could be wiped out as though you'd never existed. You must be aware of that. And yet, you come in here and talk to me glibly about insurance for your life, about letters, tape recordings."

I said quickly: "Your suggestion, not mine."

"Something else then? And I'm expected to spend the rest of my life with this menace hanging over me? If you get run over by a street car, it's to be the end of my operation, is that it? How can you be sure that what Wentworth told you was the truth? Or all of it? Or even a part of it that is not generally known? He wasn't my closest associate, you know."

"But close enough."

"Was it he who told you about Patachiaow?"

I said casually: "No. He was more concerned with Valenski."

There was a little silence behind me; I wished I could have seen the muscles on his face twitch.

He said again: "I see." In a little while he came round to face me, and said: "All right, I'm convinced that you know more than you should know, and I'm convinced that your death would be a disaster for me. Is this, then, the end of our conversation?"

I said: "Not quite. Now tell me where Sally Hyde is? Tell me that, and I'll give you back your lieutenant."

He spread his hands wide, protesting. "But I don't *know* where she is! Believe me, Cain, I'm tempted to ask your help in finding her, for my own sake. She obviously knows a great deal too much about my organization, more than I suspected. It's imperative now that I find her, more imperative than ever."

"Find her and...?"

He sat down again and looked at me hard. "Can we do business, Cain? Does money tempt you?"

"No, on both counts."

"You can't be bought and you can't be frightened, is that it?"

"Let's say I'm not prepared to sell you my conscience."

"Oh my God! I never thought that you'd be such an old-fashioned man, Cain! The world's not what it used to be, and you may as well resign yourself to the fact that the honest man is a moribund breed. Moribund, or already dead."

"You move in the wrong circles, Mr. Ming."

"Yes, undoubtedly I do. But do you think I could work so freely, so successfully, if I found, anywhere, the kind of morality you're trying to peddle? It's a sick world, Mr. Cain, as you must agree. I didn't make it sick, though, yes, I profit from its sickness." He said dryly: "When a man finds chaos all around him, he's a fool to sit back and watch someone else making the money."

I said: "Forty years ago it wasn't sick. That's when your kind of galloping cancer took hold."

He laughed, a pleasant, genuinely amused laugh. "They tell me you're a studious sort of man, Mr. Cain, so go back to your books and read the history of opium! It's had a hold, as you call it, as long as there's been a history. And the corruption I profit from, are you suggesting that's new too? No. Adam was the first liar, and the first murderer was another man named Cain. The wicked have been with us for a very long time."

We could have been discussing food or wine or the theater; he was quite at ease now, an imposing sort of man with a great deal of authority. He waved a cigar case at me, and when I shook my head lit one for himself, a thin Papetela Quintero. He was reading my thoughts, and he smiled and said:

"I am an evil man, Mr. Cain, but you weren't thinking that, were you?"

I said: "No, I wasn't. I was trying to relate you to evil. Frankly, I find it a hard thing to do."

"I'm glad. Someone else's approbation, even if it's temporary and faulty, is a very gratifying thing."

"Can I see Markle Hyde?"

"No, I'm afraid not."

"Then he's dead."

"No." There was a slight, self-satisfied smile on his face. "Hyde knows very well what plans I have for him. First, his son. Now...his daughter." The evil was now more apparent.

I said: "Not any more, Ming Sin-san."

Now he leaned back in his chair and looked at me, the blue smoke curling above his white hair. He said very deliberately: "You hold a very good trump, Mr. Cain. Don't overplay it, or you'll lose your advantage."

I said: "If Sally Hyde gets run over by a street car too."

"You are driving a very hard bargain. Too hard, perhaps. I don't even know what's in your hand."

"But you can guess. Or, more correctly, you dare not run too big a risk."

"You may, but I may not, is that the position?"

I shrugged. "I'm running no risk at all."

"That's not true. In the course of time, one way or another, I'll find out everything Wentworth told you. Are we in agreement so far?"

"We are."

"All right. And when I do, what is the problem? I get rid of the men whose names he mentioned. I change the meeting place he spoke of. I divest myself, so to speak, of all my compromised holdings." He shrugged. "A few names might have to be changed, a few passports purchased, a few sites abandoned. He knows of perhaps three poppy fields, four at the most. I control more than thirty, did he tell you that too?"

I said: "Among other things. But the figure wasn't thirty, precisely."

"Of how many did he give you the location?"

I brushed it aside. "We were talking mostly about Laos." I could see now the twitch to his face; he didn't like the sound of Laos a bit; it was a shot in the dark that found a target and hurt him.

He said: "Tell me...tell me how much persuasion you had to use to get him to talk so much? A great deal? Or none at all?" He knew his man well.

I said: "None at all. How did a weakling like that ever get so close to you?"

"Personal loyalty, Mr. Cain. I was once greatly indebted to him. You see, I do have my virtues. And you see also that virtue is a luxury I can ill afford. Have you wondered how long it will take me to find out the extent of your information?"

"A few days."

"And after that?"

"After that, my life is once again in jeopardy. But for the moment it is not."

"You're very sure of yourself."

"I can afford to be, under the circumstances. What about Sally Hyde?"

He shook his head slowly, smiling at me.

I said: "You don't believe my threat?"

He was on top of the meeting now, the Chairman of the Board in full control. He said slowly: "If she's even run over by a street car? Yes, I believe you. I believe that if she turns up dead, whatever information you may have will be handed over to the people who can hurt me the most." He shrugged. "A limited hurt, but serious, none the less. To avoid that hurt, I will keep my hands off you, Mr. Cain. All right? Does that make you happy? But in the case of Sally Hyde, I am dealing with an old enemy, not just an arrogant upstart who thinks he can get in my way. To satisfy that vendetta—and that means the destruction of Sally Hyde for her father to see—not even the danger of that hurt will stand in the way." He shrugged that careless shrug again. "So I go down too. It will be worth it."

I said: "I could understand your hatred if it were more passionate and less calculated."

"I am an Oriental, Mr. Cain." He said it with the greatest dignity in the world; and as though it answered all the questions. Somehow, I almost began to admire him a trifle.

He said again, insisting: "Believe me, Mr. Cain. If I find Sally

Hyde tomorrow, and do with her what I plan to do with her, then I'm quite prepared to take the risk of exposure, to the full extent of your knowledge. In your own case, I'll hold back, because frankly you're not worth the risk. But she is. I'm an American. Mr. Cain, but my spiritual home is with my people, in Kirin. And there, we do not take our vendettas lightly. I have a debt to pay Ben Stirani, to pay in my own way. And I'm going to pay it, and be damned to you."

"Even if it costs you your freedom? Or your life?"

"First they'll have to catch me." He said, frowning: "No, I have no worries on that score. A dozen police forces all over the world are looking for me, have been looking for me for a long time quite hopelessly. Your threat is that I might have to break up my organization and start again from scratch, and that I'm not prepared to do unless it becomes necessary to the satisfaction of my vendetta. Killing you merely because you had the impertinence to try to unseat me—no, you are right, it's not worth it, not at the moment. But only for the moment, Cain. As soon as I find out the extent of your knowledge, the position will change radically." He smiled, a dry little smile, and said "I have no way of insisting that you keep your word, have I?"

I said: "About Wentworth?"

"You did promise to return him to me if I'd see you. Am I to rely only on your good will? On that conscience you spoke of?"

I said casually: "You can have him. He's of no further use to me."

He was watching me carefully, wondering why it didn't seem to matter to me one way or the other. I knew that at this very minute his minions were out there somewhere trying to pick up Wentworth themselves. All this was just a game, *o jeito*. And it behooved me not to stay there too long, not to push my luck.

The sun was coming up over the water, throwing its pale yellow light into the big room. The lights were going off automatically, one by one, on a daylight-sensitive switch somewhere. As they blinked out and little pools of shadow fell in the corners, it gave the impression that somewhere someone was controlling all that we two were doing there, as though what was happening was not of my own volition or even of Ming's. It was an eerie feeling.

I stood up, and Ming stopped me. He said, a hand raised: "Let us understand each other, Mr. Cain. I'm getting Wentworth back?"

I shrugged. "Of course. I've nothing further to say to him."

"Even though you realize that our armistice is over when he's elucidated a few matters for me?"

"Even so."

"To undo the damage he's done will take a day or two, no more. And as for Sally Hyde, you'd better find her before I do. Or all your trouble will have been for absolutely nothing."

I went to the door and turned back. The other men scattered about the room were more alert than ever; they too were waiting. I said: "As a point of purely academic interest, what would happen if I went straight to the police and told them you were here?"

He laughed. "As long as it's only academic, I'll tell you. First of all, they wouldn't believe you. One of their most trusted informers has just told them that I am in Manila, and they've sent a telegram so advising the Philippine police. Secondly, if you happened to tell the wrong man—one of the wrong men—he would promptly throw you in jail on a trumped-up charge while he warned me that a raid was coming. And if by chance you found the right man, and he believed you, and he in turn spoke to the right man, then they'd send a squad of their best men round to arrest me, maybe twenty or thirty of them armed to the teeth with rifles and pistols and maybe even some tear gas. But I've got forty-eight men on these grounds, and one of my junks is standing offshore with another twelve men aboard. We're armed with heavy caliber machine-guns, recoilless rifles, and grenades; there's even a mortar for emergencies. There'd be a massacre, is that what you want? Even in Macao, Mr. Cain, a slaughter of such proportion is not liked at all." He said with an amused smile: "And, on top of all this, five minutes after you've left the grounds I'll be gone too. So don't waste your time."

I said mildly: "I just wondered."

In the corridor, armed men were prowling. Ming came with me to the front door; more armed men. He said simply:

"You see? It's essential you realize the size and scope of this organization. It's not a question of a gang of street hoodlums any more. We're as big as General Motors and as deadly as the Marines, so don't add to this poor colony's tragedies by senseless obstinacy. The police indeed!" His great frame shook with his laughter.

I said: "I won't. You're sure you don't know where Sally Hyde is?"

He stopped and stared at me. "Really, Mr. Cain, you are stubborn! Is there nothing I can say to convince you?"

I said: "Nothing. Nothing at all. Good day, Ming Sin-san."

I could feel his eyes on me as I walked down the pathway to the big iron gates. One of the armed men threw them open for me, unsmiling, uncaring, unmoved—like a hireling letting out the gardener and locking the gates behind him.

A helicopter was circling overhead, low enough for its roar to blot out the early-morning sounds. There was a big letter "M" painted in scarlet on its bright green flanks. The fishermen on the beach were staring up at it, and as passed them they turned back to their work; I heard one of them muttering, and his eyes flickered briefly towards me and back again.

I walked quickly along the esplanade under the broad leafed trees, listening as the helicopter landed in the grounds behind me. It took off again before I'd gone another hundred yards, rising straight up and then wheeling round fast and heading west towards the Chinese mainland and the island of Siang-chu.

It had been an interesting meeting. I'd never heard so many lies told so expertly, all in a row. I came away with one thing certain, and that thing was all that really mattered.

Ming had Sally Hyde, or knew where she was.

I shuddered when I thought about what might be happening to her.

CHAPTER 11

From the roof of Bonelli's place, the Navy night-glasses were strong enough to pick out the island clearly, dark in a darker sea against the moonlight that shone on the hills of China.

Three miles from the mainland coast, it was a fortress built by the adherents of the White Lotus Society. That must have been back in 1797, when the anti-Manchu forces were gathering on the coast for the final showdown that turned, at last, into the Tai Ping rebellion. I remembered that a hundred years later, Sir Robert Hart, the great Irish-Chinese statesman, had mapped the coastline around Canton—till then a shoreline almost unknown to the West—in an effort to deny the security of their hideouts to the opium smugglers whose silver drain was having a chaotic effect on the Chinese economy. His success at stabilizing the government's source of income had been largely due to his memorable attention to the smallest possible detail, and the records he had left—the few that survived—were masterly. Hart's pro-Manchu energy had earned him the vicious enmity of the pirates, the gangsters, and the smugglers who still operated openly along the coast in the name of some obscure political fanaticism. The Boxers had burned his house down with all its priceless records, all, that is, except the diary he had kept for forty years, and the maps of the coast which he had presented to the Emperor.

I was thinking, suddenly, of the map in Bonelli's office, knowing now what that chord was, that its delicate penmanship had evoked. Just a worthless fake, Bonelli had said. But at that time we hadn't known each other very well, and the little lie, which I was sure it was, had perhaps been necessary for the sake of an intelligent security.

Now, the name of the unscrupulous Dowager Empress Tzu Hsi kept knocking at the back of my mind, clamoring for some sort of notice; and when I'd sorted out the bits and pieces, I remembered that her son, the Emperor T'ung Chi, was an amateur cartographer and had, in turn, donated all his maps to one of the Canton museums. His collection was a famous one; did it include, I wondered, any of the rare Robert Hart maps? It was a probability, at least.

On the island, there was no sign of life. The rocky massif was dark, and I fancied that the powerful glasses were bringing it close enough for me to hear any sounds if sounds there were on it; the stillness and the clarity of the night made the fancy irresistible. But the great stones were silent as death. It was hard to recognize them as a fortress; from this distance, they were a jumble of granite blocks set against granite cliffs and washed with the spray of the granite sea.

I went downstairs to find Bonelli in his own little fortress. He was at the great teak desk in a corner of the main fan-tan room, paying large wads of notes to a small and somber Chinese who watched carefully as the notes were counted, a thin and alert old man who waited till the paying was done, not taking his eyes from the money, and then looked up at me and said, in tolerably good Portuguese: "I have to thank you for this, Cain Sin-san." He turned away and placed the money on one of the tables, and Bonelli got up and said cheerfully, taking my arm and guiding me away:

"A great deal of money is riding on your well-being, Cain. If you stay alive for a few more days, I will be ruined."

I didn't believe it. I knew that he was shrewd enough to bet heavily on my continued survival, and I wondered how he'd feel when I told him what I was planning. I said: "Remember the T'ung Chi map collection? I have an idea it was sold to the Portuguese, but I can't remember when. Or even if that's a fact."

He looked at me in surprise. There was a touch of suspicion there too. "How should I know a thing like that?"

I said: "How could you possibly not know? That's the collection your Robert Hart came from."

"Oh."

We were moving into his office, and he stood in the doorway watching me as I went to the fine old map that was over the divan. Its penmanship was splendid.

I said: "I never really did believe that this was a fake."

He said, seeming surprised: "Did I say it was a fake? What a foolish thing to do! But then, you had only just arrived, and I did not really know very much about you, did I? I said to myself: I will trust this man completely, but only when I know him a little better. So you will forgive me?"

"Of course."

"And if you're interested in maps, I have much better ones. In my vault, there's a half-section of Peutinger's Tabula, the only one in the world outside the great museums."

The Hart map was of the area around Amoy, more than three hundred miles too far north to interest me at the moment.

I said: "I'm more interested in the T'ung Chi collection."

Bonelli frowned, a distant look in his eyes. "The Emperor she placed on the throne before she died, what was his name?"

"Kuang Hsu."

"Ah yes, Kuang Hsu's entire estate was broken up when he died, and part of it was presented to the Portuguese here in Macao more than a hundred years ago." He shrugged. "In those days; you may know, it was essential for the Chinese that the colony retain its *status quo* as an outlet to the West. Hong Kong, you remember, was just beginning to thrive, and the Cantonese saw the eventual decline of Macao as a result. So they tried to bribe the Portuguese to build bigger harbors here, to strengthen the colony as a counterweight to the British influence in Hong Kong. It was not a very successful overture, but part of the price the Manchus paid was Kuang Hsu's collection of jade, twelfth-century armor, and maps. Somewhere around 1843, I think."

"And the Robert Hart maps were part of the collection?"

He podded. "And they're still here in the museum."

I said: "Where's Mai?"

He looked at me in surprise. "You do not wish to hear how I acquired one of them? It was really quite a coup. Just the faintest touch of illegality, and quite a brilliant stroke of double-dealing."

"Is there a map of Siang-chu island in the collection?"

"There must be. The purpose of Sir Robert's maps was to further his fight against the Boxers. And Siang-chu, in those days, was a collection point for Boxer weapons smuggled in from Japan. So, provided that he was able to gain access to the island he must have mapped it with his customary efficiency." He looked hard at me and said: "But there's nothing on Siang-chu any more, nothing but an old fortress which is slowly crumbling into the decay that comes even to the best of us in time."

"No military outpost of the Canton defenses?"

"Nothing, nothing at all."

"How sure are you of that?"

Bonelli raised his oh-so-elegant shoulders. "I am *perfectly* sure. One of my junks was driven ashore there in the last typhoon we had, and the crew spent the night on the island before we were able to rescue them."

I said sharply: "But that's mainland territory. The Reds didn't try to stop you landing there to pick them up?"

He said very slowly: "No, they didn't. I must admit, I wondered about that at the time. I still wonder about it. If you consider how touchy they are about territorial rights...Yes, I *still* wonder about it." His white hands were waving about like butterflies in the breeze. "And now, no doubt, you have learned something about Siang-chu that intrigues you. Would you mind telling me what it is?"

I said: "That's where Ming disappears to when he drops out of sight."

He stared. He said at last: "That's a very dangerous piece of knowledge to have, Cain! If it's true. And will you give me leave to doubt it?"

I said: "Of course, if you'll tell me why."

"We-e-ell...first of all, Red China could not so easily be fooled if someone had taken over their abandoned little fortress. Even though there's no military presence there of any sort..." He broke off. "Are you suggesting that the Chinese know about it and choose to leave him alone? To turn a blind eye?"

I could hear the wheels turning in his mind, and I let him talk. He sat down primly on the edge of the divan, his knees close together, and a finger to his cheek, and he said thoughtfully:

"For them it would be merely a case of turning a blind eye to what's going on, would it not? And Ming, no doubt, is useful to them from time to time. He supplies them with hijacked military equipment once in a while. Yes, perhaps it just might be possible. Some minor official who needn't really be particularly corrupt, if someone higher up the echelon had told him: *Leave alone the man who sells us so much that we need.* Yes, it's possible. It might even perhaps be likely."

I said: "In short, he's harming their mortal enemies, so why should they make it difficult for him?"

"Their mortal enemies?"

"Ming is a thorn in the side of honest Western governments in their search for peace on earth and goodwill towards men."

Bonelli said, tilting his chin up ridiculously: "I would give your comments more thought, Cain, if I did not detect a note of sardonic ill-humor in that comment. Why is it that your people can only regard as mortal enemies anyone who does not agree with them?" He crossed over to the bar and poured some cognac. Remy Martin Fine Champagne, and when he handed me the glass, he said, frowning: "Yes, now that I come to think of it, it would explain a lot that has always been inexplicable."

I said: "The skipper who was washed ashore on the island. It wasn't by chance Theophilo?"

"Indeed it was."

"And no one disturbed him? No one at all?"

"No one."

"Surely he'd take a look at the fortress while he was there?"

Bonelli's eyes were taking on a very shrewd, alert sort of look, the look of a man who has something to hide and who fears you may be on to it. But it occurred to me that almost any comment you might make in Bonelli's secret world would have him worried if he weren't absolutely sure what you were looking for.

He said slowly: "No, there was a typhoon raging. It would have been impossible to climb up off the lower level. When we finally got a dinghy in there to take them off, they'd washed themselves to the rocks to keep from being washed away." He made a decision. He smiled and said softly: "And now, the next step is really the deadly one, is it not? Are you really going to take it?"

"With your help, yes. I'm going to take it."

He sighed. "That's what I feared. But not tonight, I beg of you. If anything should happen to you tonight, really, it's a most infelicitous time for me."

"The lottery?"

"Yes. Any time after tomorrow at four o'clock. If you insist on getting killed off, I beg of you, do it tomorrow after four o'clock."

I said: "Get Theophilo up here for me, will you? Can you do that for me?"

He drifted across the room, clicking his tongue, and I went to find Mai. I was getting rather fond of Mai in a puzzling, inexplicable sort of way, and I thought she might like to visit the museum, that we might go there together, almost, but not quite, like tourists who are determined to see everything there is to see in a strange and exciting town.

We broke into the museum with not the slightest bit of trouble. It was comforting to know that even if we were caught, some kindly judge would lecture us and fine us a few thousand patacas, but we were quite careful none the less. I picked the lock on the door that led to the cellars, and we crept through the corridors silently enough not to disturb the somnolent guards we saw dozing over their little teak tables; one of them had an alarm clock to wake him when it was time to make his rounds again; I pushed the alarm button home to stop it from ringing at its appointed time, and we crept silently on like thieves in the night, which is what we were for the moment. A patrolling guard, ill-shaven and half-asleep, passed us by as we took cover behind a twelfth-century chest of ivory-inlaid ebony that was supposed to be by Lu Sing-chu but looked to me like a fake; it lacked the great master's emphasis on the fine incised line as a transpository device; it was probably by his lesser known pupil Su Ling. We found the map room, put a chair under the door handle, just in case, drew the heavy drapes and switched on the lights.

I found the map I wanted in ten minutes: it was somewhat stylized in the fashion of the day, but well detailed and marvelously intricate. And knowing Robert Hart's passion for precision, I was sure that it was accurate as well. I rolled it up carefully, and we went out together the way we had entered.

And an hour after we had left it, we were back in Bonelli's office. Theophilo was there, waiting for me, his scarred old face wreathed in smiles and his voice a little thick with too much whisky. I told him what we had to do, and watched the smile grow broader as he listened.

There was a sharp, cold wind whipping up the tops of the waves as the junk sailed slowly west in the darkness. There were no lights showing, and the only sound was the abominable creaking of the masts and the occasional flap of the brown sails: it was cold enough to wear heavy sweaters, and the blown spray was like ice-drops on our faces, refreshing and stimulating and somehow cleaner than I thought the job ahead of us might be.

In the darkness. Theo spoke quietly, his voice almost a whisper. I had told him very little of my thinking, because I wasn't able to explain it even to myself; all he knew was that he was going to put me ashore on Siang-chu and stand by to come running if I yelled loud enough; and from the expression on his face, I knew that he hoped I would yell at the top of my voice before he got bored sitting around as backup man. He said now:

"You go to kill Ming? Is good."

I shook my head. I said: "Ming is not the objective, though he'll probably try to run interference."

He said nothing, but stood there staring ahead into the darkness, looking up at the clouds once in a while to bless the hidden moon.

I smelled perfume, and Mai was silently beside me, turning to look up at me with a somber look in her eyes.

Another thing I could not explain to myself: a woman along on a job like this?

But Mai, somehow, was not just another woman. I thought that I might need her skills, her knowledge, her extraordinary capacity for quick and silent action. In spite of her unfeminine expertise in aggressive matters, the softness of her skin over those tight muscles, the oriental delicacy which was a counterpoint to the unexpected savagery that I knew to be there, had caused a very considerable impression on me, an impression of quite the wrong sort that had no place at all in the present circumstances. It wasn't love, or anything even remotely like it; it was a cruel and animal urge that made me want to feel her body beside me more than anything in the world. Bed had nothing to do with it either; and it wasn't platonic: I wanted to share danger, not with just any woman, but with Mai.

So there she was. When I'd told her what I was going to do, she had merely nodded, not asking me if she was supposed to come along too but just taking it for granted. It was as though her allegiance to Bettina had unaccountably been switched to me, that she was there, expectant and receptive for *anything* that I might want. I had the feeling that she understood my twisted desires more than I understood them myself; it's far easier for the Orientals to think in terms of nonlogic than it is for us, even though, inexplicably, we sometimes act as if we hadn't a brain in our heads. And for me, when emotion fights with intellect, I'll take the side that seems the better one at the moment, heart or head.

Bonelli had merely raised an expressive eyebrow when it became apparent that she was expecting to be a sort of bodyguard for me. He looked at me a little quizzically, and thought for a while, and had said at last: "A watery grave together, is that what you want?"

I'd answered him: "Together, but no grave."

"You're a romantic, Cain, did you know that?" He sounded surprised.

I said: "Well, of course I am. Not many of us left, are there?"

"And can you justify putting her life in danger for what, after all, is merely a matter, for you, of making money?"

"No." I couldn't help being short with him. "No, I can't justify it. But she's coming along anyway. She wants to."

I was quite sure that she did. I wasn't exactly quarreling with Bonelli, but we were on the edge of a fight because I knew—as he did—that what I was doing was wrong. And Mai herself had said nothing, but as we talked, she just sat there on the edge of Bettina's bed with a hand on her mistress's forehead, as if assuring herself that it was safe to leave her for a while. Seeing Bettina's eyes on both of us, Mai had told her gently: "Don't worry about me, I'll be back to take care of you." Bettina looked at me and snorted with a faintly amused contempt, as though signifying her disgust that her friend might have found a new interest.

I let it ride; I was in too weak a position to fight if Bettina had said: "First me, now her, is that it?"

Now, the scent of the fragile Chinese girl was on the night air, and she was looking at me as though waiting for me to tell her something very important, her dark eyes solemn and reflective. I bent down and kissed her, and put an arm round her narrow waist, and Theophilo laughed quietly and said in a whisper:

"Maybe we all get killed in a little while. Better you make love now, while you got the chance."

Mai broke away from me and said, her voice very low: "Have you decided how to do this thing?"

I shook my head. "We go in there and see what there is to see. It might be just a wild goose chase with nothing but crumbling ruins at the end of it." I thought of the geese in the warehouse, of how well we had worked together there, I said: "When I spoke to Ming, he said he had not seen Sally Hyde, that he didn't know where she was. And I was pretty damn sure that at that moment he was lying. We sat and talked our heads off, and each of us was playing *o jeito*, the game, for all it was worth. He told me some truths, and he told me some lies, and I came away convinced that he knows precisely where she is. And if he's got her tucked away somewhere, Siang-chu is where she'll be."

"You can't be sure of that."

"No. But it's a likelihood."

"She might be dead."

"If she were, Ming would not be able to resist the temptation to tell her father just how she died. That's where the real fight is, between those two. Everything else hinges on that. Come below with me for a while."

Not questioning, she nodded. I saw Theo's grin in the half-light, and I turned back to him and asked: "How long have we got?"

He shrugged. "Maybe twenty minutes we be in close enough, then ten minutes more while I find where to hide this pork-barrel. We take down sails, no?"

"No. Keep her mobile."

"Then better maybe stand further offshore. I don't like them rocks there too much." We could already hear the waves pounding on them.

I took Mai's arm and said roughly: "Let's take another look at the map."

We went below to the tiny cabin; there was just five feet of headroom, so even Mai had to stoop slightly; and we spread the stolen museum map out on the table under the pale light of the kerosene lamp. One arm around her, I stubbed a finger on the delicate tracery and said: "There, through the vents, if they haven't been closed up in the last hundred years or so, that's where we go in."

Sir Robert had done a fine, meticulously precise job. His own pen had scratched the words in Chinese ink: *Escape route used by Sumanu Fu during Manchu raid. February third, 1801.* There was another comment: *Northeast face of cliff cannot be scaled without ropes.*

Well, I'd brought ropes along with me, and half a dozen pitons as well. (Have you ever tried to find climbing equipment, in the middle of the night, in a place where there's scarcely a cliff in sight? But the junks carried all kinds of stuff, and Theo had found it for me.) We had no grappling hooks, but I hoped that the small anchor from the dinghy would serve as well as anything else.

And the good skipper had also armed the junk with a medley of the oddest looking, most ill-assorted weapons I had ever seen. There were modern Mauser rifles, and there was a homemade breech-loader that looked like a culverin and took any kind of shot that could be crammed into its barrel; there were new Luger automatics, and there was a huge and stubby cannon made of bronze and inscribed in Turkish with the legend: *Face to face with my enemies*; its carved breech-block was inscribed: *Constantinople, 1796.*

Mai said, her fingers tracing a pattern along my spine: "And when we are inside?"

My hand was on her hip, and I could feel cool flesh under the rough cord of her denim slacks. I said: "Inside, we play it off the cuff." It was hard to concentrate on the map. I indicated the place where the air vent on the northeast face led into the main store. In the days of the Boxers, the dynamite which had created such havoc in Canton's streets had been stored there.

I said: "Here, we follow the line of the service corridors to the lower level, keep moving down till we see lights, or hear sounds, or even smell food cooking. If there's anyone there at all, that's where they'll be, on the lower levels. Fix this chart in your mind, indelibly, because once we're inside we work in absolute darkness." She nodded, but her eyes were on me, not on the map. I said: "Keep close behind me, all the time. Anything comes to your attention, anything doesn't seem right, touch me on the shoulder."

She nodded again, not taking her eyes off me. My hand was at her waist, then moving up the small breasts, and she was pressing herself into me and trembling, and the next minute we were rolling on the hard teak floor together, clasped in each other's arms, and the tight-muscled legs were wrapping themselves around me.

And all the time I was asking myself: is this what I really want of Mai?

We went back on deck a little later, holding hands like young lovers and not talking very much, and Theo was there in the prow, pointing ahead to the black-and-white line of the surf. The stars were coming out from behind the clouds, and the moon was clearing, and I didn't like the light at all, but he whispered, seeing me glance up at the sky: "We hide under the headland there. Nobody see us at all." He turned to scowl at a sound from further down the deck where the dinghy was being lowered, and whispered an angry order. The small latten mast forward was flapping in the wind, and he scowled at that too.

I whispered: "Any junks use these waters?"

He nodded. "When they smuggle arms into China, they land here sometimes."

"An onshore watch?"

He shrugged. "Nothing we have no worry about. If Ming come here like you say, he got to have junks too, no? They leave him alone. They don't look too close either what we are doing, no?"

Watch the wall, my darling, while the gentlemen go by...

It made sense. The orders on the mainland were in all

likelihood to see, say, and hear nothing of what went on among the rocks of Siang-chu.

We laid out our equipment on the deck and checked it over for the third time: two hundred feet of knotted nylon-rope, two small flashlights. Mai's little Walther pistol and Bonelli's Luger, a sharp hunting-knife with a four-inch blade that Theo had insisted I take along with me, two tear-gas grenades, a tiny Japanese walkie-talkie (the other end of it to stay on board), and three sticks of dynamite with short fuses in them. I felt like a pirate, but there was no denying that we had to be ready for all kinds of trouble ahead of us.

We climbed down silently into the dinghy, and Theo leaned over and whispered, grinning: "You need help, Senhor Cain, you yell. We come fast."

"I'll do that, Theo."

"Don't you wait too long, dead man don't yell too good."

"I won't."

"Any help you want, you got."

"I know that, Theo. You're a good man." I didn't like to remind him that the trouble was going to be inside the fortress, where yelling wouldn't do much good.

An ancient crewman with red hair was at the oars, which I was glad to see had been rag-wrapped at the oar-locks for silence; and in five silent minutes, Mai and I were splashing ashore on the rocks at the base of the northeast cliff-face. I took the small anchor and lashed it to the end of the rope, nodded to the boatman, watched while he rowed into a creek where the boulders hid all sight of him (I'd told him to wait a while before going back to the junk); I told Mai in a whisper to wait, and then began the steep climb up the cliff.

Sir Robert had been right; it *was* unscalable.

I pulled up short below a bulky overhang of rock that loomed out over the dark sea, darker than the night itself. My exploring fingers found that it was smooth granite, devoid of any kind of recess which would afford a footing, however hazardous. I wound one leg round an upshooting pinnacle of stone and leaned out, then tugged up the anchor on the end of the long rope; I swung it back and forth and then hurled it up as high as I could reach; it clanged horribly in the silence, and then came tumbling down again to reach the rocks below with another loud clang. As I clung to the cliff-face, I could only hope that the wind, strong and vicious here, would drown out the noise or at least carry it far from waiting ears.

On the third try, the rope snagged itself into a jagged V-shape of incised stone twenty yards to my right and above me. I tugged hard and found that the anchor was holding firm, so I let myself swing on the rope for a moment and then pushed hard with both feet against the wall and sent myself swinging far over to one side; my fingers found a hold and I dragged myself tight in, wondering if I'd exchanged a safe perch for a dangerous one.

Below me, the white tops of the waves were pounding against the black rocks in Kafkaesque fury; they were a terribly long way down, and I had not realized I had climbed so far. I held on by one hand and worked a piton slowly into a crevice, wiggling it and forcing it in and wishing it was safe to use a hammer. But the piton was tight, deep-lodged in the cleft, and I put a clove-hitch on it and tugged hard and found it firm. I swung myself up onto the now taut rope, balancing uneasily on the thin nylon and seeking the cliff-face for stability, and I groped around till I found another hand-hold, firmer here and in a much more broken surface.

The darkness was a terrible handicap. I could not see whether or not I was even going in the best direction, whether or not there were other insuperable barricades ahead of me; I was wondering if I should have tried the southwest side where the slope was gentler—and therefore, it seemed to me—more likely to be under surveillance if the island were indeed under the kind of tight security I would have expected.

I found a narrow ledge and crept along it in absolute silence, moving a foot at a time and then waiting a long while, ears alert, before moving on again. It seemed that I was over the hump, so to speak, so I crawled back and unsnagged the rope, pulling it back with me and letting the anchor at its end swing gently free; I left the piton where it was; I thought it might be needed for a descent.

The silence was astonishing now; even the sound of the waves below seemed muted when the wind, unaccountably, suddenly dropped. I moved back with infinite care along the ledge.

And now, now I could hear a faint sound that shouldn't have

been there at all. It was the sound of a man's breathing.

How far will such a slight sound travel? A few feet? A few yards? He was close beside me somewhere then, waiting as I was waiting, watching as I too strained my eyes in the darkness. The wind came up again as suddenly as it had dropped and the sound was gone with it. I crouched, waiting and ready and tried hard to pinpoint the source; there, above me and a little ahead. Gently I pulled up the anchor till I felt its thirty-two pounds of iron in my hands, and I held it ahead of me like an animal trainer's chair. I leaned into the cliff and peered ahead.

A shadow moved, a man's head moving away from the darkness of the cliff and silhouetted momentarily against the sky. It did not seem to me that waiting around now would be any good so I pushed forward hard with both hands and flung the anchor at him. I saw the shadow grow larger as the arms came out and then it was gone, and there was a fierce and sudden tug at the rope that nearly hauled me off my feet. But I was waiting for it, bracing myself for a tug of war, and the harder he pulled from round that bend or wherever he was, the harder I pulled back. And then I suddenly let go the rope and leaped forward blindly, hoping that there might be somewhere to put my feet, there was.

I found myself on a flat outcrop just outside a small cave where my adversary had been waiting. He'd heard the abominable sound of the anchor striking the rock, and had come out to see what was going on; and there he was now on his back in the darkness, almost over the edge and falling into space, his arms flailing as he tried to recover his balance before I should reach him. If I'd pushed with my foot, he'd have gone over to smash himself to a bloody pulp on the rocks below. But instead, I drove the points of my fingers hard into his solar plexus—it was like hitting solid steel—and fell on him with my knee in his stomach. He grunted and twisted his head round, which was what I was hoping he'd do, so I hit again with my fingerpoints. I aimed at the superficial cervical, striking it hard enough to put him out momentarily, which was long enough for me to take my time and apply pressure to the auricular and the posterior scapular. I also bore down hard on the posterior thoracic, which would have killed him if I'd kept up the pressure for more than a second or two. But I had no quarrel with him; he was merely doing his job and telling me, incidentally, that all this trouble (if the trouble had really started yet!) was not, indeed, for nothing. There were other things than ghosts and devils on Siang-chu *they* don't put out sentries.

Once he was completely unconscious, I used my flashlight to see just who I'd been fighting with in the darkness: a big Chinese with a bull-neck and short-cropped hair, and dragons tattooed all over his arms. A Northerner. I stripped off his belt and bound his arms behind his back in case he came round too quickly—though I didn't think he would in much less than a couple of hours—and ripped his shirt and used it to gag him. I tied his thumbs together as well as his pinkies and finally put a clove-hitch around his ankles and his knees, doubling his legs back up to fasten the loose ends of rag around his neck. It was mostly improvisation, but it would take him a long, long time to wrestle himself free.

I used my light again and examined the cave very thoroughly. A small crevice in the rocks was about all it was, but there was a big demijohn of drinking water, a bottle of rice-wine, a half-eaten loaf of bread with some scraps of pork wrapped in a cloth, a length of light cord with a wicket basket on the end of it. I measured the cord and estimated that it was just long enough to reach the rocks on the beach if someone passed by there from time to time with victuals.

But there was no sign of what I was searching for; a telephone line or a radio, or any other means of communication. Whatever my unconscious friend had deduced from the clanging of that damned anchor, there was no one he could communicate his worries to. He'd been left there to cope with any worries himself, and not to bother his betters with them. It was certain that there would be other guards all over the island; and I wondered if there were many others, or indeed any others, on this route that I had chosen.

I was about to move on, when I heard a low whistle from down below there. I froze. A whistle is just about as unidentifiable a sound as you'll ever come across, but somehow I was sure it was not Mai, nor even the hidden boatman—if he was still there. I waited. In a moment, the whistle came again, more impatient-sounding now. Very quickly I took the wicker basket and snaked it down over the edge until it hit bottom. Holding the string taut, I could feel it bouncing about on the other end, and there was the whistle again. I pulled up my little load and found that a friendly benefactor had filled it up for me. I craned my neck over the edge; and though I could see absolutely nothing down there except the white caps of the waves, I clearly heard a throat-clearing cough and then a soft oath in Mandarin. I pulled back into the cave and examined the basket: more bread, more pork, another bottle of wine; I wondered how long the guard up here was meant to stay on duty.

I waited a while till I was certain the passing patrol was well in its way along the rocky beach, and then I struggled on with my climb. The going was easier now, except for one long patch where the face of the cliff was smooth as glass. But here, and without much trouble, I got the anchor swung over and wedged tight in a stand of roots among sandstone boulders. I made a little noise, but not so much as I had made on that damned granite. I swung myself over, reached up and pulled, and in a very few minutes was at the top of the cliff. I took a good look around, found nothing to alarm me, tied one end of the rope round the solid tangle of ancient, stubby roots that here, on this barren rock, had never quite succeeded in becoming trees, and dropped on it over the edge. I went down hand over hand, very quickly, and in a moment was standing back on the wet rocks of the shore again.

There was silence. I stared carefully around me, and then I saw Mai rise slowly out of the water where she had been hiding from the patrol. She came to me, dripping wet, and threw her arms round me and held me tight.

I whispered: "Did they scare you?"

She looked up at me and smiled and shook her head.

"Three men, with rifles."

"Soldiers?"

"Not soldiers."

"Good."

"They put something, food I think it was, in a basket that came down on a string, did you see? That means there's a guard up there."

I said: "It means there *was* a guard. They sent me up some pork chops and a bottle of wine."

She began to laugh then, silently but with a genuine amusement, and I said: "A rope to climb. I'll go up first."

She nodded, and I kissed her, and climbed hand over hand up that damned rope, gripping the knots in the V of my fingers and pulling myself up inch by inch. Thin nylon-rope is not the easiest thing in the world to climb; it cuts into the hands if there's any weight on it, and I weigh two hundred pounds and when I reached the top, my hands were a bloody mess I squatted on the edge and waited for Mai, and gave her a helping hand over the top, and we sat down in the dry weeds to rest for a very brief moment and get our wind back, and then I pointed, put my mouth close to her ear, and whispered: "There. The vent that leads into the fortress."

It was a black hole in the blacker earth, an incision carved in the low, steep rise of land there. The sky was dark; the earth was darker still; and the entrance to the vent was the darkest of them all.

We moved over to it carefully and felt around the smooth-cut stone it had been carved from; it was a hole not more than two feet square, a tight and alarming tunnel in the rock that might or might not lead us to where I wanted to go.

It was hard to get my shoulders into the confined space, and they scraped along the walls as I inched my way forward. I was flat on my back and using only my heels for propulsion, with my arms raised cut beyond my head, searching for whatever might be there. I could feel Mai's comforting touch on my ankles as she slid her slender body—plenty of room here for *her!*—along after me.

And then my groping arms found what I feared might be there, though it was not marked on Robert Hart's map; there was an iron grille cemented into the solid granite just ahead of us, a grille of three one-inch bars in each direction, horizontal and vertical. But, judging by the rustless feel of them, they hadn't been there for very long, a year or two at the most.

It seemed, for the moment at least, to be the end of the line.

I said: "Well, I'll be damned if *that's* going to stop us."

CHAPTER 12

I risked using the flashlight.

The heavy bars were welded at the cross-joints and cemented at the right-angled corners into the granite in which the vent had been cut. I examined the cementing carefully; as I suspected, the one-inch iron lugs had been slid into two-inch drilled holes, which could only mean that the lugs were straight and not bent over at the ends as they ought to have been, and perhaps would have been, if the cliff had not seemed to be unclimbable. It looked as though the cement were Portland, and the fresh waters on the coast here are heavily alkali—a bad combination; they should have used Portland-Pozzolana, which would have given better adhesion.

I said to Mai: "I can't get back past you, can you lug the anchor in here?"

In the darkness, I could not even hear her slithering away, but in a moment there was the horrible noise of the anchor dragging on the floor of the passage as she pushed it ahead of her. I dragged it up past my legs, wedged the bill of the fluke firmly under the bars. It was a Martin's anchor, close-stowing type—which was fortunate. (There was no room to maneuver a standard Admiralty-pattern anchor, but these were not used much on the junks for lack of suitable space.) On the Martin's, the flukes swing through an angle of 43 degrees, and with the pea tucked under a bar, there was good leverage on the shank; I worked it out rapidly in my head, more as an academic exercise than anything else, and came up with the answer that, given an angle of about forty percent at the fulcrum, a shank about thirty-six inches long, a coefficient of shrinkage in the cement of about 0.0765, then I should require about two hundred pounds of pressure at the end of the lever, or maybe two hundred and twenty if I took into account the curve of the bill. It didn't matter very much, but it kept me busy while I was getting the setup at just the right angle.

Mai whispered: "Can you shift it, you think?"

I said: "Yes, I can. Move back."

She slithered out of my way so that I could slide along into a better position. I put one flat hand against the granite above the grille, took hold of the end of the shank in the other, and merely pushed with one hand and pulled with the other. It wasn't as easy as it sounds, (maybe I was wrong about that coefficient of shrinkage, though I don't think so), and the upper bar started to bend a little as I sweated. This was not going to help, since it would merely tighten up the lug by twisting it, so I shifted the bill up to the corner and tried again. I wished I were facing the other way and could have used my legs, but while I was wondering if I should back out and start over arsy-tarsy, the iron bar suddenly bent at the corner and the lug came clear out. I was sweating profusely in the confined space, and my hands were wet. I dried them off on my sweater, shifted the anchor round to the second upper-corner, and repeated the process. This one was easier—the cement had been carelessly rammed in here—and it came free in less than three minutes. And five minutes later, Mai was backing out behind me with the grille in her hands. She brought the rope when she came back.

We both slithered through in the darkness until, leading the way, I came to an abrupt falling-off into nothingness. Robert Hart had given the height of the vent in the storage room as ten feet six inches from the ground, and I didn't expect that he would be wrong. But it occurred to me that all kinds of things might be down there that might impede our landing, so I lowered my hunting knife on the end of a measured ten feet-six rope, touched it to the surface delicately, and heard the soft-hard sound of metal on granite—clear but muted by the lightness of the touch. I found a small cleft in the vent wall, wedged a knot tight in it, coiled the rope there ready for an emergency, and then slipped over the edge, held on by my hands for a moment, and dropped.

Hard floor. I fell lightly on the balls of my feet, held out my arms, and waited. In a moment Mai's lightweight body was tight in my arms. I kissed her quickly, lowered her to the floor, and we set off together in the absolute blackness and silence, moving slowly on rubber-soled feet, a step at a time, a small wait, another step.

The image of the map was burned into my mind, and after eighteen paces I began to feel for the right-hand turn which ought to be here, with a gentle slope leading down. The turn was there, and so was the slope; and the steps down, twenty-one of them, were precisely where they were supposed to be too. I began to bless Sir Robert Hart's love of precision. And there, at the bottom, was a glimmer of light. The passage was long and narrow, and the light was at the end of it, casting a pale reflection along the corridor; we crept towards it.

At the end, the passage opened into a small chamber, and to the left, there was a wide doorway with no door in it, and the light was a quite pale neon strip, set into its lintel. It gave off an eerie glow down here, deep in the granite rocks, where you would think there ought to be nothing but old-fashioned flares and suits of armor waiting for the medieval troops to step into them.

Neon? It didn't seem right. And it was also suspicious. Why would they want a light kept burning here, placed just so? A camera set up nearby? Closed-circuit television perhaps? The lonely, ancient aura of the place made these fears seem absurd; but we were not dealing with the Manchus now; we were dealing with one of the wealthiest and most determined criminal organizations in all history. I listened for, and fancied I heard, the distant hum of machinery. A generator? I whispered to Mai: "You hear it?" She nodded, and in the half-light, she pointed down to the lower part of the doorway.

Her eyes were sharp. There was the tiniest scar on the smooth face of the rock, about twelve inches from the ground. I signaled her to wait, and went over to examine it, keeping close to the wall and feeling carefully for any tripwires as I moved round the chamber. I dropped to my knees by the doorway, and looked for what there was to see.

The scar was an incision in the rock, and there was a minute pinpoint of black light coming out of it, barely strong enough to reach the facing wall, the kind of thing, on a miniaturized scale, that opens a supermarket door. I worried about the height, a mere foot off the ground, too easy to step over. And, searching, I found the second one, even less visible except through careful search, three feet above it. I crept quietly back to Mai.

My lips close to her ear, I whispered: "A trip-light one foot off the ground, another four feet off the ground. That means we have to dive through them, perfectly horizontal, you get the idea?"

Her lovely eyes were bright, amused, expectant, excited. She nodded, and we went to the doorway together, and I pointed out the two eyes that were waiting to watch us go through them. Beyond, there was just enough light to see that the corridor continued out into the darkness again. I bent down close to the wall, held one hand at the level of the lower light and the other at the upper, just to give her a better visual aiming-point, holding my arms apart as though she were to dive through them but a little to one side. She stepped back a few paces and threw herself forward, passing neatly and lithely between my two hands, like a diver heading for the pool. On the other side, I saw her double up and roll over, and she was on her feet and waiting for me in a split second. I stepped back, worried about it just long enough to be sure of accuracy—my bulk was a problem here—and then followed her.

No bells rang, no lights flashed, no portcullis came clanging down; and we were through; and still there was no sign of any life at all. There was only the faint hum, more distinctive now, and just the whiff of diesel oil on the air, hardly noticeable to any but the keenest nose. I suddenly had a craving for a glass of good cognac; I'd brought none with me.

For half an hour we explored those caverns and passages, keeping the picture of the map well in our imaginations; they were clean, aseptic, and air-conditioned, with none of the traces of hundred-year-old dust you would have expected. Then, at last, we came to the area that was described on the map as the lower armories, the quarters that had once been used as the personal suite of the wicked Sumanu Fu, the pirate who had fought the Manchus for nearly sixty years till they finally chopped off his eighty-three-year-old head in 1809.

The old sybarite had liked good living, and I'd somehow suspected that if Ming did indeed use the old fortress for a hideout, the

Sumanu Fu suite, so to speak, would have offered the best possibilities for conversion into the kind of place Ming would demand—a place he could defend if necessary and yet would offer the kind of comfort not usually found on a barren rock.

And what else did I expect to find here? It didn't seem very likely, but somehow I had a premonition that I would find Sally Hyde in much the same kind of torment as that which had been Bettina's when I'd found her in the warehouse cellar. I dreaded to think of what I just might have to tell her father.

I took a little time out to stop and think; it's so easy to rush in when the going seems to be good. We were on the verge of entering a fortress; and had the protection, up to this point, been as good as it ought to have been? That was the question.

Or had we simply found the obstacles that we were expected to find? And were there, therefore, others?

There'd been an un-scalable cliff, a guard halfway up its face, an iron grille set in granite, a nearly invisible trip-light to warn of entry. And, above all, there was the undeniable fact that no one was supposed to know that the crumbling old fortress was functioning again there, at its lowest levels.

But wait a moment; if the Red Chinese knew that Ming was using it, and if they were keeping quiet about their knowledge, just how quiet could they be? How good was their own security? I thought it over and decided that Ming could count on at least an adequate protection, a combination of secrecy with security, if the secrecy alone should fail.

I said to Mai, whispering: "We're here, and they don't know we could possibly have done it. It's good." I hoped I was right.

And now, there was the door leading to the suite that I knew would hold; one way or the other; all the answers to all the questions.

I'd begun to use my flashlight again, because the corridors here were short and bisected everywhere by other passages, and it seemed that I'd hear danger first; rather than see it. I found the door, which was made of finely finished teak and studded with iron nails, just where the map said it ought to be. And there was a pinpoint of light coming through the keyhole. I bent down and peeked through it; I could see no living thing, but the room was comfortably furnished in

American rather than Oriental style. I could see the end of a green velvet sofa, a pale blue velvet chair, an oak refectory table on which there was a pink princess-telephone. As I looked, I heard the sudden sound of its ring muted by the heavy timber of the door, I waited, and the ring went on. I badly wanted to see who would answer it. Nobody did. It was singing to itself there in the lonely, femininely plush room.

It stopped ringing, and I waited a while, and then quickly picked the lock and went inside, signaling to Mai to wait for me in the corridor. I closed the door softly and looked around.

There were no windows here—we were deep underground—but drapes of pale mauve silk had been hung over simulated shutters where windows would normally be placed. There was another velvet sofa, this one in bright yellow, and three more velvet chairs in pastel shades of apricot, salmon, and burnt sienna. A pair of emerald satin drapes hung over a doorway, and the high ceiling was stained the same color. The net effect was extraordinary, a riot of color straight out of one of the women s magazines that teach the bored housewife the finer points of what is loosely called "decorating"; there was a riot of color, and most of it told me this was not the sort of place where I would find a man like Ming.

A Dual 1019 turntable with a Fischer amplifier was in a recessed alcove, and the albums scattered around it were modern, up-to-the-minute, and offbeat, the kind that require no studied knowledge of music to enjoy. There was a shelf of books, a small one, containing nothing but Gothic romances—again, not very likely to be Ming's choice at all.

And there was something that interested me more than anything else in the room—the only item there of any possible and very considerable value; it was a neatly framed case on the wall that contained, under glass, three postage stamps.

One of them was the Penny Black from England, undated, but which I knew to have been issued in 1840, the first adhesive stamp ever made. The second was a circular Brazil Thirty, the first stamp from the Western Hemisphere. And the third was, incredibly, the famous "inverted center" 24-cent airmail stamp from the U.S.A, with the biplane in the center printed upside down.

I thought that all the case needed was a Penny Magenta from

British Guiana, and there'd be a cool quarter million dollars right there. It was a marvelous display, and somehow it made me suddenly realize just who had been lying and who had been telling the truth. There was a great sadness in the realization; and at this moment I knew, somehow, exactly what the next step would be.

And it came, almost at once.

As I was looking at the beautiful Penny Black with its wonderful portrait of Queen Victoria, a voice behind me, hard and metallic but still feminine, said sharply in the silence: "Keep absolutely still. Don't even turn round."

I said: "Sally Hyde? I'm glad to know you. I'd thought for a while that you were a prisoner. I should have known better."

I turned round and was about to say: I'm Cabot Cain. But I couldn't speak. The woman standing there was indeed Sally Hyde, a gun in hand—a foolish little .32 revolver with too short a barrel, the kind of thing that would make a big enough hole in you ten feet away but had no range at all—with her eyes an angry fire and her body tensed and excited. It couldn't have been anybody else.

The words froze in my throat with a sudden shock of something that was closely akin to anguish.

She was tall and angular, and so indescribably thin that there wasn't enough sympathy anywhere in the world for her. Her face was a yellow-painted skull with huge, bright brown eyes that shone obscenely. Her hands were five thin twigs, her neck a piece of string. The rest of her body was covered with a loose woolen sweater and slacks, but the way she stood there, the way the clothes hung on her...I knew that if I'd been able to see the belt that was keeping her slacks up; it would have been a circle of no more than fifteen or sixteen inches. She moved quickly to one side, towards the telephone, and the illusion was heightened; the woolen sweater swayed as if there were nothing under it at all, a cover draped over a stick; a scarecrow would have had more body. I looked at the neck and could see the spine, with the Adam's apple sticking out like a chicken's giblets tight-wrapped in dried flesh.

I held up a hand and said: urgently: "No! Don't call anyone, no one, not till you hear what I have to say."

Her composure; though there was no sign of it when she had

first spoken, seemed to be coming back; the excitement was lessening, the anger growing. But she stopped the movement and stared at me, hesitant.

I said quietly: "I'm not alone, Sally. We're all over the place." I saw her eyes, mad, distorted eyes, flicker anxiously for just a second, but then she recovered and said sharply:

"But here there are just the two of us. Who are you?"

"My name is Cabot Cain. I'm a friend of your father's."

"And how did you get in here?"

"That doesn't matter now. The question is, how do we get out of here?"

"We?"

"You and I."

She hesitated, then made up her mind and reached for the telephone, but my hand was over it first, holding the receiver in place.

I said: "No, you'll have to shoot me, and I don't think you can afford to do that. Or even want to."

She said scornfully: "And why not, for God's sake?"

"Because of the others. And because you want to know what brought me here."

The phrase the others had her worried. She was trying to listen for any noises beyond the door, trying to keep her eyes on me and at the same time see what else there was around. How could she know it was a lie? Perhaps she did; perhaps she suspected it; but she could not be sure. There was an intelligent look in those mad eyes none the less.

She said: "What brought you here? Let me guess. My father sent you to bring me home."

"Yes, he did. Will you come?"

"No."

"Will you let me persuade you?"

"No."

"Will you at least talk to me, listen to me?"

"Not that either."

I reached out quite slowly for the gun. "Give it to me. It might go off and you wouldn't like that." She thrust it further forward, angrily, her finger on the trigger. I shot out a hand and gripped it hard by the chamber, preventing the chamber from turning and therefore the hammer from going back; I wanted to see if she'd apply—or try to—the necessary pressure, but she didn't. She just struggled, and took it away from her without any trouble and slipped it into my pocket. She stepped back and glared at me as though she were going to spring at me with her fingernails, ripping at my eyes, and then she opened her mouth wide to scream, but I had a band over her mouth before any sound could come; it was like closing my hand over a dry skull.

I said urgently: "I'm not here to hurt you, can't you understand that?"

She struggled for a moment, but there was no muscle there, only skin and bone and no blood to sustain the energy. In a moment she stopped struggling and went limp, and I set her down on that overly soft and feminine sofa; her body made almost no impression on the down cushions. All the fight had gone from her. She stared at me and said:

"A year ago I could have torn your eyes out, big as you are."

I said: "Your father wants you back, Sally. I'm here to take you to him."

"Let him go to hell and rot, the way I've rotted."

"So that's it."

"That's it."

"He's not to blame, you know. He loves you. You're the only thing he has."

"Don't talk nonsense. He's got everything in the world except me."

I said: "And he's sure that his love for you is returned. He's absolutely sure that you love him as much as he loves you."

There was a terrible contempt in her voice: "Love him? Maybe I did, when I was a child—he tried hard enough to make me. But when I grew older, it began to fade...You don't have to ask me why. And why should he need me? The kind of money narcotics brings in—he had everything else there was to have."

"He gave up the drug business a long time ago." An unlikely sort of thought came to me, and I said, not liking it: "Or did he?"

"Yes, he gave it up. He gave it up at a time when I'd learned all about it when the damage was done. It was too late then. Mr....Cain, or whatever your name is."

"Cain is right. What do you mean, too late?"

My gun and hers tucked away out of sight. I sat beside her, keeping an eye on the other door, the one with the green drapes over it. It was an unnecessary question, somehow; I already knew what she meant.

She said scornfully: "It was easy for him to pull out. He'd collected all the millions together, and it wasn't necessary to make more."

"And since then, he's spent them trying to make up for what he did in the past."

The scorn in her voice was terrible, "He spent some of them. You mean he's a poor man living in the gutter?"

"No, I know that."

"He kept back plenty to live on, the way he'd always lived, only without the danger, without the excitement any more. And I'd learned, for years, that this was one way to make a dollar. And when he told me how evil it was, did he really expect me to believe that my own father, whom I'd once worshipped, was an evil man? No, of course I didn't! It's only now I realize just how right he was; but then it was too late."

I said: "That's a little bit incoherent, Sally. But you know that, don't you?" Before she could answer, angrily, I said: "Is this your personal room?"

"Yes. Yes, it is."

"And who's likely to come here?"

She was quite at ease now, leaning back and talking as though we'd been friends for a long time, as though it was time she should say politely: Would you care for a drink?

Her eyes glistened, and she said: "Suppose you tell me instead just who 'the others' are?" I knew it had been worrying her.

I said carelessly, watching her: "The whole place is lousy with them. Cops, mostly."

She frowned. "This is Red China, have you forgotten that?"

I lied some more. "No. We're just hoping that the Reds won't find out until it's too late. Once we're gone, they can scream their heads off for all they're worth, but they won't. They are not going to admit that they've been sheltering Ming and his friends, not to anybody. And where is Ming now, by the way?"

She said promptly: "In Turkey."

I knew this was not true either. *O jeito* again, only Sally, in spite of that high intelligence—or perhaps because of it—didn't know how to play the game with any degree of persuasion. I heard the slightest sound at the door I'd come through, so slight that had I not been waiting for it and straining my ears I would have missed it. I made a mental note to tell Mai later on that she ought to learn how to open a door in *absolute* silence, the next best thing isn't good enough; if you're going to be heard at all, even by someone waiting for the sound, you may as well make a noise like a thunderstorm and have done with it.

But Sally heard nothing; her watery brown eyes were still on me, and she was wondering just how much of what I was saying was true, wondering if, now that I was seated and couldn't move so fast, she should try for a good loud scream again.

I said: "Tell me when you first started truly hating your father?"

"When my brother died, that's when."

"Your father's fault, you think?"

"Well, of course! The whole idea of heroin for the kids, my father practically invented it! If he'd been an insurance salesman, you think his kids would have grown up in a world where drugs were as common as apple pie? They were the source of our spending money, something we knew was bad but not so bad that it had to be rejected. Now I know better, and that's why I hate him. Now I know that if we'd been brought up in a normal way, without all that money—and without the disgrace of it being discreetly tucked out of sight and not talked about unnecessarily, and even then in a deprecating sort of way—then it all might have been very different. But it's too late now."

"You're still on them?" I didn't believe she was, and she shook her head.

She said: "No. I'm not. But look at me, Mr. Cain. Just take one look and sicken yourself. I'll be like this till the day I die, and that won't be far off either. So until then...till then, I'm going to taste the power that *he* had, and I'm going to enjoy it just as much." Her voice had taken a fierce kind of desperation.

I said gently: "Not enjoy it."

She said savagely, insisting, persuading herself more easily than she could persuade me: "Enjoy it! There's nothing in the world I can't have now, except my health. That's gone. So I'll have everything else instead! Most of all, I'll have the power to make this happen to others. I'm not going to be the only skeletal wreck in this world."

"You think that's a good philosophy?"

"No. But it's the only one I have. Here, no one can see me, ever again, except those who are afraid to stare, to laugh, to snicker. And here, I pull strings and people dance, they dance or die, and I'm a kind of skeletal god, a god for everyone except myself. No, it's not a good philosophy, but you can't tempt me to look for anything else."

"And you're happy to work for a man like Ming?"

She stared at me in genuine surprise. "To work for Ming?" There was even a laugh in her voice, a harsh and terrifying laugh. "I thought you'd guessed! I don't work for *him*. He works for *me* now. It took me less than a month to persuade him that my brains are better than his, that I can offer him more than he can offer me. And in that time, our output's tripled, did you know that? The Turkish fields have quadrupled their yield. We've doubled our sales force, and we're on the way to bigger and better things. Before I die, Mr. Cain, I'm going to put this enterprise into the top market. It's going to make General Motors look like a one-man business. I'm going to make every government in the world realize just how powerful the poppy is when someone with my brains waves it around. Do you realize that this racket is made up entirely of hoodlums? The ignoramus who dropped out of school when he was twelve years old, the punk with no learning who's picked up what he has to know and has gotten where he is because he is tough...Do you realize what the addition of a little true erudition can do to a setup like this? I learned *how* to learn in the best schools in the world, and I've got something they can never acquire. I've got *learning*." She said again: "And every government in the world is beginning to jump to the sound of it."

I said quickly, searching for hope: "To make them fight the harder? A kind of suicide? Is that your subconscious hope?"

The fire went from her at once, and I caught a glimpse of the honest, intelligent woman she once had been. She said slowly: "Keep your dilettante psychiatry to yourself, Mr. Cain, and don't try to impute altruistic motives to me, not any more. Not any more, Mr. Cain. I'm god, an evil god, with all the power in the world in my hand, and I'm going to push it till the whole damn thing blows up. And I don't give a damn what happens when it does." She sank into silence for a while, and then said thoughtfully: "No, not to make them fight harder. To wallow in the only thing I know about. The poppy field. A child running through the pretty flowers with bare feet, with the dew still shining on them, crimson poppies and scarlet, and the green-brown hills..."

She broke off and was silent. So was I. How do you tell a sad, mad woman that *everything* has gone?

There was one thing I had to know. I asked her: "Tell me how your ex-husband comes into all this? He's not somehow the kind of man I'd pick for you. And yet..."

Her voice was full of loathing. "Him! Almost the only mistake I ever made in my adult life."

"But you went back to him."

She was genuinely surprised. "Went back to him?"

"At least, you were corresponding."

"Of course! I had to find out where Ming was. After I'd told him who my father really was, I was pretty sure that he'd tell Ming about that, once the great Markle Hyde had ruined him. That's the kind of man he is. So I used him. And, having used him, I just dropped out of his sight along with everyone else's. A nasty piece of work, Mr. Cain, not worthy of your attention, or mine."

"Yes. Yes, I'd noticed that." It was good to hear her talking sense again.

There was still no sound, but Mai was in the room. I did not want to turn my head or even flicker my eyes, but I knew she was there, directly behind Sally and to my right, up against the wall somewhere. I knew that she was sizing up the position, since she too realized that time might be running out. I knew she wanted to urge me to get moving, to get out of here fast while the fates were still with us.

And she was right, of course.

I said heavily: "Sally, it might be too late, I don't know, but I'm taking you back to your father. He'll know what to do for you."

The moment of sadness had gone, and there was a dreadful sardonic anger there instead. "Take me back? To begin all over again?"

"No. To try to end it."

"No hope, Mr. Cain. And you can't take me back either. I'm going to shout for help."

A woman who is going to scream doesn't tell you all about it first; she wanted to know what I would do if she did.

I said calmly: "Go ahead. I'll have you out of here before the sound has gone six inches."

"Through the lights?" I waited, and she said: "You must have somehow jumped through them. I told them it could be done, but they thought the cliff...But try and drag me through there and see what happens."

I thought we could face that problem when we came to it. Less than two minutes to get back to the vent and out onto the face of the cliff, thirty seconds to secure the rope, twenty seconds to climb down, in under three minutes I'd be whistling for the boatman. And then? Three minutes for him to row ashore, with guns covering him if necessary.

I was about to stand up and tell her: Let's get going; and then, the door with the green drapes opened and Ming was there. I'd heard the sound a fraction of a second before the fact, not long enough to do much more than whip out the Luger and aim it.

He stood there with a look of shocked surprise on his face—he was already in the room before he realized I was there. A shadow behind him moved, and it was another man, too vaguely seen to be more than a nebulous menace moving back out of the line of fire, stepping back with an instinctive movement of alarm.

I had to fire. There was nothing else I could do, though it was something I had badly wanted to avoid.

I saw the shadow crumple, and when it fell into the patch of light that was cast on the floor, I saw it was one of the Northern Chinese that Ming liked to keep around him. He was grabbing at his shattered shoulder and yelling his head off. The time for silence had gone. Mai had already dashed to the doorway we had used and was holding it open, her little gun leveled at Ming. She said, quite quietly: "I've got him. Carry her." She seemed to know exactly what to do, and she was right.

I swooped over Sally and scooped up her featherweight in my arms. She was even lighter than I had suspected, and I let her scream as I ran with her out of there, fast. There was just time to see the surprise go quickly from Ming's face, to hear him call out mockingly: "A cadaver, Cain, before you've gone fifty yards."

Mai slammed the door shut behind me and stood there coolly and said: "I'll hold it. Move." I ran as far as the doorway with the lights, stopped, looked back at Mai who was standing there waiting for someone to open the door, and I called out: "Now!"

Not waiting a split second, she turned and ran towards me, and I said quickly: "Both of us through this thing together, just in case." Side by side, we ran through it.

And then, all the expertise, the efficiency, the mechanical know-how that was implicit in an operation like Ming's—like Sally's—came rushing into immediate action. Somewhere, a bright light went on ahead of us, a searchlight that cast its strong beam all down the corridor. I put it out with my first shot, and a bell was ringing, and there was already the sour stench of chlorine in the air.

I yelled: "Gas!" and we ran like hell for the stone stairway. More lights were coming on, and I was glad of them; it would have been impossible to move so fast in the darkness with the struggling bundle under my arm that was showing a surprising burst of desperate strength. Sally was kicking her legs wildly and trying to ram a heel into my face, and I swung her round with her arms in front of me, and that was worse, because she promptly grabbed me in a very sensitive place and squeezed hard, so I swung her back again and yelled at her: "Cut it out!"

The gas was behind us, on the other side of the lights, where we'd have been if we'd set off the alarm going in instead of coming out; but it was seeping along the corridor and even finding its way slowly up the stairs. But it meant one thing: there'd be no one behind us unless hampered with a gas mask. The lights were everywhere now, small bulbs, mostly, set inside cutouts in the granite roof, too many of them to try and shoot out once we were on the upper level and knew where we were going.

We headed fast for the vent, and there was a guard there,

running up and unshouldering a Bren gun as he ran. Mai fired once, and he fell, and then I dropped my angry bundle on the floor and said to her: "I need both hands, do I have to hit you?"

I didn't wait for a reply, knowing that for one reason or another she'd lie where I put her. I hoisted Mai by the ankles as she held herself stiff and straight, and she grabbed the overhang of the vent and pulled herself up, and then the rope came snaking down and I heard her call: "Behind you!"

I spun round just fast enough to see a thin Chinese pull back round the corner of the passage, fast enough to see his submachine-gun cradled just so, with the sling over his shoulder and the barrel leveled.

Mai called down: "I'll cover. Hurry."

I wrapped an end of rope round Sally's middle and told her, speaking fast and urgently: "This will hurt. Don't fight it." But she did. She struggled as Mai pulled her up, tried to kick herself free of the rope, tried to pull at the slipknot as it bit into her frail bones. I heard her screams, and then she was over the edge and suddenly silent.

Mai called: "All right, you're still covered."

I fired a quick shot at the angle of granite, just to let them know I was still awake, grabbed the thin rope, and swarmed up it. A burst of gunfire sounded, and I saw the bullets make an upward-moving arc over the walls and roof as the gun ran away from a dead gunners dead hands; I hadn't heard Mai's shot in the frightful maelstrom of gunfire in the confined and hollow rock, but there was the man out from under cover and lying dead or dying on the ground with his gun still running away till the magazine was empty.

Sally was up there, lying still and silent and showing no sign of whatever it was that Mai had done to her. Mai slipped along the passage ahead of me, dragging the rope (she never missed a thing, that girl!), and I followed with Sally's impossibly thin wrists in my hands. And a moment later, we were both sliding down the rope to the rocks of the beach.

I looked up at the top of the cliff. There, silhouetted against the lightening sky of the dawn, were ten, twelve, fifteen men, strung out like soldiers and peering out towards the sea.

But of Theo's junk, there was no sign at all.

CHAPTER 13

The bullets started coming a moment later.

It was as though the whole of Red China had erupted into sudden and well-accustomed violence. I threw myself at Mai as the rocks chipped noisily right beside our bodies, and I forced her tight into the overhang of the cliff face, knowing that the same bluff that had given me so much trouble on the climb would now be our salvation. In the noisy, bullet-whining darkness, I took out at last the walkie-talkie I'd brought. I flicked it on and said: "All right, Theo, where the hell are you now that I need you?"

His voice came back, calm yet excited, soothing yet distant. He said: "Senhor Cain? Run to the north, five hundred yards. You do this for me, you make me very happy man."

I said: "Me too, brother Theo," and switched off.

Sally was coming round, her eyes opening in the darkness, open enough to glare at me with a terrible savagery; I was hoping that the time might have come for complete resignation, but this wasn't a resigning kind of woman. She echoed Ming's words and said: "All right, another fifty yards, so you measure your life in the distance you can travel?"

Her wrist in my hand was a painfully fragile stick as we ran along the shore, stumbling over the wet boulders, listening to the roar of the waves. From up on top of the cliff, the bullets were coming fast, but we were close in under its protection. At an open space where the protection was gone, I sent the two girls on ahead while I turned and fired a few rounds from the Luger, glad of the weapons long range. They were following us along up there, running along the top of the cliff as we scooted along at the bottom; somewhere, I was sure, there'd be a way down. I saw one man in the moonlight, trying to make the difficult descent alone, his gun slung over his shoulder; I could only admire his courage, but this was hardly the time for mercy; he fell, yelling, when I fired.

We stepped now into deep water, and Sally screamed; Mai was there immediately to help, though it wasn't at all necessary. Ahead of us, up against the sky, a rope ladder was being thrown over the steep cliff, a suicide mission if ever I saw one, and as we rounded a curve in the broken shoreline, there was the silhouette of the junk against the cold red-bronze of the eastern horizon. I could still see the lights of Macao, impossibly close and impossibly far away. I was ready with the Luger for the first sign of anyone on the top of the ladder, but then a frightening booming sound crashed out, and there was a sheet of fire shooting out from the junk. I heard rocks shattering, mixed in with the twanging sounds of metal on granite, and I said "For God's sake!" It was as though a great bomb had blown up on board the junk, but I knew that it was something else; it was hard not to laugh.

Now they were swarming down the rope ladder, six, seven, eight of them all at once. I fired in the hope of discouraging them, and two men fell, but the Chinese are not easily discouraged when they're aroused; their anger is always emotional rather than intellectual, and that makes them savage and dangerous enemies. I'd used my gun eight times, so there was one round left in the breech; I shoved Sally ahead of me while I changed the magazine hurriedly, and then a man rose up out of the rocks in front of me and shoved a rifle in the pit of my stomach. I wondered how he'd got there so fast.

I threw myself sideways and lashed out with one foot as the shot screamed through my side, just raking the flesh; he went spinning into the water, his arms thrown out wide, and I heard the crack of his head against a rock, but he recovered quickly and was pulling himself out of the water again when I kicked him once more, just hard enough to make sure that this time he stayed there for a while.

And then another of them was rushing at Mai, his rifle held horizontally and pointed at her stomach. I fired, not taking time to aim;

and the rifle went spinning from his hands; but he still came on, and I saw that Mai's gun was jammed in the open position, meaning that its last shot had been fired and it was time to reload. I saw her drop it, almost calmly; and then, so help me...

It was time to fire again. But somehow, I wanted to see what would happen now. I could not justify, even to myself, what I was thinking. But it was something to do with the legend of the magnificent; I thought of that ancient Hispano-Suiza again and heard myself telling myself: All right, now's the moment to open the throttle and see what she can really do down the autobahn.

It was quite unforgiveable, but I'd seen the look in Mai's face as she put down the gun and sized up her opponent at the same time, and the look there was of absolute self-control, a look of the coolest possible assurance; so much so that I could only gape and think of legends that now or never would prove themselves.

All right, it was a moment of aberration, and a dreadful way to behave; but we all have our weaknesses, even the best of us. And my confidence in the legend was more than justified; the horsepower was still all there, and more. Mai dropped to one knee, which he was waiting for, of course, then stood up straight again without completing the move as he pulled back his shoulders to avoid the throw he must have thought was coming. And then, she dug her fingers into his exposed solar plexus, hit him under the ear with the flat of her hand as he doubled up, kicked an ankle out from under him as he tried for new balance, seized his wrist, and sent him hurtling through the air; I heard his skull crack open on a rock. It was all over in a split second.

I was still staring at her; my mouth, no doubt, was not hanging open; but it felt as though it were. She turned to me calmly and said: "Impressed?" and gathered up her gun and ran on.

I swallowed hard and followed her, grabbing at Sally again and dragging her with me through the rock-strewn water, splashing over the sharp barnacles and feeling the heavy tug of the receding waves.

The red-headed boatman was there, close into the rocks, and so help me, he was lighting a cigarette; I wondered if the light was to show us the way or whether it was just a show of bravado; it didn't immediately occur to me that, for these pirates, this was the norm of their lives. You step into a world that is not your own, and it takes a little time to realize that other people live there all the time.

I saw Mai splash through the water and fall base-over- lovely-apex into the boat, and she was on her feet again in a flash, firing her little Walther and quickly reloading as I threw Sally aboard and jumped in after her. I put away my Luger and grabbed an oar as the boatman started to pull, using it over the stern in sampan fashion to help us along a bit faster.

The junk was close in shore, its brown sails flapping, the sheets creaking and the main mast groaning, and then the diesel roared into noisy, smelly life that was going to be our salvation, I hoped.

A machine-gun on shore began its deadly stutter, and then that damned gun on the junk fired again in an impossibly uncontrolled explosion that ought, by rights, to have sent the whole craft to the bottom. It was a roar and a sheet of flame, a cannonade straight out of the eighteenth-century histories, with shrapnel of all sorts and sizes flying haphazardly in all directions. But the machine-gunner was gone; one minute he was there, firing away in an arc that was cutting through the water and almost reaching us, and then next there was nothing. I heard the rattle of rifle-fire from the junk, orderly, organized fire that was keeping the shore empty of life with surprising efficiency.

From somewhere under cover, a bullet tore into the *boat*, and the boatman yelled and dropped one of his oars; but he kept going with the other, and between the two of us we reached the junk, and there was Theo, leaning down and grinning and helping us aboard and yelling over the din: "How you like my cannon, eh?"

There was a fearsome pain in my foot, and I fell as soon as we hit the deck, but Theo helped me up and I saw his face grow serious suddenly as he looked at Sally. He threw me a quick glance and said nothing, and then we were hurrying for cover as more and more bullets stacked into the heavy timber sides. He said calmly: "Just keep low down. We don't got nothing to worry about now. We got good junk here, not the first time we catch little bit trouble, not the last time either." The sides of the junk were heavy teak, strong as iron and eight inches thick.

The helmsman was bearing down hard on the tiller, and the motor was roaring, and the sails were taking up the wind as we swung round and away from there. All around us, along the scuppers, a dozen crewmen were kneeling, their rifles firing steadily under the watchful eye of the big Arab cook. He laughed and yelled at me: "Pretty good fighting man, I tell you." He was standing there, huge and flabby and quite unafraid, completely exposed and saying calmly, over and over, in three different dialects: "Don't wait for targets; keep firing around the ladder. That's where they are; keep them under cover." There was a stream of blood pouring down from his right forearm, but he seemed to pay no heed to it at all.

I was holding Sally down close by the dreadful cannon, and it exploded again and nearly blew the top of my head off with the force of the charge. Theo was down beside me, trying to keep Mai's head down, unsuccessfully, and I said: "For God's sake, what have you got in that thing?"

He grinned in the growing red light: "Dynamite, gelignite, I don't know for sure. Whatever we got, we use. Fill up with nails, bits of iron; anything. Make pretty damn good noise, no?" Two men were packing rusted nuts and bolts down the old barrel for another blast, and close by, the open-breech culverin was being swiveled on its homemade base. A crewman was tamping powder into it with a calloused thumb, and when it was just so, he touched his cigarette to it, closing his eyes and turning his head away. The whole damn thing blew up in his hands, and he stared at a shattered wrist with something more like frustration than pain.

We were far offshore now, and out of useful range of their rifles. I heard a bullet or two clipping through the sails, a few more still thudding hopelessly into the timbers, but there was nothing much to worry about now. I said to Theo: "How long before we're in safe waters?"

He laughed. "Chinese won't worry us none. Too many people fight each other all the time here. Pirates, smugglers, they don't care. But Ming, Ming is different. Maybe you get safe from Ming now when you go to moon. Not before that, you not going to be safe no place. Better I fix that foot for you, anybody else hurt?"

We made a quick survey. Mai was untouched, and as cool and calm as she had ever been. Sally was unhurt. I had a scratch in the side and a painful wound in my right foot where a bullet had ripped open the ankle. The big cook was sitting down on the deck and grinning at the terrible mess a pattern of machine-gun slugs had made of his left thigh. Two other men had been slightly wounded, and nobody seemed in the least concerned about it; it was part of the pattern of their daily lives.

And then, I beard the roar of the helicopter.

There was nothing to see at first; there was just the monstrous sound of it coming across the water. I looked at Theo, and the smile had gone. He said slowly: "Better we get the senhoritas below deck, I think, no?"

I said: "I suppose it's too much to hope for an antiaircraft gun in this comic arsenal of yours?"

He shook his head. "Anything on the water, we fight it good, we win good. But up there..." He jerked a thumb at the lightening sky. "We don't never have to fight airplanes before. Maybe next time." I was glad he thought there was going to be a next time.

I told Mai: "Take Sally below, will you? Look after her?"

She hesitated. "If you give me a rifle..."

I said: "No, we'll manage, Get life-belts for both of you."

The resignation I was waiting for had come over Sally. She was sitting dejectedly on an upturned wicker-basket, her hands hanging listlessly at her sides, her glazed eyes staring at the teak boards of the deck. I had believed her when she said she was still off the drugs, and I believed her still; but there was a terrible, listless look to her eyes; the pupils were swollen to twice their normal size, and I remembered what she had said about the damage being permanent.

I said gently: "Better go below, Sally. There's more trouble ahead."

She said, not unkindly now: "More trouble than you know, Cain, for all of us."

"As long as you realize that."

"I know."

"To get back at me, he won't worry too much that you're on board. Whatever you've done to strengthen his kingdom, it's a likelihood he'd like to have it back for himself."

She said heavily: "I know that too. I've known it all the time." It was a good sign.

Mai took her arm silently, almost wincing when she felt there was nothing but a thin bone, and led her below.

We could see the helicopter now, rising up over the island. The gray sky was streaked with red and yellow as the helicopter wheeled over to the west and began to rise. Theo was binding a dirty length of cloth round the wounded cook's fat thigh, and the cook forced himself to his feet, leaning against the bulkhead and still grinning. "Am okay, skipper, *kulshi tamam*, is all okay." He spat into the water and laughed and looked at me and said: "Skipper think I fall down because I get hurt, but not so, is a little bit drunk still from last night." He threw back his head and roared with laughter, and then yelled suddenly, in Cantonese: "Get that gun on its back!"

The helicopter was wheeling towards us. Theo, staring up at it, said: "He don't know we got no antiaircraft. Maybe he waste little bit time making sure, no? What you think?"

I said: "I think we'd better get every rifle trained on him the moment he comes anywhere near us. I hope to God your men know how to shoot straight."

"They shoot pretty good, you see."

Four or five of the crew were struggling with the cannon, pulling it away from its embrasure and trying to wedge the barrel into an upright position. I said: "Good God, you can't fire that thing like that. It'll blow a hole in the deck. If it doesn't run away and kill us all instead."

Theo frowned, his mind working in unaccustomed academic exercise. "I don't know, maybe you right, maybe it fire pretty good."

"The recoil will blow it clean down to the bottom of the ocean."

"I don't think you right, Senhor Cain. We got pretty good decks on this ship."

"You have now. I don't know how long they'll last."

"We try, we find out, no?"

I shrugged. "It's your ship, Theo."

"No. Is Senhor Bonelli's ship. He got plenty money. We lose it, he not get too damn mad."

I sighed. It was a long swim home.

Now, the copter was swooping down towards us on a trial run. I looked at the cook. His arm was raised and he was watching the copter as he leaned against the bulwarks with his flabby face creased with pain. Under the cover of every obstruction on deck was a rifleman, his rifle raised high. Waiting. It hovered a moment out there, a hundred yards away and five hundred feet up, and then it swooped and came roaring in, almost at water level. The men on deck scurried to better positions against the side, and then the cook yelled: "*Udrubbu!*" and a dozen shots rang out in simultaneous precision.

It was close enough for me to see a burst of sudden holes in the helicopters fabric, and then the man in the passenger seat was slung round with a bazooka poked out over the side. I heard the shell come and yelled: "Cover!" as it slammed into the base of the mast and exploded, and I heard Theo yell: "Get the mainsail down!"

Two men were there already with their knives, slashing at the sheets, and the patched brown sail flapped loose and trailed in the water behind us as the junk swung round in answer to the urgent tiller. The helicopter was rising now, and I grabbed the binoculars that Theo had slung round his neck and watched it. It was too directly above me to make sure who was on board; but as it had wheeled in, I'd seen Ming at the controls and two other men with him, one who seemed to be an American—the one with the bazooka—and the other a Chinese.

The skipper was close beside me. I heard him shout as I watched: "We hit him good, you see?"

I nodded. He was high above us now, hovering, getting into position directly overhead. I could see no armament fitted to the craft, no bomb-bays or anything really nasty, and I said: "We just might have a chance to hold him at bay till we get close enough to Macao to scare him off."

Someone was cutting away the trailing mainsail, lightening our load, and the prow was slicing through the waves with a fine turn of speed. Mai was there suddenly, dragging away a man who had been wounded by the shell; and I said angrily: "Mai, get below!" She said calmly: "A man is hurt. I will take care of him."

"Sally?"

"She'll give us no trouble." I didn't press the point.

The helicopter was slowly, almost imperceptibly, dropping down. I took a rifle from one of the crew and asked Theo: "Does this thing shoot straight?" He laughed. "All our guns shoot straight, you see."

It was a Magnum .45 with a shell in it that would knock an elephant over. I sighted carefully on the underbelly of the helicopter, taking my time and holding the aim until I was sure I was dead on target, and then I fired. I took the glasses again and saw the hole where the bullet had landed, just where I'd put it, and said: "He's got armor plating under the seats. That means he's safe above us, but I'll bet you he won't come in at water level again."

I saw an arm come out of the craft above us, and called out again: "Take cover, grenade!" I heard the crew scurrying for shelter; a dozen mad characters in rags, with colored clothes around their middles and oddly assorted head coverings that ranged from coolie hats of straw to knitted caps of gaudy wool to knotted kerchiefs of brilliant Japanese print. They wore tire-soled sandals or heavy army boots, and some of them had bare feet; and there wasn't a decently shaved face among them. I dived down by the hatch cover; the grenade landed in the water close beside us, harmlessly, and then another came down and landed on the deck, but there was nobody exposed within its range, and all it did was tear a few holes in what was left of the sails.

Theo was setting up the ancient cannon just so, and he ordered everyone out of the way and said: "Now, we see, no?" He applied a match to the breech, and there was a tremendous sheet of flame, and the gun went wild, running free of its moorings and shooting across the deck, to land with a dreadful, rasping thud in the scuppers. The shot had gone wild, and there was a gaping hole along the bulwarks where the cannon had hit, and Theo said calmly: "Okay, so we know, this is no good, eh?"

I said: "The theory was fine, but the practice was wrong. You should have lashed it in position. There was too much play at the fulcrum."

Some men were already struggling with the wheels to get it back into its accustomed place, and then a hail of machine-gun bullets came thudding into the deck from up there, pinning us down, sweeping the decks with a terrifying fire. Theo had dived in beside me, and I said: "All he's got to do is keep that gun firing, keep us under cover till he can get low enough to use the bazooka again."

Theo said, worried: "That first time we hit him, we hit him

good. How come nobody get hurt?"

As if in answer to his question, there was a bundle being thrust out of the helicopter high above us. I wondered what it was, but only briefly.

In a moment, it was free of the plexiglas door and hurtling down; a body; the Chinese. I said: "We killed one of them, and he's lightening the load." The body crashed into the sea close beside us, disappeared, and then floated back into sight again, a gray-clad, spread-eagled body staining the water with its blood, I wondered who it might have been, but whoever it was, there was no time for any misplaced sympathy for any of Ming's crowd.

The helicopter was dropping down again, and the bazooka was outside the door, aiming straight down with nothing in sight behind it. I yelled: "Aim at the bazooka!" and the shell crashed into the deck, hitting home amidships as a dozen shots answered it; but it was a tiny target, and I saw it withdrawn and then come out again, much closer now. Another shell hit home and blew a gaping hole in the deck, and miraculously no one was hurt.

We were halfway across the straits now, and Macao was comfortingly close; but now there was steam gushing out from the hole in the deck, and I realized that it was peril ously close to the engine. The diesel took on another note; it was laboring, and then stopped suddenly, and the men on deck were firing wildly from under whatever cover they could find as hand grenades came dropping down onto the deck, fragmenting horribly all over the place. The junk slued round in the wind, and Theo, close beside me by the hatch and pressing himself into the timbers, said softly: "Now, the son of a bitch, he got us good, no?" The junk had stopped and was swinging round listlessly with the current.

I said; "No, not yet, he's too damn vulnerable so close in."

I could see our bullets thudding uselessly into, the underside of the craft, and I even fancied I could hear the clang of them hitting against solid armor, and then it wheeled away and over to one side the machine-gun still rattling at us, though its bullets were strafing the sides rather than the decks now. The copter was low, near the water again, but now up-tilted at an angle so that the tail propeller was almost dragging in the water; it was coming at us with its belly raised and pushed forward ahead, so that the armor was still out in front. Our own men had ceased firing, knowing that in this position they were wasting their ammunition. I saw two of them scurrying across to the other side of the junk, bent low and racing from one cover to the next, ready for the moment of truth when the rear end of the copter would be exposed to their fire, and I shouted out: "The tail propeller!"

The junk was stopped now, and the tail end of the copter was so close; as it swept past us, that it missed the top of the split mast by inches. We all fired at once, and I saw pieces of metal fly and the prop stopped turning with a sudden sound that was almost a shriek of anguish. But the main motor was still in good shape, and the copter was rising fast, high into the sky directly over us. I wondered how good a pilot Ming was, and it occurred to me that he was probably an expert.

It hung there in the sky, directly over our heads, five hundred feet up; and we rocked gently on the sea directly below; and for the moment, both of us were stymied.

But not for long. I knew that he could still fly, with limited but adequate maneuverability, as long as his main rotor was turning. And I knew that in the course of time, from his invulnerable overhead position, he could sink us with his grenades or his bazooka. Or worse...I wondered why he hadn't done it already; was it the pride of personal vendetta? Did he feel the urge to finish this off himself?

I said to Theo: "He must have friends on shore. He must have a radio. Why doesn't he call for help? A lightly armed launch could sink us in two minutes now."

Theo shook his head. The engineer, grease-stained and bloodied, poked his head up, and they held a whispered consultation, and Theo said glumly: "Engine seized up, two grenades in engine room. Looks like we stay here long time now. Unless you got any bright ideas?"

The bazooka fired again. The shell crashed into us amidships and blew a hole in the deck, and then another one followed and enlarged it, and then a third that missed us altogether. He wasn't aiming very carefully, because all he could do was hold the barrel over the edge of the craft and fire; but he didn't have to line his eyes up behind it at such close range. Two more shells missed, and another slammed into the deck, and then another one—the one we had all been waiting for—went through an existing hole and slammed into the hull of the junk. In a few moments we heard the sound of rushing water, and the ship took on an alarming list.

I said to Theo: "Do you have any hand grenades?"

He looked at me, puzzled. "Sure, we got plenty. But how you going to get them up there where they do some good? You tell me that." He caught on before I could answer, and his eyes lit up, and he laughed suddenly and said: "Like I tell you, is bloody good cannon."

Yelling for someone to help him, he jumped to his feet and raced towards the cannon. I took hold of one wheel, and two men were lugging at the other. We rolled it down into the scuppers, reversed to take advantage of the list, and raised the barrel as high as it would go. We began to lash the wheels this time with stout ropes; and now the machine-gun up there started firing, but the gunner wasn't taking any risks with careful aim, just sticking the muzzle out and firing blindly; and I sent three rapid shots up there to make him keep his head in behind the armor. A bullet caught one of our men in the knee, and he fell, screaming, and Mai was there to drag him away, and I knew it was no good trying to stop her.

Another shell landed, and the crippled mast crashed down suddenly, and two of the men leaped overboard to avoid it.

I said: "Now...or never."

Theo was ramming powder into the ugly muzzle of the cannon, ramming rags down on top of it, and he looked at me and grinned and said: "This work, maybe, you think?"

I said: "It'll work. Just a question of putting a projectile in the air, and that's what this thing was made for. Only we have a different kind of projectile this time. I must admit..." I took time off to fire three rapid rounds at the helicopter to discourage him from examining too closely what we were up to, and went on: "I must admit, I've never fired hand grenades from an eighteen century cannon before. And I hope I never will again. You know we've got to wait for the right moment?"

Above us, the helicopter was swaying back and forth, wounded but still deadly, getting too far ahead and then backing up to correct its position. The barrel of the ancient cannon, now, was pointed straight up, and all we could do was seize the moment.

I said: "If this doesn't work, we're all of us dead."

Theo grinned. "Some time, we all die, even people like us, Senhor Cain."

The hand grenades were there, ready for us; a box of Mills'. I set two of them close beside the gun, took another one in each hand, and wondered what would happen if they all wouldn't go down the ugly muzzle at one time. I said: "Keep the men firing, for God's sake. We've got to stand here exposed till he's in exactly the right position. Make sure the gunner up there can't poke his face out." He yelled an order, and I heard the cook swearing vociferously, and the firing started again.

Up there, he was ignoring the bullets; he could afford to. Well armored on the underside, all he had to do was stay overhead as best he could, maneuvering himself with his main rotor till he was where he wanted to be, and keep on firing shells over the side till, by the very force of quantity, a sufficient number of them hit home, enlarged the hole in our hull, and sent us to the bottom. The dinghy was gone, and we'd be in the water with no rifles to keep him at bay, and the rest would be easy. So, from his safe position, knowing he need not watch to aim, he just went on dropping his deadly missiles, knowing the end could not be far off.

And he was right.

It was all a question of timing. I nodded to Theo, and he yelled for the men to clear the decks. They went hurrying below, and the deck was all ours, just the two of us huddled there, terribly exposed and waiting for just the right moment of time.

I crouched by the gun while Theo held a lit taper ready. It was all a matter of guesswork now; and I'm much better at mathematical calculation; I thought about it for a moment, but there just isn't a formula available.

I watched the helicopter. He was behind us now, a hundred feet or more, coming in slowly for another round. The junk was swaying slightly, the list increasing. The moment when the list and the swing were just right...

He passed overhead, but the list was wrong, and ignoring the two shells that went into the sea on this pass, I wanted for him to back up again. And now he was coming into position and so was the angle of the junk. I said quietly: "Ready."

My eyes were on the helicopter, straining, watching while I tried to calculate. I thought: This is a hell of a long way from the Norden bombsight.

I pulled the two pins with my teeth, dropped the grenades down the muzzle, snatched up the other two, pulled their pins, dropped them down too, and yelled:

"Now! For God's sake, now!"

Theo was holding the taper to the breech, quite calm. I saw there was going to be more time than I'd thought, and I worried about angles and inclinations while I hurriedly grabbed two more grenades and stuffed them home. The tiny fuse caught and spluttered, and we both dived through the hole in the deck, not caring how far we dropped, landing in a horrible mess on the bottom.

And then, it went off.

It was the last time that cannon would fire. She broke free of her moorings and crashed through the bulwarks and over the side, and I rolled over on my back and looked up and there, high in the sky above me, were five live hand-grenades hurtling straight for the helicopter; five black and deadly specks against the blue sky; I never did learn where the sixth one went. Two of them were soaring off to the left, one was dead center, and two more were angling off to the right. Any one of them, I thought, would do the job if they went off at roughly the right moment; anywhere above or below, and within a couple of hundred feet.

I counted, mentally, from the moment I pulled the first pin, but I was late pulling back; was it perhaps fascination with the improvised weapon?

I saw one of them, the first, explode well to one side, and a black flower opened up on the helicopter's green painted side. Stray pieces of shrapnel came raining down around us, and one buried itself deep into my calf as the second grenade went off. And then the last three exploded almost simultaneously, and at that precise moment the roar of the copter's motor ceased.

Theo and I struggled to our feet and reached up to clamber quickly back on deck. The men had come up from under cover, and they were standing there in the open, a ragged, uncouth, loyal army of villains yelling their heads off in a variety of languages, waving their rifles like savage dervishes, slapping their thighs and clapping each other on the back.

And the helicopter was plunging slowly into the sea. It was catching fire, the flames spreading outwards on a sheet of falling gasoline, then seeming to turn back and engulf the craft itself. I fancied I heard a terrible long drawn out scream. It toppled over and gathered speed and crashed into the water close beside us, its twisted framework scraping our hull as it went down.

I ran to the side and looked over, and there below me was the cold, dead face of Alexander Ming; the eyes were open and the face was blackened, and in death he was staring straight at me, accusingly. The black smoke covered the stare, and he was gone. Of the other men there was no sign. And then the flames took over, and the black smoke, and then the water. And all that was left on the surface was a charred piece of green metal with the letter "M" in scarlet on it.

Theo was beside me, scratching his head. He said: "Now, how we get this junk into port, we only got little bit sail left, you want to tell me that?"

I said: "You'll find a way, skipper."

He grinned at me, and I went below to find Mai.

Sally was stretched out on a bunk, her eyes glazed, silent and morose and listless. There were four wounded men, whom Mai had bandaged, lying on the floor and slowly getting drunk on the wine she had found for them.

I said: "All over now. We'll be home soon."

Mai nodded, looking at me with solemn, somber eyes. She said: "Next door."

"I know."

I took her hand and we went into the tiny cabin to while away the time till we should arrive in port.

CHAPTER 14

I said: "In the course of time, she'd have killed Ming and herself too. You're going to have your work cut out to patch things up again."

Markle Hyde nodded. He said, wondering: "How did she get so close to him and still stay alive? That's what I can't understand."

I shrugged. "Too long, too involved a story. One day, perhaps, Sally will tell you that herself. But I shouldn't press her for it, not too hard. And not for a while yet."

He knew that I was keeping something back, knew too that he would never get it out of me.

We sat together in the fine old living room of Bonelli's house at Penha Point, with the yellow sun streaming in through the open windows, and the cool breeze blowing off the waters. Sally was there too, standing still and silent by the window and looking out across the water, with her back turned to us. She looked round at me and said nothing.

I said to him: "What will you do now? The whole world will know who Markle Hyde really is. Does that matter to you?"

He shook his head. "Not anymore." He was a tired old man, with all the fire gone out of him. "I can't go back to the States, of course. But somewhere out here, there ought to be room for me. I don't know. When all this..." He groped for the words. "When all this has settled down—wherever Sally wants to go."

"She'll find the best treatment in the world out here. In Hong

Kong, or Singapore, or Rangoon."

"Yes. Yes, I know that. Maybe there is something we can do. At least we can try."

Sally moved away from the open window and came and sat on the floor next to her father, like a child, her head against his knees. He put a hand on her shoulder and touched it, and she took his hand in hers, and I felt that this was no place to stay any longer.

I got up and went over to her, and I bent down and raised her chin and kissed her just once, and she looked at me and said nothing.

And as I turned at the door, I saw that she was crying quietly.

Somehow, the tears were the most comforting thing I could have wished for. I closed the door softly behind me and went back to the fan-tan house.

Bettina was there, and so was Mai, and so was Bonelli. There were a couple of loose ends still to be tied up, and I said to Bonelli:

"Whatever happened to our dear friend Wentworth?"

He shrugged. "The police were delighted to get him; and now that Ming is dead, there is, no doubt, a great deal he will tell the worthy captain."

"Captain?"

"Melindo. I arranged for him to make the arrest, and they were so delighted that he is now a captain."

I said politely: "That be nice for you, won't it?"

"Of course. All it requires is a little manipulation. And you, my dear Cain?"

"Me? Back to San Francisco."

I looked at Mai, and she lowered her eyes and said nothing. I said to Bettina: "Are you ready for Hong Kong now?"

She said, hinting broadly: "Of course. That's where the money is now that I'm a free woman again."

Bonelli was opening a bottle of champagne, Boulinger 1959, and pouring it into beautiful tulip-shaped glasses; they were deeply engraved and were made, I suspected, at Louis Vaupel's New England Glass Company about seventy-five years ago.

I said to him: "There's an awful lot of Markle Hyde's money to be used up. And a lot of people who'll need it. The men on Theo's junk. Theo himself, Bettina, Mai."

Mai said sharply: "No money. I have my work with Bettina. I do not need it."

Bettina said: "Take it and give what you don't want to me. Don't be a bigger fool than God made you."

I saw Mai smile suddenly, and she looked at me and said: "Or do you want to take me back to the States with you?"

"No. Not really."

"I didn't think you would."

"Would you have come if I'd asked you?"

She did not hesitate, "No. Of course not. And you must have known that."

"Yes, I knew that."

Bettina was staring glumly at her champagne, and I said: "I don't really feel like celebrating." She pushed the glass away and said to Bonelli, almost wistfully: "Could I have Scotch instead? Champagne gives me a rash on my belly."

I sat and drank with them for a while, and then I wrote a note to Harry Mann-Crawford in Hong Kong, reminding him of the Queen's pardon for Bettina and thanking him for his help; I told him:

...And when this fellow Wentworth has finished all he has to say, no doubt there'll be some tidying up to be done at your end too. I didn't really come here to break up a crime syndicate, but it seems that, with help, that's what we've done. So sweep up all the refuse, and may your career thereby be enhanced. . . .

We drove over to the airport in Bonelli's car, and we put the two of them on the plane, and we stood there, saying nothing as the Caravelle took off sharply. We watched it climb and wondered why it should be so hard to bring to an end something that had caused so many people so much grief.

We turned away and, as we walked slowly back to the car, Bonelli glanced up at me sideways and asked softly: "Is it hard to see her go?"

"Yes. Very hard."

"If you ever want to come back..."

"Yes, I know that."

"And sadness makes better men of us, did you know that?"
"Yes, I know that too. It doesn't help very much, does it?"
"In the course of time..."
"Uh-huh."
There was a plane leaving for the States that night, and I bought myself a ticket, and we spent the waiting hours walking round the colorful town together, looking at the brilliantly painted signs, listening to the raucous noises, pushing our way through the restless crowds: and I knew that, with Mai, a little of my life had drained away.

And then, the sun went down and the evening came, and then the darkness pierced by the bright and shining lights; and the sounds of the town rose in their nightly crescendo.

And soon, Macao was only a memory.

THE END

ABOUT THE AUTHOR

Alan Lyle-Smythe was born in Surrey, England. Prior to World War II, he served with the Palestine Police from 1936 to 1939 and learned the Arabic language. He was awarded an MBE in June 1938. He married Aliza Sverdova in 1939, then studied acting from 1939 to 1941.

In January 1940, Lyle-Smythe was commissioned in the Royal Army Service Corps. Due to his linguistic skills, he transferred to the Intelligence Corps and served in the Western Desert, in which he used the surname "Caillou" (the French word for 'pebble') as an alias.

He was captured in North Africa, imprisoned and threatened with execution in Italy, then escaped to join the British forces at Salerno. He was then posted to serve with the partisans in Yugoslavia. He wrote about his experiences in the book *The World is Six Feet Square* (1954). He was promoted to captain and awarded the Military Cross in 1944.

Following the war, he returned to the Palestine Police from 1946 to 1947, then served as a Police Commissioner in British-occupied Italian Somaliland from 1947 to 1952, where he was recommissioned a captain.

After work as a District Officer in Somalia and professional hunter, Lyle-Smythe travelled to Canada, where he worked as a hunter and then became an actor on Canadian television.

He wrote his first novel, *Rogue's Gambit*, in 1955, first using the name Caillou, one of his aliases from the war. Moving from Vancouver to Hollywood, he made an appearance as a contestant on the January 23 1958 edition of *You Bet Your Life*.

He appeared as an actor and/or worked as a screenwriter in

such shows as *Daktari*, *The Man From U.N.C.L.E.* (including the screenwriting for *"The Bow-Wow Affair"* from 1965), *Thriller*, *Daniel Boone*, *Quark*, *Centennial*, and *How the West Was Won*. In 1966-67, he had a recurring role (as Jason Flood) in NBC's *"Tarzan"* TV series starring Ron Ely. Caillou appeared in such television movies as *Sole Survivor* (1970), *The Hound of the Baskervilles* (1972, as Inspector Lestrade), and *Goliath Awaits* (1981). His cinema film credits included roles in *Five Weeks in a Balloon* (1962), *Clarence, the Cross-Eyed Lion* (1965), *The Rare Breed* (1966), *The Devil's Brigade* (1968), *Hellfighters* (1968), *Everything You Always Wanted to Know About Sex* (*But Were Afraid to Ask)* (1972), *Herbie Goes to Monte Carlo* (1977), *Beyond Evil* (1980), *The Sword and the Sorcerer* (1982) and *The Ice Pirates* (1984).

Caillou wrote 52 paperback thrillers under his own name and the nom de plume of Alex Webb, with such heroes as Cabot Cain, Colonel Matthew Tobin, Mike Benasque, Ian Quayle and Josh Dekker, as well as writing many magazine stories.

Several of Caillou's novels were made into films, such as *Rampage* with Robert Mitchum in 1963, based on his big game hunting knowledge; *Assault on Agathon*, for which Caillou did the screenplay as well; and *The Cheetahs*, filmed in 1989.

He was married to Aliza Sverdova from 1939 until his death. Their daughter Nadia Caillou was the screenwriter for the film *Skeleton Coast*.

Alan Caillou died in Sedona, Arizona in 2006.

LOOKING FOR ACTION AND ADVENTURE
AUTHOR ALAN CAILLOU
NOVELS DELIVER!

WWW.CALIBERCOMICS.COM

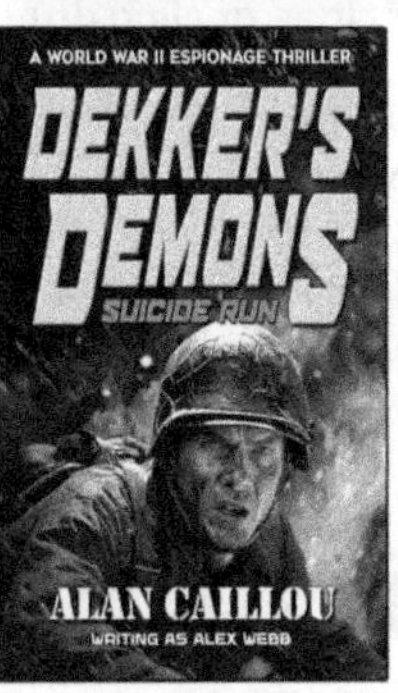

AVAILABLE IN PAPERBACK OR EBOOK

DON'T MISS ANY OF MICHAEL KASNER'S HARD HITTING MILITARY NOVEL SERIES

BLACK OPS

Formed by an elite cadre of government officials, the Black OPS team goes where the law can't - to seek retribution for acts of terror directed against Americans anywhere in the world.

3 BOOK SERIES

Armed with all the tactical advantages of modern technology, battle hard and ready when the free world is threatened - the Peacekeepers are the baddest grunts on the planet.

4 BOOK SERIES

CHOPPER COPS

America is being torn apart as criminal cartels terrorize our cities, dealing drugs and death wholesale. Local police are outgunned, so the President unleashes the U.S. TACTICAL POLICE FORCE. An elite army of super cops with ammo to burn, they swoop down on the hot spots in sleek high-tech attack choppers to win the dirty war and take back America!

4 BOOK SERIES

FROM CALIBER BOOKS

www.calibercomics.com

DON'T MISS ANY OF NEIL HUNTER'S NOVELS FROM CALIBER BOOKS

Reporter Les Mason is completing an expose on the Long Point Nuclear Plant. But before he can finish he dies an agonizing death. The doctors are baffled—and there are similar cases to follow...Chris Lane, his girlfriend, and organizer of the Long Point Protestors, discovers Mason's notes, and decides to find out for herself what the plant has to hide.

2 BOOK SERIES

In middle of the 21st century America – over-populated decaying cities are ruled by hi-tech gangs pushing every vice and wastelands are controlled by bands of mutants. Ordinary citizens are oppressed and face a hopeless future. But Marshal T.J. Cade is a new breed of law enforcer. Teamed with his cyborg partner, Janek, Cade takes on these criminals and works in the gray areas of the law to get the job done.

3 BOOK SERIES

The village of Shepthorne England wasn't being gripped, but strangled by a winter's blanket of heavy snow and Arctic temperatures. The trouble began innocently enough with a massive pile-up of autos on frozen roads leading to and from the village. Then, from the sky, a military transport plane with its top secret cargo of devastation crashed down towards the center of the village. Hell was just beginning to touch Shepthorne and its unsuspecting citizens...

FROM CALIBER BOOKS

www.calibercomics.com

CALIBER COMICS GOES TO WAR!
HISTORICAL AND MILITARY THEMED GRAPHIC NOVELS

WORLD WAR ONE: MO MAN'S LAND

ISBN: 9781635298123

A look at World War 1 from the French trenches as they faced the Imperial German Army.

CORTEZ AND THE FALL OF THE AZTECS

ISBN: 9781635299779

Cortez battles the Aztecs while in search of Inca gold.

TROY: AN EMPIRE UNDER SIEGE

ISBN: 9781635298635

Homer's famous The Iliad and the Trojan War is given a unique human perspective rather than from the God's.

WITNESS TO WAR

ISBN: 9781635299700

WW2's Battle of the Bulge is seen up close by an embedded female war reporter.

THE LINCOLN BRIGADE

ISBN: 9781635298222

American volunteers head to Spain in the 1930s to fight in their civil war against the fascist regime.

EL CID: THE CONQUEROR

ISBN: 9780982654996

Europe's greatest warrior attempts to unify Spain against invading foreign and domestic armies.

WINTER WAR

ISBN: 9780985749392

At the outbreak of WW2 Finland fights against an invading Soviet army.

ZULUNATION: END OF EMPIRE

ISBN: 9780941613415

The global British Empire and far-reaching influence is threatened by a Zulu uprising in southern Africa.

AIR WARRIORS: WORLD WAR ONE #V1 - V4   Take to the skies of WW1 as various fighter aces tell their harrowing stories.
ISBN: 9781635297973 (V1), 9781635297980 (V2), 9781635297997 (V3), 9781635298000 (V4)

CALIBER COMICS PRESENTS
The Complete
VIETNAM JOURNAL

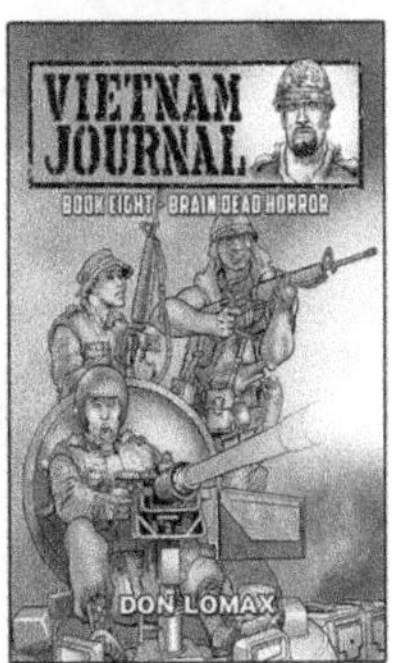

8 Volumes Covering the Entire Initial Run of the Critically Acclaimed Don Lomax Series

And Now Available
VIETNAM JOURNAL SERIES TWO
"INCURSION", "JOURNEY INTO HELL", "RIPCORD"

All new stories from Scott 'Journal' Neithammer as he reports durings the later stages of the Vietnam War.

CALIBER COMICS   WWW.CALIBERCOMICS.COM

FROM AWARD-WINNING COMIC WRITER AND ARTIST
WAYNE VANSANT

COMES TALES FROM WORLD WAR II

An action/adventure tale of the French Legionnaire soldier, Battron, who is involved with the liberation of a freebooting French ship, the Martel, from a heavily guarded Vichy French port during WWII. The Allies want the ship destroyed; the Germans have sent serious resources and firepower to save it. But a critical security leak in British intelligence could jeopardize not only the mission but Battron's life. The key is the beautiful former mistress of the Martel's captain, enlisted in the hope she can convince him to join the Free French movement with his ship. But has she told the Allies all she knows? And can Battron and his skillful commandos complete their dangerous mission in time under the luming shadow of the pending Allied invasion of North Africa?

Collection of tales involving the German Waffen SS from acclaimed creator and comic artist Wayne Vansant. These stories deal with the German Panzer troops during World War II and collects the highly acclaimed Battle Group Peiper story, Witches' Cauldon saga, along with three short tales. Knights of the Skull covers the war experiences of young German troops on the Eastern Front to the massacre of American troops near Malmedy Belgium to the harsh conditions of a crushing winter and engagements against an unrelenting Soviet troop onslaught.

The epic and incredible telling of the early days of the United States during the Second World War. Days of Darkness covers the darkest days of WWII for the US, when the country went from the tragedy of Pearl Harbor to the triumph at Midway. Covering in detail is the attack of the US Naval base and the devastation of the fleet in Hawaii, then the action moves to the evacuation and fall of the Philippines to the horror of the Death March of Bataan, and finally to the dramatic Battle of Midway which stopped the Japanese juggernaut in the Pacific.

"Heavy on authenticity, compellingly written and beautifully drawn." - Comics Buyers Guide.

WWW.CALIBERCOMICS.COM

CALIBER COMICS GOES TO THE EDGE!
Science Fiction and Horror themed graphic novels

DEADWORLD
ISBN: 9781942351245

RENFIELD
ISBN: 9781942351825

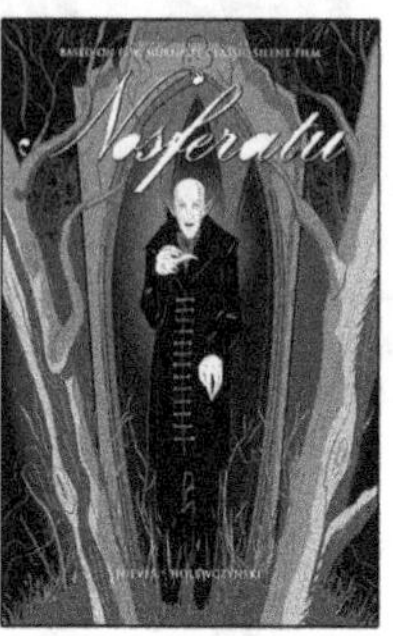

NOSFERATU
ISBN: 9781942351931

**LOVECRAFT:
THE EARLY STORIES**
ISBN: 9781942351634

**THE WAR OF THE WORLDS:
INFESTATION**
ISBN: 9781942351962

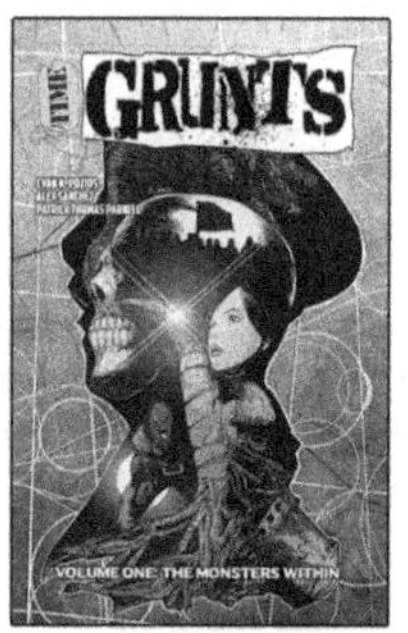

TIME GRUNTS
ISBN: 9781635299472

DRACULA
ISBN: 9780996030649

**DRACULA:
THE SUICIDE CLUB**
ISBN: 9781635299571

**JACK THE RIPPER
ILLUSTRATED**
ISBN: 9781942351917

THE SEARCHERS
ISBN: 9781942351979

A.A.I. WARS
ISBN: 9781635299168

**AUTUMN: TERROR IN THE
LONDON UNDERGROUND**
ISBN: 9781544624020

www.calibercomics.com

ALSO AVAILABLE FROM CALIBER COMICS

QUALITY GRAPHIC NOVELS TO ENTERTAIN

THE SEARCHERS: VOLUME 1
The Shape of Things to Come

Before *League of Extraordinary Gentlemen* there was *The Searchers*. At the dawn of the 20th Century the greatest literary adventurers from the minds of Wells, Doyle, Burroughs, and Haggard were created. All thought to be the work of pure fiction. However, a century later, the real-life descendents of those famous characters are recuited by the legendary Professor Challenger in order to save mankind's future. Series collected for the first time.

"Searchers is the comic book I have on the wall with a sign reading - 'Love books? Never read a comic? Try this one! ....money back guarantee..." - Dark Star Books.

WAR OF THE WORLDS: INFESTATION

Based on the H.G. Wells classic! The "Martian Invasion" has begun again and now mankind must fight for its very humanity. It happened slowly at first but by the third year, it seemed that the war was almost over... the war was almost lost.

"Writer Randy Zimmerman has a fine grasp of drama, and spins the various strands of the story into a coherent whole... imaginative and very gritty."
- war-of-the-worlds.co.uk

HELSING: LEGACY BORN

From writer Gary Reed (Deadworld) and artists John Lowe (Captain America), Bruce McCorkindale (Godzilla). She was born into a legacy she wanted no part of and pushed into a battle recessed deep in the shadows of the night. Samantha Helsing is torn between two worlds...two allegiances...two families. The legacy of the Van Helsing family and their crusade against the "night creatures" comes to modern day with the most unlikely of all warriors.

"Congratulations on this masterpiece..."
- Paul Dale Roberts, Compuserve Reviews

DEADWORLD

Before there was The Walking Dead there was Deadworld. Here is an introduction of the long running classic horror series, Deadworld, to a new audience! Considered by many to be the godfather of the original zombie comic with over 100 issues and graphic novels in print and over 1,000,000 copies sold, Deadworld ripped into the undead with intelligent zombies on a mission and a group of poor teens riding in a school bus desperately try to stay one step ahead of the sadistic, Harley-riding King Zombie. Death, mayhem, and a touch of supernatural evil made Deadworld a classic and now here's your chance to get into the story!

DAYS OF WRATH

Award winning comic writer & artist Wayne Vansant brings his gripping World War II saga of war in the Pacific to Guadalcanal and the Battle of Bloody Ridge. This is the powerful story of the long, vicious battle for Guadalcanal that occurred in 1942-43. When the U.S. Navy orders its outnumbered and out-gunned ships to run from the Japanese fleet, they abandon American troops on a bloody, battered island in the South Pacific.

"Heavy on authenticity, compellingly written and beautifully drawn."
- Comics Buyers Guide

SHERLOCK HOLMES:
THE CASE OF THE MISSING MARTIAN

Sherlock is called out of retirement to London in 1908 to solve a most baffling mystery: The British Museum is missing a specimen of a Martian from the failed invasion of 1899. Did it walk away on its own or did someone steal it?

Holmes ponders the facts and remembers his part in the war effort alongside Professor Challenger during the War of the Worlds invasion that was chronicled in H.G. Wells' classic novel.

Meanwhile, Doctor Watson has problems of his own when his wife steals a scalpel from his surgical tool kit and returns to her old stomping grounds of Whitechapel, the London

CALIBER PRESENTS

The original Caliber Presents anthology title was one of Caliber's inaugural releases and featured predominantly new creators, many of which went onto successful careers in the comics' industry. In this new version, Caliber Presents has expanded to graphic novel size and while still featuring new creators it also includes many established professional creators with new visions. Creators featured in this first issue include nominees and winners of some of the industry's major awards including the Eisner, Harvey, Xeric, Ghastly, Shel Dorf, Comic Monsters, and more.

LEGENDLORE

From Caliber Comics now comes the entire Realm and Legendlore saga as a set of volumes that collects the long running critically acclaimed series. In the vein of The Lord of The Rings and The Hobbit with elements of Game of Thrones and Dungeon and Dragons.

Four normal modern day teenagers are plunged into a world they thought only existed in novels and film. They are whisked away to a magical land where dragons roam the skies, orcs and hobgoblins terrorize travelers, where unicorns prance through the forest, and kingdoms wage war for dominance. It is a world where man is just one race, joining other races such as elves, trolls, dwarves, changelings, and the dreaded night creatures who steal the night.

TIME GRUNTS

What if Hitler's last great Super Weapon was – Time itself! A WWII/time travel adventure that can best be described as *Band of Brothers* meets *Time Bandits*.

October, 1944. Nazi fortunes appear bleaker by the day. But in the bowels of the Wenceslas Mines, a terrible threat has emerged . . . The Nazis have discovered the ability to conquer time itself with the help of a new ominous device!

Now a rag tag group of American GIs must stop this threat to the past, present, and future . . . While dealing with their own past, prejudices, and fears in the process.

CALIBER
COMICS